**THROUGHOUT THE BUS A DEEP
CHANGE HAD BEGUN TAKING PLACE,
AND LIKE HIS EXPERIMENT IN THE
STORE IT DID NOT FIT; IT WAS NOT
WHAT HE WANTED.**

Damn you, he thought. Fade away!

The sides of the bus became transparent. He saw out into the street, the sidewalk and stores. Thin support struts, the skeleton of the bus. Metal girders, an empty hollow box. No other seats. Only a strip, a length of planking, on which upright featureless shapes like scarecrows had been propped. They were not alive. The scarecrows lolled forward, back, forward, back. Ahead of him he saw the driver; the driver had not changed. The red neck. Strong, wide back. Driving a hollow bus.

The hollow men, he thought. We should have looked up poetry.

Philip K. Dick

Time Out of Joint

A ROC BOOK

ROC

Published by the Penguin Group
Penguin Books Ltd, 27 Wrights Lane, London W8 5TZ, England
Penguin Books USA Inc., 375 Hudson Street, New York, New York 10014, USA
Penguin Books Australia Ltd, Ringwood, Victoria, Australia
Penguin Books Canada Ltd, 10 Alcorn Avenue, Toronto, Ontario, Canada M4V 3B2
Penguin Books (NZ) Ltd, 182–190 Wairau Road, Auckland 10, New Zealand

Penguin Books Ltd, Registered Offices: Harmondsworth, Middlesex, England

First published in the USA by Lippincott 1959
Published in Penguin Books 1969
10 9 8 7 6 5

Printed in England by Clays Ltd, St Ives plc
Set in Monotype Plantin

I

From the cold-storage locker at the rear of the store, Victor Nielson wheeled a cart of winter potatoes to the vegetable section of the produce department. In the almost empty bin he began dropping the new spuds, inspecting every tenth one for split skin and rot. One big spud dropped to the floor and he bent to pick it up; as he did so he saw past the check-out stands, the registers and displays of cigars and candy bars, through the wide glass doors and on to the street. A few pedestrians walked along the sidewalk, and along the street itself he caught the flash of sunlight from the fender of a Volkswagen as it left the store's parking lot.

'Was that my wife?' he asked Liz, the formidable Texas girl who was the checker on duty.

'Not that I know of,' Liz said, ringing up two cartons of milk and a package of ground lean beef. The elderly customer at the check-out stand reached into his coat pocket for his wallet.

'I'm expecting her to drop by,' Vic said. 'Let me know when she does.' Margo was supposed to take Sammy, their ten-year-old, to the dentist for x-rays. Since this was April – income tax time – the savings account was unusually low, and he dreaded the results of the x-rays.

Unable to endure the waiting, he walked over to the pay phone by the canned-soup shelf, dropped a dime in, dialled.

'Hello,' Margo's voice came.

'Did you take him down?'

Margo said hectically, 'I had to phone Dr Miles and postpone it. About lunchtime I remembered that this is the day Anne Rubenstein and I have to take that petition over to the Board of Health; it has to be filed with them today, because the contracts are being let now, according to what we hear.'

'What petition?' he said.

'To force the city to clear away those three empty lots of old house foundations,' Margo said. 'Where the kids play after school. It's a hazard. There's rusty wire and broken concrete slabs and –'

'Couldn't you have mailed it?' he broke in. But secretly he was relieved. Sammy's teeth wouldn't fall out before next month; there was no urgency about taking him. 'How long will you be there? Does that mean I don't get a ride home?'

'I just don't know,' Margo said. 'Listen, dear; there's a whole flock of ladies in the living room – we're figuring out last-minute items we want to bring up when we present the petition. If I can't drive you home I'll phone you at five or so. Okay?'

After he had hung up he wandered over to the check-out stand. No customers were in need of being checked, and Liz had lit a cigarette for a few moments. She smiled at him sympathetically, a lantern-like effect. 'How's your little boy?' she asked.

'Okay,' he said. 'Probably relieved he's not going.'

'I have the sweetest little old dentist I go to,' Liz chirruped. 'Must be nearly a hundred years old. He don't hurt me a bit; he just scrapes away and it's done.' Holding aside her lip with her red-enamelled thumbnail, she showed him a gold inlay in one of her upper molars. A breath of cigarette smoke and cinnamon whisked around him as he leaned to see. 'See?' she said. 'Big as all get out, and it didn't hurt! No, it never did!'

I wonder what Margo would say, he wondered. If she walked in here through the magic-eye glass door that swings open when you approach it and saw me gazing into Liz's mouth. Caught in some fashionable new eroticism not yet recorded in the Kinsey reports.

The store had during the afternoon become almost deserted. Usually a flow of customers passed through the check-out stands, but not today. The recession, Vic decided. Five million unemployed as of February of this year. It's getting at our business. Going to the front doors he stood watching the sidewalk traffic. No doubt about it. Fewer people than usual. All home counting their savings.

'We're in for a bad business year,' he said to Liz.

'Oh what do you care?' Liz said. 'You don't own the store; you just work here, like the rest of us. Means not so much work.' A woman customer had begun unloading items of food on to the counter; Liz rang them up, still talking over her shoulder to Vic.

6

'Anyhow I don't think there's going to be any depression; that's just Democratic talk. I'm so tired of those old Democrats trying to make out like the economy's going to bust down or something.'

'Aren't you a Democrat?' he asked. 'From the South?'

'Not any more. Not since I moved up here. This is a Republican state, so I'm a Republican.' The cash register clattered and clanged and the cash drawer flew open. Liz packed the groceries into a paper bag.

Across the street from the store the sign of the American Diner Café started him thinking about afternoon coffee. Maybe this was the best time. To Liz he said, 'I'll be back in ten or so minutes. You think you can hold the fort alone?'

'Oh sholly,' Liz said merrily, her hands making change. 'You go ahead on, so I can get out later and do some shopping I have to do. Go on, now.'

Hands in his pockets, he left the store, halting at the curb to seek out a break in the traffic. He never went down to the crosswalk; he always crossed in the middle of the block, directly to the café, even if he had to wait at the curb minute after minute. A point of honour was involved, an element of manliness.

In the booth at the café he sat before his cup of coffee, stirring idly.

'Slow day,' Jack Barnes the shoe salesman from Samuel's Men's Apparel said, bringing over his cup of coffee to join him. As always, Jack had a wilted look, as if he had steamed and baked all day in his nylon shirt and slacks. 'Must be the weather,' he said. 'A few nice spring days and everybody starts buying tennis rackets and camp stoves.'

In Vic's pocket was the most recent brochure from the Book-of-the-Month Club. He and Margo had joined several years ago, at the time they had put a down payment on a house and moved into the kind of neighbourhood that set great stock by such things. Producing the brochure he spread it flat on the table, swivelling it so Jack could read it. The shoe salesman expressed no interest.

'Join a book club,' Vic said. 'Improve your mind.'

'I read books,' Jack said.

'Yeah. Those paperback books you get at Becker's Drugs.'

Jack said, 'It's science this country needs, not novels. You know darn well that those book clubs peddle those sex novels about small towns in which sex crimes are committed, and all the dirt comes to the surface. I don't call that helping American science.'

'The Book-of-the-Month Club also distributed Toynbee's *History*,' Vic said. 'You could stand reading that.' He had got that as a dividend; although he hadn't quite finished it he recognized that it was a major literary and historical work, worth having in his library. 'Anyhow,' he said, 'bad as some books are, they're not as bad as those teen-age sex films, those drag-race films that James Dean and that bunch do.'

His lips moving, Jack read the title of the current Book-of-the-Month selection. 'A historical novel,' he said. 'About the South. Civil War times. They always push that stuff. Don't those old ladies who belong to the club get tired of reading that over and over again?'

As yet, Vic hadn't had a chance to inspect the brochure. 'I don't always get what they have,' he explained. The current book was called *Uncle Tom's Cabin*. By an author he had never heard of: Harriet Beecher Stowe. The brochure praised the book as a daring exposé of the slave trade in pre-Civil War Kentucky. An honest document of the sordid outrageous practices committed against hapless Negro girls.

'Wow,' Jack said. 'Hey, maybe I'd like that.'

'You can't tell anything by the blurb,' Vic said. 'Every book that's written these days is advertised like that.'

'True,' Jack said. 'There's sure no principles left in the world any more. You look back to before World War Two, and compare it to now. What a difference. There wasn't this dishonesty and delinquency and smut and dope that's going around. Kids smashing up cars, these freeways and hydrogen bombs . . . and prices going up. Like the price you grocery guys charge for coffee. It's terrible. Who's getting the loot?'

They argued about it. The afternoon wore on, slowly, sleepily, with little or nothing happening.

At five, when Margo Nielson snatched up her coat and car keys and started out of the house, Sammy was nowhere in sight.

Off playing, no doubt. But she couldn't take time to round him up; she had to pick up Vic right away or he'd conclude she wasn't coming and so take the bus home.

She hurried back into the house. In the living room her brother, sipping from his can of beer, raised his head and murmured, 'Back already?'

'I haven't left,' she said. 'I can't find Sammy. Would you keep your eye open for him while I'm gone?'

'Certainly,' Ragle said. But his face showed such weariness that at once she forgot about leaving. His eyes, red-rimmed and swollen, fastened on her compellingly; he had taken off his tie, rolled up his shirt-sleeves, and as he drank his beer his arm trembled. Spread out everywhere in the living room the papers and notes for his work formed a circle of which he was the centre. He could not even get out; he was surrounded. 'Remember, I have to get this in the mail and postmarked by six,' he said.

In front of him his files made up a leaning, creaking stack. He had been collecting material for years. Reference books, charts, graphs, and all the contest entries that he had mailed in before, month after month of them . . . in several ways he had reduced his entries so that he could study them. At this moment, he was using what he called his 'sequence' scanner; it involved opaque replicas of entries, in which the point admitted light to flash in the form of a dot. By having the entries fly by in order, he could view the dot in motion. The dot of light bounced in and out, up and down, and to him its motions formed a pattern. To her it never formed a pattern of any sort. But that was why he was able to win. She had entered the contest a couple of times and won nothing.

'How far along are you?' she asked.

Ragle said, 'Well, I've got it placed in time. Four o'clock, p.m. Now all I have to do – ' he grimaced, 'is get it in space.'

Tacked up on the long plywood board was today's entry on the official form supplied by the newspaper. Hundreds of tiny squares, each of them numbered by rank and file. Ragle had marked off the file, the time element. It was file 344; she saw the red pin stuck in at that point. But the *place*. That was harder, apparently.

'Drop out for a few days,' she urged. 'Rest. You've been going at it too hard the last couple of months.'

'If I drop out,' Ragle said, scratching away with his ballpoint pen, 'I have to drop back a flock of notches. I'd lose – ' He shrugged. 'Lose everything I've won since January 15.' Using a slide rule, he plotted a junction of lines.

Each entry that he submitted became a further datum for his files. And so, he had told her, his chances of being correct improved each time. The more he had to go on, the easier it was for him. But instead, it seemed to her, he was having more and more trouble. Why? she had asked him, one day. 'Because I can't afford to lose,' he explained. 'The more times I'm correct, the more I have invested.' The contest dragged on. Perhaps he had even lost track of his investment, the mounting plateau of his winnings. He always won. It was a talent, and he had made good use of it. But it was a vicious burden to him, this daily chore that had started out as a joke, or at best a way of picking up a couple of dollars for a good guess. And now he couldn't quit.

I guess that's what they want, she thought. They get you involved, and maybe you never live long enough to collect. But he had collected; the *Gazette* paid him regularly for his correct entries. She did not know how much it came to, but apparently it ran close to a hundred dollars a week. Anyhow it supported him. But he worked as hard – harder – than if he had a regular job. From eight in the morning, when the paper was tossed on the porch, to nine or ten at night. The constant research. Refining of his methods. And, over everything else, the abiding dread of making an error. Of turning in a wrong entry and being disqualified.

Sooner or later, they both knew, it had to happen.

'Can I get you some coffee?' Margo said. 'I'll fix you a sandwich or something before I go. I know you didn't have any lunch.'

Preoccupied, he nodded.

Putting down her coat and purse, she went into the kitchen and searched in the refrigerator for something to feed him. While she was carrying the dishes out to the table, the back door flew open and Sammy and a neighbourhood dog appeared, both of them fluffed up and breathless.

'You heard the refrigerator door,' she said, 'didn't you?'

'I'm real hungry,' Sammy said, gasping. 'Can I have one of

those frozen hamburgers? You don't have to cook it; I'll eat it like it is. It's better that way – it lasts longer!'

She said, 'You go get into the car. As soon as I've fixed Uncle Ragle a sandwich we're driving down to the store and pick up Dad. And take that old dog back out; he doesn't live here.'

'Okay,' Sammy said. 'I bet I can get something to eat at the store.' The back door slammed as he and the dog departed.

'I found him,' she said to Ragle when she brought in the sandwich and glass of apple cider. 'So you don't have to worry about what he's doing; I'll take him downtown with me.'

Accepting the sandwich, Ragle said, 'You know, maybe I'd have been better off if I'd got mixed up playing the ponies.'

She laughed. 'You wouldn't have won anything.'

'Maybe so.' He began reflexively to eat. But he did not touch the apple cider; he preferred the warm beer from the can that he had been nursing for an hour or so. How can he do that intricate math and drink warm beer? she asked herself as she found her coat and purse and rushed out of the house to the car. You'd think it would muddle up his brain. But he's used to it. During his stint in the service he had got the habit of swilling warm beer day in, day out. For two years he and a buddy had been stationed on a minuscule atoll in the Pacific, manning a weather station and radio transmitter.

Late-afternoon traffic, as always, was intense. But the Volkswagen sneaked through the openings, and she made good time. Larger, clumsier cars seemed bogged down, like stranded land turtles.

The smartest investment we ever made, she said to herself. Buying a small foreign car. And it'll never wear out; those Germans build with such precision. Except that they had had minor clutch trouble, and in only fifteen thousand miles . . . but nothing was perfect. In all the world. Certainly not in this day and age, with H-bombs and Russia and rising prices.

Pressed to the window, Sammy said, 'Why can't we have one of those Mercs? Why do we have to have a dinky little car that looks like a beetle?' His disgust was manifest.

Feeling outraged – her son a traitor right here at her bosom – she said, 'Listen, young man; you know absolutely nothing about cars. You don't have to make payments or steer through this darn traffic, or wax them. So you keep your opinions to yourself.'

Grumpily, Sammy said, 'It's like a kid's car.'

'You tell your father that,' she said, 'when we get down to the store.'

'I'm scared to,' Sammy said.

She made a left turn against traffic, forgetting to signal, and a bus beeped at her. Damn big buses, she thought. Ahead was the entrance to the store's parking lot; she drifted down into second and drove up across the sidewalk, past the vast neon sign that read

LUCKY PENNY SUPERMARKET

'Here we are,' she said to Sammy. 'I hope we didn't miss him.'

'Let's go in,' Sammy cried.

'No,' she said. 'We'll wait here.'

They waited. Inside the store, the checkers finished up with a long line of miscellaneous persons, most of whom pushed the stainless-wire baskets. The automatic doors flew open and shut, open and shut. In the lot, cars started up.

A lovely shiny red Tucker sedan sailed majestically by her. Both she and Sammy gazed after it.

'I do envy that woman,' she murmured. The Tucker was as radical a car as the VW, and at the same time wonderfully styled. But of course it was too large to be practical. Still . . .

Maybe next year, she thought. When it's time to trade in this car. But you don't trade in VWs; you keep them forever.

At least the trade-in is high on VWs. We can get back our equity. At the street, the red Tucker steered out into traffic.

'Wow!' Sammy said.

She said nothing.

2

At seven-thirty that evening Ragle Gumm glanced out the living room window and spied their neighbours, the Blacks, groping through the darkness, up the path, obviously over to visit. The street light behind them outlined some object that Junie Black carried, a box or a carton. He groaned.

'What's the matter?' Margo asked. Across the room from him, she and Vic watched Sid Caesar on television.

'Visitors,' Ragle said, standing up. The doorbell rang at that moment. 'Our neighbours,' he said. 'I guess we can't pretend we're not here.'

Vic said, 'Maybe they'll go when they see the TV set on.'

The Blacks, ambitious to hop up to the next notch of the social tree, affected a loathing for TV, for anything that might appear on the screen, from clowns to the Vienna Opera performance of Beethoven's *Fidelio*. Once Vic had said that if the Second Coming of Christ were announced in the form of a plug on TV, the Blacks would not care to be involved. To that, Ragle had said that when World War Three began and the H-bombs started falling, their first warning would be the conelrad signal on the TV set . . . to which the Blacks would respond with jeers and indifference. A law of survival, Ragle had said. Those who refused to respond to the new stimulus would perish. Adapt or perish . . . version of a timeless rule.

'I'll let them go in,' Margo said. 'Since neither of you are willing to bestir yourselves.' Scrambling up from the couch she hurried to the front door and opened it. 'Hello!' Ragle heard her exclaim. 'What's this? What is it? Oh – it's hot.'

Bill Black's youthful, assured voice: 'Lasagne. Put on some hot water – '

'I'll fix café espresso,' Junie said, passing through the house to the kitchen with the carton of Italian food.

Hell, Ragle thought. No more work for tonight. Why, when they get on some new kick, do they have to trot it over here? Don't they know anybody else?

This week it's café espresso. To go with last week's fad: lasagne. Anyhow, it dovetails. In fact it probably tastes very good . . . although he had not gotten used to the bitter, heavy Italian coffee; to him it tasted burned.

Appearing, Bill Black said pleasantly, 'Hi, Ragle. Hi, Vic.' He had on the ivy-league clothes customary with him these days. Button-down collar, tight pants . . . and of course his haircut. The styleless cropping that reminded Ragle of nothing so much as the army haircuts. Maybe that was it: an attempt on the part of sedulous young sprinters like Bill Black to appear regimented,

13

part of some colossal machine. And in a sense they were. They all occupied minor status posts as functionaries of organizations. Bill Black, a case in point, worked for the city, for its water department. Every clear day he set off on foot, not in his car, striding optimistically along in his single-breasted suit, beanpole in shape because the coat and trousers were so unnaturally and senselessly tight. And, Ragle thought, so obsolete. Brief renaissance of an archaic style in men's clothing . . . seeing Bill Black legging it by the house in the morning and evening made him feel as if he were watching an old movie. And Black's jerky, too-swift stride added to the impression. Even his voice, Ragle thought. Speeded up. Too high-pitched. Shrill.

But he'll get somewhere, he realized. The odd thing in this world is that an eager-beaver type, with no original ideas, who mimes those in authority above him right to the last twist of necktie and scrape of chin, always gets noticed. Gets selected. Rises. In the banks, in insurance companies, big electric companies, missile-building firms, universities. He had seen them as assistant professors teaching some recondite subject – survey of heretical Christian sects of the fifth century – and simultaneously inching their path up with all their might and main. Everything but sending their wives over to the administration building as bait . . .

And yet, Ragle rather liked Bill Black. The man – he seemed young to him; Ragle was forty-six, Black no more than twenty-five – had a rational, viable outlook. He learned, took in new facts and assimilated them. He could be talked to; he had no fixed store of morals, no verities. He could be affected by what happened.

For instance, Ragle thought, if TV should become acceptable in the top circles, Bill Black would have a colour TV set the next morning. There's something to be said for that. Let's not call him 'non-adaptive', just because he refuses to watch Sid Caesar. When the H-bombs start falling, conelrad won't save us. We'll all perish alike.

'How's it going, Ragle?' Black asked, seating himself handily on the edge of the couch. Margo had gone into the kitchen with Junie. At the TV set, Vic was scowling, resentful of the interruption, trying to catch the last of a scene between Caesar and Carl Reiner.

'Glued to the idiot box,' Ragle said to Black, meaning it as a parody of Black's utterances. But Black chose to accept it on face value.

'The great national pastime,' he murmured, sitting so that he did not have to look at the screen. 'I'd think it would bother you, in what you're doing.'

'I get my work done,' Ragle said. He had got his entry off by six.

On the TV set, the scene ended; a commercial appeared. Vic shut off the set. Now his resentment turned toward advertisers. 'Those miserable ads,' he declared. 'Why's the volume level always higher on ads than on the programme? You always have to turn it down.'

Ragle said, 'The ads usually emanate locally. The programme's piped in over the co-ax, from the East.'

'There's *one* solution to the problem,' Black said.

Ragle said, 'Black, why do you wear those ridiculous-looking tight pants? Makes you look like a swabbie.'

Black smiled and said, 'Don't you ever dip into the *New Yorker*? I didn't invent them, you know. I don't control men's fashions; don't blame me. Men's fashions have always been ludicrous.'

'But you don't have to encourage them,' Ragle said.

'When you have to meet the public,' Black said, 'you're not your own boss. You wear what's being worn. Isn't that right, Victor? You're out where you meet people; you agree with me.'

Vic said, 'I wear a plain white shirt as I have for ten years, and an ordinary pair of wool slacks. It's good enough for the retail-produce business.'

'You also wear an apron,' Black said.

'Only when I'm stripping lettuce,' Vic said.

'Incidentally,' Black said, 'how's the retail sales index this month? Business still off?'

'Some,' Vic said. 'Not enough to matter, though. We expect it to pick up in another month or so. It's cyclic. Seasonal.'

To Ragle, his brother-in-law's change of tone was clear; as soon as business was involved – his business – he became professional, close-mouthed, tactical in his responses. Business was never really off, and always on the verge of improving. And no matter how low the national index dropped, a man's personal individual business was unaffected. Like asking a man how he feels, Ragle thought. He has to say he feels fine. Ask him how business is, and he either automatically says terrible or improving. And neither means anything; it's just a phrase.

To Black, Ragle said, 'How's the retail sale of water? Market holding firm?'

Black laughed appreciatively. 'Yes, people are still bathing and washing dishes.'

Entering the living room, Margo said, 'Ragle, do you want café espresso? You, darling?'

'None for me,' Ragle said. 'I had all the coffee I can drink for dinner. Keeps me awake as it is.'

Vic said, 'I'll take a cup.'

'Lasagne?' Margo asked the three of them.

'No thanks,' Ragle said.

'I'll try some,' Vic said, and Bill Black wagged his head along with him. 'Need any help?'

'No,' Margo said, and departed.

'Don't tank up too heavily on that Italian stuff,' Ragle said to Vic. 'It's rich. A lot of dough and spices. And you know what that does to you.'

Black chimed in, 'Yeah, you're getting a little bulgy around the middle there, Victor.'

Jokingly, Ragle said, 'Well what do you expect from a bird who works in a grocery store?'

That seemed to nettle Vic. He glared at Ragle and murmured, 'At least it's a real job.'

'Meaning what?' Ragle said. But he knew what Vic meant. At least it was a salaried job, to which he set out every morning and returned home from every night. Not something he did in the living room. Not a puttering about with something in the daily newspaper . . . like a kid, Vic had said one day during an argument between them. Mailing in boxtops from cereal packages and a dime for his Magic Decoder Badge.

Shrugging, Vic said, 'I'm not ashamed to work in a supermarket.'

'That's not what you meant,' Ragle said. For some obscure reason he savoured these insults directed toward his preoccupation with the *Gazette* contest. Probably because of an inner guilt at frittering his time and energies away, a wanting to be punished.

So he could continue. Better to have an external source berating him than to feel the deep internal gnawing pangs of doubt and self-accusation.

And then, too, it gave him a kick that his daily entries earned him a higher net income than Vic's slavery at the supermarket. And he didn't have to spend time riding downtown on the bus.

Walking over beside him, Bill Black lowered himself, pulled up a chair, and said, 'I wondered if you saw this, Ragle.' He unfolded, in a confidential manner, a copy of the day's *Gazette*. Almost reverently he opened it to page fourteen. There, at the top, was a line of photos of men and women. In the centre was a photo of Ragle Gumm himself, and under it the caption:

Grand all-time winner in the Where Will the Little Green Man Be Next? contest, Ragle Gumm. National champion leading for two straight years, an all-time record

The other persons shown were lesser greats. The contest was national, with newspapers participating in strings. No local paper could afford to pay the tab. Costs ran higher – he had figured one day – than the famous Old Gold contest of the mid-thirties or the perennial 'I use Oxydol soap *because* in twenty-five words or less' contests. But evidently it built circulation, in these times when the average man read comic books and watched . . .

I'm getting like Bill Black, Ragle thought. Knocking TV. It's a national pastime in itself. Think in your mind of all the homes, people sitting around saying, 'What's happened to this country? Where's the level of education gone? The morality? Why rock-and-roll instead of the lovely Jeanette MacDonald and Nelson Eddy *Maytime* music that we listened to when we were their age?'

Sitting close by him. Bill Black held on to the paper, jabbing at the picture with his finger. Obviously he was stirred by the sight of it. By golly, old Ragle Gumm's picture in newspapers coast to coast! What honour! A celebrity living next door to him.

'Listen, Ragle,' Black said. 'You're really making a mint out of this "green man" contest, aren't you?' Envy was rampant on his face. 'Couple of hours at it, and you've got a week's pay right there.'

With irony Ragle said, 'A real soft berth.'

'No, I know you put in plenty of work at it,' Black said. 'But it's creative work; you're your own boss. You can't call that "work" like working at a desk somewhere.'

'I work at a desk,' Ragle said.

'But,' Black persisted, 'it's more like a hobby. I don't mean to knock it. A man can work harder on a hobby than down at the office. I know when I'm out in the garage using my power saw, I really sweat at it. But – there's a difference.' Turning to Vic, he said, 'You know what I mean. It's not drudgery. It's what I said; it's creative.'

'I never thought of it like that,' Vic answered.

'Don't you think what Ragle's doing is creative?' Black demanded.

Vic said, 'No. Not necessarily.'

'What do you call it, then, when a man carves his own future out by his own efforts?'

'I simply think,' Vic said, 'that Ragle has an ability to make one good guess after another.'

'Guess!' Ragle said, feeling insulted. 'You can say that, after watching me doing research? Going over previous entries?' As far as he was concerned, the last thing to call it was 'guessing'. If it were a guess he would merely seat himself at the entry form, close his eyes, wave his hand around, bring it down to cover one square out of all the squares. Then mark it and mail it. And wait for the results. 'Do you guess when you fill out your income tax return?' That was his favourite analogy for his work on the contest. 'You only have to do it once a year; I do it every day.' To Bill Black he said, 'Imagine you had to make out a new return every day. It's the same thing. You go over all your old forms; you keep records, tons of them – every day. And no guessing. It's exact. Figures. Addition and subtraction. Graphs.'

There was silence.

'But you enjoy it, don't you?' Black said finally.

'I guess so,' he said.

'How about teaching me?' Black said, with tension.

'No,' he said. Black had brought it up before, a number of times.

'I don't mean so I can compete with you,' Black said.

Ragle laughed.

'I mean just so I can pick up a few bucks now and then. For

18

instance, I'd like to build a retaining wall in the back, so in the winter that wet dirt doesn't keep slopping down into our yard. It would cost me about sixty dollars for the materials. Suppose I won – how many times? Four times?'

'Four times,' Ragle said. 'You'd get a flat twenty bucks. And your name would go on the board. You'd be competing.'

Vic spoke up. 'Competing with the Charles Van Doren of the newspaper contests.'

'I consider that a compliment,' Ragle said. But the enmity made him uncomfortable.

The lasagne did not last long. They all dipped into it. Because of Bill Black's and Ragle's remarks, Vic felt impelled to eat as much as possible. His wife watched him critically as he finished.

'You never eat what I cook the way you ate that,' Margo said.

Now he wished he hadn't eaten so much. 'It was good,' he said gamely.

With a giggle, Junie Black said, 'Maybe he'd like to live with us for a while.' Her pert, miniature face took on a familiar knowing expression, one that was sure to annoy Margo. For a woman who wore glasses, Vic thought, Junie Black could look astonishingly depraved. Actually, she was not unattractive, But her hair, black, hung down in two twisted thick braids, and he did not like that. In fact he was not drawn to her at all. He did not like tiny, dark, active women, especially those who giggled, and, like Junie, who insisted on pressing against other women's husbands on the strength of a single gulp of sherry.

It was his brother-in-law who responded to Junie Black, according to Margo's gossip. Both Ragle and Junie, being home all day, had plenty of free time on their hands. That was a bad business, Margo said now and again. A man being home all day in a residential neighbourhood, where all the other husbands were away at the office and only the wives remained behind. So to speak.

Bill Black said, 'To confess, Margo – she didn't whip this stuff up. We got it on the way home. At some catering place on Plum Street.'

'I see,' Margo said. 'Well, how nice.'

Junie Black, not embarrassed, laughed.

After the two women had cleared the table, Bill suggested a few hands of poker. They haggled for a while, and then the chips were brought out, and the deck of cards, and presently they were playing for a penny a chip, all colours worth the same. It was a twice-weekly matter between them. Nobody could remember how it had gotten started. The women, most likely, had originated it; both Junie and Margo loved to play.

While they were playing, Sammy appeared. 'Dad,' he said, 'can I show you something?'

'I wondered where you were,' Vic said. 'You've been pretty quiet this evening.' Having folded for the round, he could take a moment off. 'What is it?' he asked. His son wanted advice most likely.

'Now keep your voice down,' Margo warned Sammy. 'You can see we're playing cards.' The intense look on her face and the tremor in her voice indicated that she held a reasonably good hand.

Sammy said, 'Dad, I can't figure out how to wire up the antenna.' Beside Vic's stack of chips he set down a metal frame with wires and electronic-looking parts visible on it.

'What's this?' Vic said, puzzled.

'My crystal set,' Sammy said.

'What's a crystal set?' he said.

Ragle spoke up. 'It's something I got him doing,' he explained. 'One afternoon I was telling him about World War Two and I got to talking about the radio rig we operated.'

'Radio,' Margo said. 'Doesn't that take you back?'

Junie Black said, 'Is that what he's got there, a radio?'

'A primitive form of radio,' Ragle said. 'The earliest.'

'There's no danger he'll get a shock, is there?' Margo said.

'None whatever,' Ragle said. 'It doesn't use any power.'

'Let's have a look at it,' Vic said. Hoisting the metal frame he examined it, wishing he knew enough to assist his son. But the plain truth was that he knew nothing at all about electronics, and it certainly was obvious. 'Well,' he said haltingly, 'maybe you have a short-circuit somewhere.'

Junie said, 'Remember those radio programmes we used to listen to before World War Two? "The Road of Life." Those soap operas. "Mary Martin." '

' "Mary Marlin", ' Margo corrected. 'That was – good lord. Twenty years ago! I blush.'

Humming *Clair de Lune*, the theme for 'Mary Marlin,' Junie met the last round of raises. 'Sometimes I miss radio,' she said.

'You've got radio plus vision,' Bill Black said. 'Radio was just the sound part of TV.'

'What would you get on your crystal set?' Vic asked his son. 'Are there any stations still transmitting?' It had been his impression that radio stations had folded up several years ago.

Ragle said, 'He can probably monitor ship-to-shore signals. Aircraft landing instructions.'

'Police calls,' Sammy declared.

'That's right,' Ragle said. 'The police still use radio for their cars.' Holding out his hand he accepted the crystal set from Vic. 'I can trace the circuit later, Sammy,' he said. 'But I've got too good a hand right now. How about tomorrow?'

Junie said, 'Maybe he can pick up flying saucers.'

'Yes,' Margo agreed. 'That's what you ought to aim for.'

'I never thought of that,' Sammy said.

'There's no such thing as flying saucers,' Bill Black said testily. He fiddled with his cards.

'Oh no?' Junie said. 'Don't kid yourself. Too many people have seen them for you to dismiss it. Or don't you accept their documented testimony?'

'Weather balloons,' Bill Black said. Vic was inclined to agree with him, and he saw Ragle nodding. 'Meteors. Meteorological phenomena.'

'Absolutely,' Ragle said.

'But I read that people had actually ridden in them,' Margo said.

They all laughed, except Junie.

'It's true,' Margo said. 'I heard it over TV.'

Vic said, 'I'll go as far as admitting that there seems to be some sort of odd-ball stuff going on up there.' He remembered one experience of his own. The summer before, during a camping trip, he had watched a bright object flash across the sky at such velocity that no plane, even a jet-propelled plane, could have matched it. The thing had more the manner of a projectile. In an instant it had whisked off over the horizon. And occasionally, at

21

night, he had heard rumblings, as if heavy vehicles were passing at reduced velocity across the sky. Windows had vibrated, so it had not been head-noises, as Margo had decided. In an article in a digest medical magazine she had read that head-noises indicate high blood pressure, and after that she had wanted him to visit their health-plan doctor for a check-up.

He gave the half-finished radio back to his son and resumed playing cards; the next hand had already been dealt and it was time for him to ante up.

'We're going to install this crystal set as our official club equipment,' Sammy informed him. 'It'll be locked up in the clubhouse, and nobody can use it but authorized personnel.' In the back yard the neighbourhood kids, banding together in response to the herd instinct, had built a sturdy but ugly building out of boards and chickenwire and tarpaper. Mighty doings were conducted several times a week.

'Fine,' Vic said, studying his hand.

'When he says "fine",' Ragle said, 'it means he's got nothing.'

'I've noticed that,' Junie said. 'And when he throws down his cards and walks away from the table, it means he's got four of a kind.'

At the moment he felt a little like leaving the table; the lasagne and café espresso had been too much for him, and inside him the compound – that and his dinner – had begun to act up. 'Maybe I have four of a kind now,' he said.

'You look pale,' Margo said. To Ragle she said, 'Maybe he does have something.'

'More like the Asian flu,' Vic said. Pushing his chair back he got to his feet. 'I'll be right back. I'm not out. Just getting something to calm my stomach.'

'Oh dear,' Junie said. 'He did eat too much; you were right, Margo. If he dies it's my fault.'

'I won't die,' Vic said. 'What'll I take?' he asked his wife. As mother of the household she was in charge of the medicines.

'There's some Dramamine in the medicine cabinet,' she answered, preoccupied, discarding two cards. 'In the bathroom.'

'You don't take tranquillizers for *indigestion*, do you?' Bill Black demanded, as he left the room and started down the hall. 'Boy, that is carrying it too far.'

'Dramamine isn't a tranquillizer,' Vic answered, half to himself. 'It's an anti-motion pill.'

'Same thing,' Black's voice came to him, along the hall, following after him as he entered the bathroom.

'Same thing hell,' Vic said, his indigestion making him surly. He groped above him for the light cord.

Margo called, 'Hurry on back, dear. How many cards for you? We want to play; you're holding us up.'

'All right,' he muttered, still groping for the light cord. 'I want three cards,' he called. 'It's the top three on my hand.'

'No,' Ragle called. 'You come back and pick them. Otherwise you'll claim we got the wrong ones.'

He still had not found the light cord that dangled in the darkness of the bathroom. His nausea and irritation grew, and he began thrashing around in the dark, holding up both arms, hands together with thumbs extended and touching; he rotated his hands in a wide circle. His head smacked against the corner of the medicine cabinet and he cursed.

'Are you okay?' Margo called. 'What happened?'

'I can't find the light cord,' he said, furious now, wanting to get his pill and get back to play his hand. The innate propensity of objects to be evasive . . . and then suddenly it came to him that there was no light cord. There was a switch on the wall, at shoulder level, by the door. At once he found it, snapped it on, and got his bottle of pills from the cabinet. A second later he had filled a tumbler with water, taken the pill, and come hurrying out of the bathroom.

Why did I remember a light cord? he asked himself. A specific cord, hanging a specific distance down, at a specific place.

I wasn't groping around randomly. As I would in a strange bathroom. I was hunting for a light cord I had pulled many times. Pulled enough to set up a reflex response in my involuntary nervous system.

'Ever had that happen to you?' he said, as he seated himself at the table.

'Play,' Margo said.

He drew three new cards, bet, met the raises that went around, lost, and then leaned back lighting a cigarette. Junie Black raked in the winnings, smiling in her inane fashion.

'Ever had what happen?' Bill Black said.

'Reached for a switch that didn't exist.'

'Is that what you were doing that took so long?' Margo said, irked at having lost the hand.

'Where would I be used to a light cord hanging from above?' he said to her.

'I don't know,' she said.

In his mind he chronicled all the lights he could think of. In his house, at the store, at friends' houses. All were wall switches.

'You hardly ever run into a cord hanging down any more,' he said aloud. 'That suggests an old-fashioned overhead light with a string.'

'Easy enough,' Junie said. 'When you were a child. Many, many years ago. Back in the 'thirties when everybody lived in old-fashioned houses that weren't old-fashioned yet.'

'But why should it crop up now?' he said.

Bill said, 'That is interesting.'

'Yes,' he agreed.

They all seemed interested.

'What about this?' Bill said. He had an interest in psycho-analysis; Freudian jargon cropped up in his conversation, a sign of his being familiar with cultural questions. 'A reversion to infancy due to stress. Your feeling ill. The tension of the sub-conscious impulses to your brain warning you that something was amiss internally. Many adults revert to infancy during ill-ness.'

'What rubbish,' Vic said.

'There's just some light switch you don't remember con-sciously,' Junie said. 'Some gas station where you used to go when you had that old Dodge that used so much gas. Or some place you visit a few times a week, year after year, like a laundry or a bar, but outside your important visits, like your home and store.'

'It bothers me,' he said. He did not feel like going on with the poker-playing, and he remained away from the table.

'How does your innard feel?' Margo asked.

'I'll live,' he said.

They all seemed to have lost interest in his experience. All except Ragle, perhaps. Ragle eyed him with what might have been cautious curiosity. As if he wanted to ask Vic more, but for some obscure reason refrained from doing so.

'Play,' Junie urged. 'Whose deal is it?'

Bill Black dealt. The money was tossed into the pot. In the other room the TV set gave off dance music, its screen turned down to dark.

Upstairs, in his room, Sammy laboured over his crystal set. The house was warm and peaceful.

What's wrong? Vic wondered. *What did I stumble on, in there? Where have I been that I don't remember?*

3

Thump!

Shaving himself before the bathroom mirror, Ragle Gumm heard the morning paper land on the porch. A muscular spasm shook his arm, at his chin his safety razor burred across his flesh and he drew it away. Then he took a deep breath, closed his eyes for a moment, and, opening his eyes, continued shaving.

'Are you almost done in there?' his sister called through the closed door.

'Yes,' he said. He washed his face, patted on after-shave lotion, dried his neck and arms, and opened the bathroom door.

In her bathrobe, Margo materialized and went immediately past him into the bathroom. 'I think I heard your paper,' she said over her shoulder as she shut the door. 'I have to drive Vic down to the store; could you push Sammy out the front door? He's in the kitchen – ' Her voice was cut off by the sound of water in the washbowl.

Entering his bedroom, Ragle finished buttoning his shirt. He passed judgement on his various ties, discriminated from the group a dark green knit tie, put it on, put his coat on, and then said to himself,

Now the newspaper.

Before he went to get it he began dragging out his reference books, files, graphs, charts, scanning machinery. Today, by dealing with them first, he managed to delay contact with the paper by eleven minutes. He set up the table in the living room – the room was cool and damp from the night, and smelled of cigarettes – and then he opened the front door.

There, on the concrete porch, lay the *Gazette*. Rolled up, held by a rubber band.

He picked it up and slid the rubber band off. The rubber band sprang away and vanished into the bushes by the porch.

For several minutes he read the news items on the front page. He read about President Eisenhower's health, the national debt, moves by cunning leaders in the Middle East. Then he folded the paper back and read the comics page. Then he read the letters to the editor. While he was doing that, Sammy pushed by him and outside.

'Good-bye,' Sammy said. 'See you this afternoon.'

'Okay,' he said, hardly aware of the boy.

Margo appeared next; she hurried by him and to the sidewalk, her key extended. Unlocking the Volkswagen she slid inside and started up the motor. While it heated she wiped moisture from the windshield. The morning air was crisp. Along the street a few children trotted in the direction of the grammar school. Cars started up.

'I forgot about Sammy,' Ragle said, when Vic stepped out of the house and on to the porch beside him. 'But he left on his own power.'

'Take it easy,' Vic said. 'Don't work too hard on your contest.' His coat over his shoulder he descended the steps to the path. A moment later Margo put the Volkswagen into gear, and she and Vic thundered off toward the through-street leading downtown.

Those little cars make a lot of noise, Ragle thought to himself. He remained on the porch reading the newspaper as long as he could; then the cold morning air got the better of him and he turned and went back inside, to the kitchen.

As yet he had not looked at page 16, the page on which the *Where-Will-the-Little-Green-Man-Be-Next?* entry -form appeared. Most of the page belonged to the form; beyond it there was little but instructions and comments on the contest, news of previous winners. The tally-sheet of standings; everybody who was still competing was there, represented in the smallest typeface the newspaper could obtain. His name, of course, was huge.

Unique. In a box by itself. Every day he saw it there. Below his name, other names had' a transient existence, not quite at the threshold of consciousness.

For each day's contest the newspaper presented a series of clues, and these always got read by him as a preliminary to the task of solving the problem itself. The problem, of course, was to select the proper square from the 1,208 in the form. The clues did not give any help, but he assumed that in some peripheral fashion they contained data, and he memorized them as a matter of habit, hoping that their message would reach him subliminally – since it never did literally.

'A swallow is as great as a mile.'

Some oblique stream of association process, perhaps . . . he let the crypticism lie about in his mind, sinking down layer by layer. To trip reflexes or whatever. Swallow suggested the process of eating. And of course flying. Wasn't flying a symbol of sex? And swallows returned to Capistrano, which was in California. The rest of the phrase reminded him of, 'A miss is as good as a mile.' Why great then, instead of good? Great suggested whales . . . the great white whale. Ah, association at work. Flying over the water, possibly toward California. Then he thought of the ark and the dove. Olive branch. Greece. That meant cooking . . . Greeks operate restaurants. Eating, again! Sensible . . . and doves were a gourmet's delight.

'The bell tolled on tee-hee.'

That stuck in his craw. Gibberish, certainly. But it suggested homosexuality. 'Bell.' And the 'tee-hee', the effeminate laugh of the queer, the belle. And the John Donne sermon with the line 'For whom the bell tolls'. Also a Hemingway book. Tee might be tea. Ring bell, get tea served. Tiny silver bell. Mission! The mission at Capistrano, where the swallows returned to! It fitted.

While he was pondering the clues, he heard steps on the front walk. Setting down the paper, he slipped into the living room to see who it was.

Approaching the house was a tall, slim, middle-aged man wearing a baggy, tweedy suit, and smoking a cigar. He had a kindly look, like a minister or a drain-inspector. Under his arm he carried a manila folder. Ragle recognized him. The man represented the

Gazette; he had come visiting a number of times before, some-times to bring Ragle's cheque – which ordinarily was mailed – and sometimes to clear up misunderstandings about entries. Ragle felt dismay; what did Lowery want?

With no haste, Lowery stepped up on to the porch, raised his hand and touched the bell.

Bell, Ragle thought. Minister. Maybe the clues were there to tell him that the newspaper would be sending Lowery to visit him.

'Hi, Mr Lowery,' he said, opening the door.

'Hello, Mr Gumm.' Lowery beamed ingenuously; there was no gravity in his manner, nothing to suggest that any bad news was to be conveyed, or that anything had gone wrong.

'What's the visit for?' Ragle asked, sacrificing manners in the name of need.

Lowery, chewing on his Dutch Master, gazed at him and then said, 'I have a couple of cheques for you . . . the paper thought I might as well deliver them in person, since they knew I'd be driving out this way today.' He wandered about the living room. 'And I have a few things to ask you. Just to be on the safe side. About your entries for yesterday's contest.'

'I mailed in six,' he said.

'Yes, we got all six.' Lowery winked at him. 'But you failed to indicate the order of value.' Opening the manila envelope, he laid out the six entry forms; they had already been photographed, reduced to more convenient size. Handing Ragle a pencil, Lowery said, 'I know it's just an oversight on your part . . . but we have to have them numbered.'

'God damn,' he said. How could he have been in such a hurry? Swiftly, he marked them in order, from one to six. 'There,' he said, returning them. What a stupid oversight. It might have cost him the contest then and there.

Lowery seated himself, selected the entry marked *one*, and for a surprisingly long time studied it.

'Is it right?' Ragle demanded, although he knew that Lowery would not know; the entries had to be sent on to puzzle head-quarters in New York or Chicago, wherever it all was done.

'Well,' Lowery said, 'time will tell. But this *is* the one you mean as your first entry. Your primary entry.'

'Yes,' he said. This was the secret compact between himself and the contest people; he was permitted to submit more than one entry for each day's puzzle. They allowed him up to ten, with the stipulation that they be numbered in order of preference. If the number one entry was incorrect, it was destroyed – as if it had never reached them – and the second was considered, and so on down to the last. Usually, he felt sure enough of the solution to limit his submissions to three or four. The fewer, of course, the better the contest people felt about it. No one else, to his knowledge, had this privilege. It was for the one simple purpose of keeping him in the contest.

They had proposed it, after he had missed the correct solution by only a few squares. His entries generally grouped about tangent squares, but once in a while he was unable to decide between squares quite far apart on the entry form. In those cases, he took a risk; his intuition was not strong. But when he felt the solution to lie in an approximate region, he was safe. One or another of the entries proved correct. In his two and a half years of submissions, he had missed eight times. On those days none of his entries had been correct. But the contest people had allowed him to continue. There was a clause in the rules that permitted him to 'borrow' against past correct entries. For every thirty correct entries he could make one mistake. And so it went. By the use of loopholes he had remained in the contest. No one outside the contest knew that he had ever missed; it was his secret and the contest people's secret. And neither of them had any motive to air it publicly.

Evidently he had become valuable from the standpoint of publicity. Why the public would want the same person to win over and over again he did not know. Obviously, if he won he won over the other contenders. But that was the manner of the public mind. They recognized his name. As it was explained to him, the theory went that the public liked to see a name they could identify. They resisted change. A law of inertia was involved; as long as he was out, the public wanted him – and everyone else – out; as soon as he was in, well, that made it self-perpetuating. The force of stasis worked on his side. The vast reactionary pressures now ran with him, not against him. 'Swimming with the tide,' as Bill Black would put it.

Lowery, seated with his legs crossed, smoking and blinking, said, 'Have you looked at today's puzzle?'

'No,' he said. 'Just the clues. Do they mean anything?'

'Not literally.'

'I know that. I mean, do they mean anything at all, in any way, shape, or form? Or is it just to convince us that somebody up at the top knows the answer?'

'What does that mean?' Lowery said, with a shade of annoyance.

'I have a theory,' Ragle said. 'Not a very serious theory, but it's fun to toy with. Maybe there's no correct answer.'

Lowery raised an eyebrow. 'Then on what basis do we declare one answer a winner and all others incorrect?'

'Maybe you read over the entries and decide on the strength of them which appeals to you the most. Aesthetically.'

Lowery said, 'You're projecting your technique on us.'

'My technique?' He was puzzled.

'Yes,' Lowery said. 'You work from an æsthetic, not a rational, standpoint. Those scanners you constructed. You view a pattern in space, a pattern in time. You try to fill. Complete the pattern. Anticipate where it goes if extended one more point. That's not rational; not an intellectual process. That's how – well, vase-makers work. I'm not disapproving. How you go about it is your business. But you don't dope it out; I doubt if you've ever solved the content of the clues. If you had you wouldn't have asked, matter of fact.'

No, he realized. I never have doped out the clues. In fact, it had never occurred to him that anybody did, that anyone read them and got concrete meanings from them. Such as lining up the first letter of each third word, adding ten, and coming out with the number of a specific square. Thinking that, he laughed.

'Why laugh?' Lowery said, with great soberness. 'This is a serious business. A lot of money is at stake.'

'I was just thinking about Bill Black.'

'Who's that?'

'A neighbour. He wants me to teach him how I do it.'

'Well, if it's done on an aesthetic basis – '

'Then I can't,' Ragle finished for him. 'He's out of luck. That's why I laughed. He'll be disappointed; he wanted to pick up a couple of bucks.'

With a suggestion of moral indignation, Lowery said, 'Does it please you to know that your talent can't be taught? That it isn't a technique in the usual sense . . . it's more a – ' He searched for the word. 'God knows. Obviously, chance plays no role.'

'I'm glad to hear somebody say that.'

Lowery said, 'Can anybody imagine in good faith that you could *guess* correctly, day after day? That's ridiculous. The odds are beyond calculation. Or at least, almost beyond. Yes, we did calculate it. A stack of beans reaching to Betelgeuse.'

'What's Betelgeuse?'

'A distant star. I use it as a metaphor. In any case, we know there's no guesswork involved . . . except perhaps in the final stage. When it's a choice between two or three squares.'

'Then I flip a coin,' Ragle agreed.

'But then,' Lowery said thoughtfully, rubbing his chin and waggling his cigar up and down, 'when it's a question of two or three squares out of over a thousand, it doesn't matter. Any of us could guess it, at that point.'

Ragle agreed.

In the garage of their home, Junie Black crouched before the automatic washer, stuffing clothes into it. Under her bare feet the concrete was cold; shivering, she straightened up, poured a stream of granules from the box of detergent into the washer, shut the little glass door, and turned on the machinery. The clothes, behind the glass, proceeded to swirl about. She set down the box, looked at her wristwatch, and started out of the garage.

'Oh,' she said, startled. Ragle was standing in the driveway.

'I thought I'd drop by,' he said. 'Sis is ironing. You can smell that fine burned-starch smell all over the house. Like duck feathers and phonograph records roasted together at the bottom of an old oil drum.'

She saw that he was peering at her from the corner of his eye. His straw-coloured, shaggy eyebrows drew together and his big shoulders hunched as he clasped his arms together. In the mid-afternoon sunlight his skin had a deep underlying tan, and she wondered how it was achieved. She had never been able to tan that well, try as she might.

'What's that you have on?' he asked.

'Slim-jims,' she said.

'Pants,' he said. 'The other day I asked myself, What's the psychological reason for my admiring women in pants? And then I said to myself, Why the hell not?'

'Thank you,' she said. 'I guess.'

'You look very good,' he said. 'Especially with your feet bare. Like one of those movies where the heroine pads over the sand dunes, her arms to the sky.'

Junie said, 'How's the contest today?'

He shrugged. Obviously he wanted to get away from it. 'I thought I'd take a stroll,' he said. And again he peered at her sideways. It was a compliment to her, but it always made her wonder if she had left a button undone; she could scarcely resist glancing furtively down. But except for her feet and midriff she was well covered.

'Open midriff,' she said.

'Yes, so I see,' Ragle said.

'You like-e?' With her, that passed as humour.

Ragle said, almost brusquely, 'I thought I'd see if you'd like to go for a swim. It's a nice day, not too cold.'

'I have all this housework to do,' she said. But the idea appealed to her; at the public park, on the north end of town, where the uncultivated hills began, were a playground and swimming pool. Naturally the kids used it mostly, but adults showed up, too, and quite often gangs of teenagers. It always made her feel good to be where teenagers were; she had been out of school – high school – only a few years, and for her the transition had been imperfect. In her mind she still belonged to that bunch which showed up in hot rods, with radios blaring pop tunes . . . the girls in sweaters and bobby socks, the boys in blue jeans and cashmere sweaters.

'Get your swimsuit,' Ragle said.

'Okay,' she agreed. 'For an hour or so; but then I have to get back.' Hesitating, she said, 'Margo didn't – see you come over here, did she?' As she had found out, Margo loved to blab.

'No,' he said. 'Margo's off on some – ' He gestured. 'She's busy ironing,' he concluded. 'Involved, you know.'

She shut off the washer, got her swimsuit and a towel, and shortly she and Ragle were striding along across town to the swimming pool.

Having Ragle beside her made her feel peaceful. She had always been attracted to big burly men, especially older ones. To her, Ragle was exactly the right age. And look at the things he had done, his military career in the Pacific, for instance. And his national fame in the newspaper contest. She liked his bony, grim, scarred face; it was a real man's face, with no trace of double chin, no fleshiness. His hair had a bleached quality, white and curled, never combed. It had always struck her that a man who combed his hair was a sissy. Bill spent half an hour in the mornings, fussing with his hair; although now that he had a crewcut he fussed somewhat less. She loathed touching crewcut hair; the stiff bristles reminded her of a toothbrush. And Bill fitted perfectly into his narrow-shouldered ivy-league coat . . . he had virtually no shoulders. The only sport he played was tennis, and that really aroused her animosity. A man wearing white shorts, bobby socks, tennis shoes! A college student at best . . . as Bill had been when she met him.

'Don't you get lonely?' she asked Ragle.

'Eh?'

'Not being married.' Most of the kids she had known in high school were now married, all but the impossible ones. 'I mean, it's fine your living with your sister and brother-in-law, but wouldn't you like to have a little home of your own for you and your wife?' She put the emphasis on *wife*.

Considering, Ragle said, 'Ultimately I'll do that. But the truth of the matter is I'm a bum.'

'A bum,' she echoed, thinking of all the money he had won in the contest. Heaven knew how much it added up to in all.

'I don't like a permanent thing,' he explained. 'Probably I picked up a nomadic outlook in the war . . . and before that, my family moved around a lot. My father and mother were divorced. There's a real resistance in my personality toward settling down . . . being defined in terms of one house, one wife, one family of kids. Slippers and pipe.'

'What's wrong with that? It means security.'

Ragle said, 'But I'd get doubts.' Presently he said, 'I did get doubts. When I was married before.'

'Oh,' she said, interested. 'When was that?'

'Years ago. Before the war.' When I was in my early twenties. I met a girl; she was a secretary for a trucking firm. Very nice girl. Polish parents. Very bright, alert girl. Too ambitious for me. She wanted nothing but to get up in the class where she'd be giving garden parties. Barbecues in the patio.'

'I don't see anything wrong with that,' Junie said. 'It's natural to want to live graciously.' She had got that term out of *Better Homes and Gardens*, one of the magazines she and Bill subscribed to.

'Well, I told you I was a bum,' Ragle grunted, and dropped the subject.

The ground had become hilly, and they had to climb. Here, the houses had larger lawns, terraces of flowers; fat imposing mansions, the homes of the well-to-do. The streets were irregular. Thick groves of trees appeared. And above them they could see the woods itself, beyond the final street, Olympus Drive.

'I wouldn't mind living up here,' Junie said. Better, she thought, than those one-storey tract houses with no foundations. That lose their roofs on the first windy day. That if you leave the hose running all night the water fills up the garage.

Among the clouds in the sky a rapidly moving glittery dot shot by and was gone. Moments later she and Ragle heard the faint, almost absurdly remote roar.

'A jet,' she said.

Scowling upward, Ragle shaded his eyes and peered at the sky, not walking but standing in the middle of the sidewalk with his feet planted apart.

'You think it's perhaps a Russian jet?' she asked mischievously.

Ragle said, 'I wish I knew what went on up there.'

'You mean what God is doing?'

'No,' he said. 'Not God at all. I mean that stuff that floats by every now and then.'

Junie said, 'Vic was talking last night about groping around for the light cord in the bathroom; you remember?'

'Yes,' he said, as they trudged on uphill once more.

'I got to thinking. That never happened to me.'

'Good,' Ragle said.

'Except I did remember one thing like that. One day I was out on the sidewalk, sweeping. I heard the phone ring inside the house. This was about a year ago. Anyhow, I had been expecting a real important call.' It had been from a young man whom she had known in school, but she did not include that detail. 'Well, I dropped the broom and I ran in. You know, we have two steps up to the porch?'

'Yes,' he said, paying attention to her.

'I ran up. And I ran up three. I mean, I thought there was one more. No, I didn't *think* there was in so many words. I didn't mentally say, I have to climb three steps. . . . '

'You mean you stepped up three steps without thinking.'

'Yes,' she said.

'Did you fall?'

'No,' she said. 'It's not like when there's three and you think there's only two. That's when you fall on your face and break off a tooth. When there's two and you think there's three – it's real weird. You try to step up once more. And your foot comes down – bang! Not hard, just – well, as if it tried to stick itself into something that isn't there.' She became silent. Always, when she tried to explain anything theoretical, she got bogged down.

'Ummm,' Ragle said.

'That's what Vic meant, isn't it?'

'Ummm,' Ragle said again, and she let the subject drop. He did not seem in the mood to discuss it.

Beside him in the warm sunlight Junie Black stretched out with her arms at her sides, on her back, her eyes shut. She had brought a blanket along with her, a striped blue and white towel-like wrapper on which she lay. Her swimsuit, a black-wool two-piece affair, reminded him of days gone by, cars with rumble seats, football games, Glenn Miller's orchestra. The funny heavy old fabric and wooden portable radios that they had lugged to the beach . . . Coca-Cola bottles stuck in the sand, girls with long blonde hair, lying stomach-down, leaning on their elbows like girls in 'I was a ninety-eight-pound scarecrow' ads.

He contemplated her until she opened her eyes. She had ditched her glasses, as she always did with him. 'Hi,' she said.

Ragle said, 'You're a very attractive-looking woman, June.'

'Thank you,' she said, smiling up at him. And then she shut her eyes once more.

Attractive, he thought, albeit immature. Not dumb so much as sheer retarded. Dwelling back in high school days . . . Across the grass a bunch of small kids scampered, shrieking and pummelling one another. In the pool itself, youths splashed about, girls and boys wet and mixed together so that all of them appeared about the same. Except that when the girls crawled out on to the tile deck, they had on two-piece suits. And the boys had only trunks.

Off by the gravel road, an ice cream vendor roamed about pushing his white-enamel truck. The tiny bells rang, inviting the kids.

Bells again, Ragle thought. Maybe the clue was that I was going to wander up here with June Black – *Junie*, as her corrupt taste persuades her to call herself.

Could I fall in love with a little trollopy, giggly ex-high school girl who's married to an eager-beaver type, and who still prefers a banana split with all the trimmings to a good wine or a good whisky or even a good dark beer?

The great mind, he thought, bends when it nears this kind of fellow creature. Meeting and mating of opposites. Yin and yang. The old Doctor Faust sees the peasant girl sweeping off the front walk, and there go his books, his knowledge, his philosophies.

In the beginning, he reflected, was the word.

Or, in the beginning was the *deed*. If you were Faust.

Watch this, he said to himself. Bending over the apparently sleeping girl, he said, ' "*Im Anfang war die Tat.*" '

'Go to hell,' she murmured.

'Do you know what that means?'

'No.'

'Do you care?'

Rousing herself, she opened her eyes and said, 'You know the only language I ever took was two years of Spanish in high school. So don't rub it in.' Crossly, she flopped over on her side, away from him.

'That was poetry,' he said. 'I was trying to make love to you.'
Rolling back, she stared at him.

'Do you want me to?' he said.

'Let me think about it,' she said. 'No,' she said, 'it would never work out. Bill or Margo would catch on, and then there'd be a lot of grief, and maybe you'd get bounced out of your contest.'

'All the world loves a lover,' he said, and bending over her he took hold of her by the throat and kissed her on the mouth. Her mouth was dry, small, and it moved to escape him; he had to grab her neck with his hands.

'Help,' she said faintly.

'I love you,' he told her.

She stared at him wildly, her pupils hot and dark, as if she thought – god knew what she thought. Probably nothing. It was as if he had clutched hold of a little thin-armed crazed animal. It had alert sense and fast reflexes – under him it struggled, and its nails dug into his arms – but it did not reason or plan or look ahead. If he let go of it, it would bound away a few yards, smooth its pelt, and then forget. Lose its fear, calm down. And not remember that anything had happened.

I'll bet, he thought, she's astonished every first of the month when the paper boy comes to collect. What paper? What paper boy? What two-fifty?

'You want to get us thrown out of the park?' she said, close to his ear. Her face, uncooperative and wrinkled, glowered directly beneath his.

A couple of people, walking by, had glanced back to grin.

The mind of a virgin, he thought. There was something touching about her . . . the capacity to forget made her innocent all over again, each time. No matter how deeply she got involved with men, he conjectured, she probably remained physically untouched. Still as she had been. Sweater and saddle-shoes. Even when she got to be thirty, thirty-five, forty. Her hair-style would alter through the years; she would use more make-up, probably diet. But otherwise, eternal.

'You don't drink, do you?' he said. The hot sun and the situation made him yearn for a beer. 'Could you be talked into stopping off at a bar somewhere?'

'No,' she said. 'I want to get some sun.'

He let her up. At once she sat up, rising forward to fix her straps and dust bits of grass from her knees.

'What would Margo say?' she said. 'She's already snooping around seeing what dirt she can dig up.'

'Margo is probably off getting her petition presented,' he said. 'To force the city to clear the ruins from its lots.'

'That's very meritorious. A lot better than forcing your attentions on somebody else's spouse.' From her purse she took a bottle of suntan lotion and began rubbing it into her shoulders, ignoring him pointedly.

He knew that one day he could have her. Chance circumstances, a certain mood; and it would be worth it, he decided. Worth arranging all the various little props.

That fool Black, he thought to himself.

Off past the park, in the direction of town, a flat irregular patch of green and white made him think again about Margo. The ruins. Visible from up here. Three city lots of cement foundations that had never been pried up by bulldozers. The houses themselves – or whatever buildings there had been – had long since been torn down. Years ago, from the weathered, cracked, yellowed blocks of concrete. From here, it looked pleasant. The colours were nice.

He could see kids weaving in and out of the ruins. A favourite place to play . . . Sammy played there occasionally. The cellars formed caves. Vaults.'Margo was probably right; one day a child would suffocate or die of tetanus from being scratched on rusty wire.

And here we sit, he thought. Basking in the sun. While Margo struggles away at city hall, doing civic good for all of us.

'Maybe we ought to go back,' he said to Junie. 'I ought to get my entry whipped into shape.' My job, he thought ironically. While Vic plugs away at the supermarket and Bill at the water company I idle away the day in dalliances.

That made him crave a beer more than ever. As long as he had a beer in his hand he could be untroubled. The gnawing unease did not quite get through to him.

'Look,' he said to Junie, getting to his feet. 'I'm going up the hill to that soft-drink stand and see if by any chance they've got any beer. It could be.'

'Suit yourself.'

'Do you want anything? Root beer? A Coke?'

'No thank you,' she said in a formal tone.

As he plodded up the grassy slope toward the soft-drink stand he thought, I'd have to take Bill Black on, sooner or later. In combat.

No telling what colour the man would turn if he found out. Is he the kind that gets down his hunting .22 and without a word sets off and shoots the trespasser of that most sacred of all a man's preserves, that Elysian field where only the lord and master dares to graze?

Talk about bagging the royal deer.

He reached a cement path along which grew green wooden benches. On the benches assorted people, mostly older, sat watching the slope and pool below. One heavy-set elderly lady smiled at him.

Does she know? he asked himself. That what she saw going on down there was not happy springtide youthful frolic at all, but sin? Near-adultery?

'Afternoon,' he said to her genially.

She nodded back genially.

Reaching around in his pockets, he found some change. A line of kids waited at the soft-drink stand; the kids were buying hot dogs and popsicles and Eskimo Pies and orange drink. He joined them.

How quiet everything was.

Stunning desolation washed over him. What a waste his life had been. Here he was, forty-six, fiddling around in the living room with a newspaper contest. No gainful, legitimate employment. No kids. No wife. No home of his own. Fooling around with a neighbour's wife.

A worthless life. Vic was right.

I might as well give up, he decided. The contest. Everything. Wander on somewhere else. Do something else. Sweat in the oil fields with a tin helmet. Rake leaves. Tote up figures at a desk in some insurance company office. Peddle real estate.

Anything would be more mature. Responsible. I'm dragging away in a protracted childhood . . . hobby, like glueing together model Spads.

The child ahead of him received its candy bar and raced off. Ragle laid down his fifty-cent piece on the counter.

'Got any beer?' he said. His voice sounded funny. Thin and remote. The counter man in white apron and cap stared at him, stared and did not move. Nothing happened. No sound, anywhere. Kids, cars, the wind; it all shut off.

The fifty-cent piece fell away, down through the wood, sinking. It vanished.

I'm dying, Ragle thought. Or something.

Fright seized him. He tried to speak, but his lips did not move for him. Caught up in the silence.

Not again, he thought.

Not again!

It's happening to me again.

The soft-drink stand fell into bits. Molecules. He saw the molecules, colourless, without qualities, that made it up. Then he saw through, into the space beyond it, he saw the hill behind, the trees and sky. He saw the soft-drink stand go out of existence, along with the counter man, the cash register, the big dispenser of orange drink, the taps for Coke and root beer, the ice-chests of bottles, the hot dog broiler, the jars of mustard, the shelves of cones, the row of heavy round metal lids under which were the different ice creams.

In its place was a slip of paper. He reached out his hand and took hold of the slip of paper. On it was printing, block letters.

SOFT-DRINK STAND

Turning away, he unsteadily walked back, past children playing, past the benches and the old people. As he walked he put his hand into his coat pocket and found the metal box he kept there.

He halted, opened the box, looked down at the slips of paper already in it. Then he added the new one.

Six in all. Six times.

His legs wobbled under him and on his face particles of cold seemed to form. Ice slid down into his collar, past his green knit tie.

He made his way down the slope, to Junie.

4

At sunset, Sammy Nielson put in a last tardy hour galloping around the Ruins. Together with Butch Cline and Leo Tarski he had dragged a mass of roofing slats into a heap to form a real swell defensive position. They could probably hold the position indefinitely. Next came the gathering of dirt clods, those with long grass attached, for superior throwing.

Cold evening wind blew about him. He crouched behind the breastwork, shivering.

The trench needed to be deeper. Taking hold of a board that stuck up from the soil, he pried and tugged. A mass of brick, ash, roofing, weeds and dirt broke away and rolled down at his feet. Between two split slabs of concrete an opening could be seen, more of the old basement, or maybe a drainage pipe.

No telling what might be discovered. Lying down, he scooped up handfuls of plaster and chickenwire. Bits covered him as he laboured.

In the half-light, straining to see, he found a soggy yellow blob of paper. A phone book. After that, rain-soaked magazines.

Feverishly, he clawed on and on.

In the living room, before dinner, Vic lounged across from his brother-in-law. Ragle had asked him if he could spare a couple of minutes. He wanted to talk to him. Seeing the sombre expression on his brother-in-law's face, Vic said,

'You want me to close the door?' In the dining room, Margo had started setting the table; the noise of dishes mixed with the six o'clock news issuing out of the TV set.

'No,' Ragle said.

'Is it about the contest?'

Ragle said, 'I'm considering dropping out of the contest voluntarily. It's getting too much for me. The strain. Listen.' He leaned toward Vic. His eyes were red-rimmed. 'Vic,' he said, 'I'm having a nervous breakdown. Don't say anything to Margo.' His voice wavered and sank. 'I felt I should discuss it with you.'

It was hard to know what to say to him. 'Is it the contest?' Vic said finally.

'Probably.' Ragle gestured.

'How long?'

'Weeks, now. Two months. I forget.' He lapsed into silence, staring past Vic at the floor.

'Have you told the newspaper people?'

'No.'

'Won't they kick up a fuss?'

Ragle said, 'I don't care what they do. I can't go on. I may take a long trip somewhere. Even leave the country.'

'My gosh,' Vic said.

'I'm worn out. Maybe after I take a rest, six months of it, I'll feel better. I might tackle some manual labour. On an assembly line. Or outdoors. What I want to clear up with you is the financial business. I've been contributing about two hundred fifty a month to the household; that's what it averages over the last year.'

'Yes,' Vic said. 'That sounds right.'

'Can you and Margo make out without it? On the house payments and car payments, that sort of business?'

'Sure,' he said. 'I guess we can.'

'I want to write you out a cheque for six hundred bucks,' Ragle said. 'Just in case. If you need it, cash it. If not, don't. Better put it in an account . . . cheques are good only for a month or so, aren't they? Start a savings account, get your four per cent interest.'

'You haven't said anything to Margo?'

'Not yet.'

At the doorway, Margo said, 'Dinner's almost ready. Why are you two men sitting there so solemnly?'

'Business,' Vic said.

'Can I sit and listen?' she asked.

'No,' both men said together.

Without a word she went off.

'To continue,' Ragle said, 'if you don't mind hearing about it. I thought about going to the VA hospital . . . I can use my veteran's status and get some kind of medical assistance. But I have doubts as to whether it lies in their province. I also thought of using the GI Bill and going up to the university and taking a few courses.'

'In what?'

'Oh, say, philosophy.'

That sounded bizarre to him. 'Why?' he said.

'Isn't philosophy a refuge and a solace?'

'I didn't know that. Maybe it was once. My impression of philosophy is something having to do with theories of ultimate reality and What is the purpose of life?'

Stolidly, Ragle said, 'What's wrong with that?'

'Nothing, if you think it would help you.'

Ragle said, 'I've read some, in my time. I was thinking of Bishop Berkeley. The Idealists. For instance – ' He waved his hand at the piano over in its corner of the living room. 'How do we know that piano exists?'

'We don't,' Vic said.

'Maybe it doesn't.'

Vic said, 'I'm sorry, but as far as I'm concerned, that's just a bunch of words.'

At that, Ragle's face lost its colour entirely. His mouth dropped open. Staring at Vic, he drew himself up in his chair.

'Are you okay?' Vic said.

'I have to think about this,' Ragle said, speaking with effort. He got to his feet. 'Excuse me,' he said. 'I'll talk to you again some time later. Dinner's ready . . . or something.' He disappeared through the doorway, into the dining room.

The poor guy, Vic thought. It certainly has got him down. The loneliness and isolation of sitting around all day . . . the futility.

'Can I help set the table?' he asked his wife.

'All done,' Margo said. Ragle had gone on by, down the hall to the bathroom. 'What is it?' Margo said. 'What's wrong with Ragle tonight? He's so miserable . . . he didn't flunk out of the contest, did he? I know he would have told me, but – '

'I'll tell you later,' he said. He put his arm around her and kissed her; she leaned warmly against him.

If he had this, he thought, maybe he'd feel better. A family. Nothing in the world is equal to it. And nobody can take it away.

At the dinner table, as they all ate, Ragle Gumm sat deep in thought. Across from him, Sammy yammered on about his club and its powerful machinery of war. He did not listen.

Words, he thought.

Central problem in philosophy. Relation of word to object . . . what is a word? Arbitrary sign. But we live in words. Our reality, among words not things. No such thing as a thing anyhow; a gestalt in the mind. Thingness . . . sense of substance. An illusion. Word is more real than the object it represents.

Word doesn't represent reality. Word *is* reality. For us, anyhow. Maybe God gets to objects. Not us, though.

In his coat, hanging up in the hall closet, was the metal box with the six words in it.

SOFT-DRINK STAND

DOOR

FACTORY BUILDING

HIGHWAY

DRINKING FOUNTAIN

BOWL OF FLOWERS

Margo's voice roused him. 'I told you not to play there.' Her tone, sharp and loud, caused him to lose his line of thought. 'Now don't play there. Mind me, Sammy. I'm serious.'

'How did it go with the petition?' Vic asked.

'I got to see some minor clerk. He said something about the city not having funds at the present time. The infuriating thing is that when I phoned last week they said contracts were being let, and work ought to start any day. That just goes to show you. You can't get them to do anything. You're helpless; one person is helpless.'

'Maybe Bill Black could flood the lots,' Vic said.

'Yes,' she said, 'and then all the children could drown instead of fall and crack their skulls.'

After dinner, while Margo washed the dishes in the kitchen and Sammy lay in the living room in front of the TV set, he and Vic talked some more.

'Ask the contest people for a leave of absence,' Vic suggested.

'I doubt if they would.' He was fairly familiar with the pack of rules and he recalled no such provision.

'Try them.'

44

'Maybe,' he said, scratching at a spot on the table top.

Vic said, 'That business last night gave me a real turn. I hope I didn't get you upset. I hope I'm not responsible for your feeling depressed.'

'No,' he said. 'If any one thing's responsible, it's probably the contest. And June Black.'

'Now listen,' Vic said. 'You can do a lot better for yourself than Junie Black. And anyhow, she's spoken for.'

'By a nitwit.'

'That doesn't matter. It's the institution. Not the individual.'

Ragle said, 'It's hard to think of Bill and June Black as an institution. Anyhow, I'm not in the mood for discussing institutions.'

'Tell me what happened,' Vic said.

'Nothing.'

'Tell me.'

Ragle said, 'Hallucination. That's all. Recurrent.'

'Want to describe it?'

'No.'

'Is it anything like my experience last night? I'm not trying to pry. That bothered me. I think something's wrong.'

'Something is wrong,' Ragle said.

'I don't mean with you or with me or with any one person. I mean in general.'

' "The time', " Ragle said, ' "is out of joint." '

'I think we should compare notes.'

Ragle said, 'I'm not going to tell you what happened to me. You'll nod gravely right now. But tomorrow or the next day, while you're standing around down at your supermarket chewing the rag with the checkers . . . you'll run out of conversation and you'll hit on me. And you'll convulse everybody with titillating gossip. I've had enough gossip. Remember, I'm a national hero.'

'Suit yourself,' Vic said. 'But we might – get somewhere. I mean it. I'm worried.'

Ragle said nothing.

'You can't clam up,' Vic said. 'I have a responsibility to my wife and my son. Are you no longer in control of yourself? Do you know what you may or may not do?'

'I won't run amuck,' Ragle said. 'Or at least I have no reason to think I will '

'We all have to live together in the same house,' Vic pointed out. 'Suppose I told you I – '

Ragle interrupted, 'If I feel I'm a menace, I'll leave. I'll be leaving anyhow, probably in the next couple of days. So if you can last that long, everything will be okay.'

'Margo won't let you go.'

At that, he laughed. 'Margo,' he said, 'will just have to let me go.'

'Are you sure you're not just feeling sorry for yourself because your love-life is fouled up?'

Ragle didn't answer that. Getting up from the table he walked into the living room, where Sammy lay watching 'Gunsmoke'. Throwing himself down on the couch, he watched too.

I can't talk to him, he realized.

Too bad. Too darn bad.

'How's the Western?' he said to Sammy, during the mid-point commercial.

'Fine,' Sammy said. From the boy's shirt pocket, crumpled white paper stuck up. The paper had a stained, weathered appearance, and Ragle leaned over to see. Sammy paid no attention.

'What's that in your pocket?' Ragle asked.

'Oh,' Sammy said, 'I was setting up defence bastions over at the Ruins. And I dug up a board, and I found a bunch of old telephone books and magazines and stuff.'

Reaching down, Ragle pulled the paper from the boy's pocket. The paper fell apart in his hands. Stringy slips of paper, and on each was a block-printed word, smeared by rain and decay.

GAS STATION
COW
BRIDGE

'You got these at those city lots?' he demanded, unable to think clearly. 'You dug them up?'

'Yes,' Sammy said.

'Can I have them?'

'No,' Sammy said.

He experienced a maniacal wrath. 'All right,' he said, as reasonably as possible. 'I'll trade you something for them. Or buy them.'

46

'What do you want them for?' Sammy said, ceasing to watch the TV set. 'Are they valuable or something?'

He answered, truthfully, 'I'm collecting them.' Going to the hall closet he reached into his coat, got out the box, and carried it back to the living room. Sitting down beside Sammy, he opened the box and showed the boy the six slips that he had already acquired.

'A dime apiece,' Sammy said.

The boy had five slips in all, but two were so badly weather-damaged that he couldn't read the word on them. But he paid him fifty cents anyhow, took the slips, and went off by himself to think.

Maybe it's a gag, he thought. I'm the victim of a hoax. Because I'm a Hero Contest Winner First Class.

Publicity by the paper.

But that made no sense. No sense at all.

Baffled, he smoothed the five slips out as best he could, and then added them to the box. In some respects he felt worse than before.

Later that evening he located a flashlight, put on a heavy coat, and set off in the direction of the Ruins.

His legs ached already from the hike with Junie, and by the time he reached the empty lots he wondered if it was worth it. At first his flashlight beam picked up only the shape of broken concrete, pits half-filled with spring rain, heaps of boards and plaster. For some time he prowled about, flashing his light here and there. At last, after stumbling and falling over a tangle of rusted wire, he came upon a crude shelter of rubble, obviously made by the boys.

Getting down, he turned his light on the ground near the shelter. And by golly, there in the light the edge of yellowed paper gleamed back at him. He wedged his flashlight under his arm and with both hands rooted until he had dislodged the paper. It came loose in a thick pack. Sammy had been right; it seemed to be a telephone book, or at least part of one.

Along with the telephone book he managed to dig loose the remains of large, slick family magazines. But after that he found himself shining his light down into a cistern or drainage system. Too risky, he decided. Better wait until day.

Carrying the telephone book and magazines from the lot, he started back to the house.

What a desolate place, he thought to himself. No wonder Margo wants the city to clear it. They must be out of their minds. One broken arm and they'd have a lawsuit on their hands.

Even the houses near the lots seemed dark, uninhabited. And ahead of him the sidewalk was cracked, littered with debris.

Fine place for kids.

When he got back to the house he carried the phone book and magazines into the kitchen. Both Vic and Margo were in the living room, and neither of them noticed that he had anything with him. Sammy had gone to bed. He spread wrapping paper on the kitchen table, and then, with care, he laid out what he had got.

The magazines were too damp to handle. So he left them near the circulating heater to dry. At the kitchen table, he began to examine the phone book.

It was not the phone book he was used to. The print had a darker quality; the typeface was larger. The margins were greater, too. He guessed that it represented a smaller community.

The exchanges were unfamiliar to him. Florian. Edwards. Lakeside. Walnut. He turned the pages, not searching for anything in particular; what was there to search for? Anything, he thought. Out of the ordinary. Something that would leap up and hit him in the eye. For instance, he could not tell how old the book was. Last year's? Ten years ago? How long had there been printed phone books?

Entering the kitchen, Vic said, 'What have you got?'

He said, 'An old phone book.'

Vic bent over his shoulder to see. Then he went to the refrigerator and opened it. 'Want some pie?' he said.

'No thanks,' Ragle said.

'Are these yours?' Vic pointed to the drying magazines.

'Yes,' he said.

Vic disappeared back into the living room, taking two pieces of berry pie with him.

Picking up the phone book, Ragle carried it into the hall, to the phone. He seated himself on the stool, chose a number at random, lifted the receiver and dialled. After a moment he heard a series of clicks and then the operator's voice.

'What number are you calling?'

He read off the number. 'Bridgeland 3-4465.'

Then a pause. 'Would you please hang up and dial that number again?' the operator said, in her lofty, no-nonsense voice.

He hung up, waited a moment, and dialled the number again.

Immediately the circuit was broken. 'What number are you calling?' an operator's voice – not the same one – sounded in his ear.

'Bridgeland 3-4465,' he said.

'Just a moment, sir,' the operator said.

He waited.

'I'm sorry, sir,' the operator said. 'Would you please look up that number again?'

'Why?' he said.

'Just a moment, sir,' the operator said, and at that point the line went dead. No one was on the other end; he heard the absence of a living substance there. He waited, but nothing happened.

After a time he hung up, waited, and dialled the number again.

This time he got the squalling siren-sound, up and down in his ear, deafening him. The racket that indicated that he had misdialled.

Choosing other numbers he dialled. Each time he got the racket. Misdial. Finally he closed the phone book, hesitated, and dialled for the operator.

'Operator.'

'I'm trying to call Bridgeland 3-4465,' he said. He could not tell if she was the same operator as before. 'Would you get it for me? All I get is the misdial signal.'

'Yes sir. Just a moment sir.' A long pause. And then, 'What was that number again, sir?'

He repeated it.

'That number has been disconnected,' the operator said.

'Would you check on some others for me?' he asked.

'Yes sir.'

He read off other numbers from the page. Each one had been disconnected.

Of course. An old phone book. Obviously. It was true; probably it was a discarded series in its entirety.

He thanked her and hung up.

So nothing had been proved or learned.

An explanation might be that these numbers had been assigned to several towns nearby. The towns had incorporated, and a new number system installed. Perhaps when the switch to dial phones was made, only recently, a year or so ago.

Feeling foolish, he walked back into the kitchen.

The magazines had begun to dry, and he seated himself with one of them on his lap. Fragments broke away as he turned the first page. A family magazine, first an article on cigarettes and lung cancer . . . then an article on Secretary Dulles and France. Then an article by a man who had trekked up the Amazon with his children. Then stories, Westerns and detectives and adventure in the South Seas. Ads, cartoons. He read the cartoons and put the magazine down.

The next magazine had more pictures in it; something like *Life*. But the paper was not as high-quality as the Luce publications' paper. Still, it was a first-line magazine. The cover was gone, so he could not tell if it was *Look ;* he guessed that it was *Look* or one he had seen a couple of times called *Ken*.

The first picture-story dealt with a hideous train-wreck in Pennsylvania. The next picture-story –

A lovely blonde Norse-looking actress. Reaching up, he moved the lamp so that it cast more light on the page.

The girl had heavy hair, well-groomed and quite long. She smiled in an amazingly sweet manner, a jejune but intimate smile that held him. Her face was as pretty as any he had seen, and in addition she had a deep, full, sensual chin and neck, not the rather ordinary neck of most starlets but an adult, ripe neck, and excellent shoulders. No hint of boniness, nor of fleshiness. A mixture of races, he decided. German hair. Swiss or Norwegian shoulders.

But what really held him, held him in a state of near-incredulity, was the sight of the girl's figure. Good grief, he said to himself. And what a pure-looking girl. How could she be so developed?

And she seemed happy to show it. The girl leaned forward, and most of her bosom spilled out and displayed itself. It looked to be the smoothest, firmest, most natural bosom in the world. And very warm-looking, too.

He did not recognize the girl's name. But he thought, There's the answer to our need of a mother. Look at that.

'Vic,' he said, getting up with the magazine and carrying it into the living room. 'Take a look at this,' he said, putting it down in Vic's lap.

'What is it?' Margo said, from the other side of the room.

'You'd be bored,' Vic said, setting aside his piece of berry pie. 'It's real, isn't it?' he said. 'Yes, you can see under it. No supports. It holds itself out like that.'

'She's leaning forward,' Ragle said.

'A girl, is it?' Margo said. 'Let me look; I won't carp.' She came over and stood beside Ragle, and all three of them studied the picture. It was full-page, in colour. Of course the rain had stained and faded it, but there was no doubt; the woman was unique.

'And she has such a gentle face,' Margo said. 'So refined and civilized.'

'But sensual,' Ragle said.

Under the picture was the caption, *Marilyn Monroe during her visit to England, in connection with the filming of her picture with Sir Laurence Olivier.*

'Have you heard of her?' Margo said.

'No,' Ragle said.

'She must be an English starlet,' Vic said.

'No,' Margo said, 'it says she's on a visit to England. It sounds like an American name.' They turned to the article itself.

The three of them read what remained of the article.

'It talks about her as if she's very famous,' Margo said. 'All the crowds. People lining the streets.'

'Over there,' Vic said. 'Maybe in England; not in America.'

'No, it says something about her fan clubs in America.'

'Where did you get this?' Vic said to Ragle.

He said, 'In the lots. Those ruins. That you're trying to get the city to clear.'

'Maybe it's a very old magazine,' Margo said. 'But Laurence Olivier is still alive ... I remember seeing *Richard the Third* on TV, just last year.'

They looked at one another.

Vic said, 'Do you want to tell me what your hallucination is now?'

'What hallucination?' Margo said instantly, glancing from him to Ragle. 'Was that what you two were talking about, that you didn't want me to hear?'

After a pause, Ragle said, 'I've been having an hallucination, dear.' He tried to smile at his sister encouragingly, but her face remained cruel with concern. 'Don't look so anxious,' he said. 'It's not that bad.'

'What is it?' she demanded.

He said, 'I'm having trouble with words.'

At once she said, 'Trouble speaking? Oh my god . . . that's how President Eisenhower was after his stroke.'

'No,' he said. 'That's not what I mean.' They both waited, but now that he tried to explain he found it almost impossible. 'I mean,' he said, 'things aren't what they seem.'

Then he was silent.

'Sounds like Gilbert and Sullivan,' Margo said.

'That's all,' Ragle said. 'I can't explain it any better.'

'Then you don't think you're losing your mind,' Vic said. 'You don't think it's in you; it's outside. In the things themselves. Like my experience with the light cord.'

After hesitating he at last nodded. 'I suppose,' he said. For some obscure reason he had an aversion toward tying in Vic's experience with his own. They did not appear to him to be similar.

Probably just snobbery on my part, he thought.

Margo, in a slow, dreadful voice, said, 'Do you think we're being duped?'

'What a strange thing to say,' he said.

'What do you mean by that?' Vic said.

'I don't know,' Margo said. 'But in *Consumer's Digest* they're always telling you to watch out for frauds and misleading advertising; you know, short weight and that sort of thing. Maybe this magazine, this publicity about this Marilyn Monroe, is all just a big bunch of hot air. They're trying to build up some trivial starlet, pretend everybody has heard of her, so when people hear about her for the first time they'll say, Oh yes, that famous actress. Personally I don't think she's much more than a glandular case.'

52

She ceased talking and stood silently, plucking at her ear in a repetitious nervous tic. Her forehead webbed with worry-lines.

'You mean maybe somebody made her up?' Vic said, and laughed.

'Duped,' Ragle repeated.

It rang a bell deep inside him. On some sub-verbal level.

'Maybe I won't go away,' he said.

'Were you going away?' Margo said. 'Nobody feels obliged to let me in on anything; I suppose you were going to leave tomorrow and never come back. Write us a post card from Alaska.'

Her bitterness made him uncomfortable. 'No,' he said. 'I'm sorry, dear. Anyhow I'm going to stay. So don't brood about it.'

'Were you intending to drop out of your contest?'

'I hadn't decided,' he said.

Vic said nothing.

To Vic, he said, 'What do you suppose we can do? How do we go about – whatever we ought to go about?'

'Beats me,' Vic said. 'You're experienced with research. Files and data and graphs. Start keeping a record of all this. Aren't you the man who can see patterns?'

'Patterns,' he said. 'Yes, I suppose I am.' He hadn't thought about his talent in this connexion. 'Maybe so,' he said.

'String it all together. Collect all the information, get it down in black and white – hell, build one of your scanners and run it through so you can view it, the way you do.'

'It's impossible,' he said. 'We have no point of reference. Nothing to judge by.'

'Simple contradictions,' Vic disagreed. 'This magazine with an article about a world-famous movie star we haven't heard of; that's a contradiction. We ought to comb the magazine, read every word and line. See how many other contradictions there are, with what we know outside the magazine.'

'And the phone book,' he said. The yellow section, the business listings. And perhaps, at the Ruins, there was other material.

The point of reference. The Ruins.

5

Bill Black parked his '57 Ford in the reserved slot in the employees' lot of the M U D O – Municipal Utility District Office – building. He meandered up the path to the door and inside the building, past the receptionist's desk, to his office.

First he opened the window, and then he removed his coat and hung it up in the closet. Cool morning air billowed into the office. He inhaled deeply, stretched his arms a couple of times, and then he dropped himself into his swivel chair and wheeled it around to face his desk. In the wire basket lay two notes. The first turned out to be a gag, a recipe clipped from some household column describing a way to fix a casserole of chicken and peanut butter. He tossed the recipe into the wastebasket and lifted out the second note; with a flourish he unfolded it and read it.

Man at the house tried to call Bridgeland, Sherman, Devonshire, Walnut, and Kentfield numbers.

I can't believe it, Black thought to himself. He stuck the note in his pocket, got up from his desk and went to the closet for his coat, closed the window, left his office and walked down the corridor and past the receptionist's desk, outside on to the path, and then across the parking lot to his car. A moment later he had backed out on to the street and was driving downtown.

Well, you can't have everything in life perfect, he said to himself as he drove through the morning traffic. I wonder what it means. I wonder how it could have happened.

Some stranger could have stepped in off the street and asked to use the phone. Oh? What a laugh that was.

I give up, he said to himself. It's just one of those deadly things that defies analysis. Nothing to do but wait and see what took place. Who made the call, why, and how.

What a mess, he said to himself.

Across the street from the back entrance of the *Gazette* building he parked and got out of his car, stuck a dime in the parking meter, and then entered the *Gazette* offices by the back stairs.

'Is Mr Lowery around?' he asked the girl at the counter.

'I don't think he is, sir,' the girl said. She moved toward the switchboard. 'If you want to wait, I'll call around and see if they can locate him.'

'Thanks,' he said. 'Tell him it's Bill Black.'

The girl tried various offices and then said to him, 'I'm sorry, Mr Black. They say he hasn't come in yet, but he ought to be in soon. Do you want to wait?'

'Okay,' he said, feeling glum. He threw himself down on a bench, lit a cigarette, and sat with his hands folded.

After fifteen minutes he heard voices along the hall. A door opened and the tall, lean, baggy-tweed figure of Stuart Lowery put in its appearance. 'Oh, hello Mr Black,' he said in his reasonable fashion.

'Guess what was waiting for me in my office,' Bill Black said. He handed Lowery the note. Lowery read it carefully.

'I'm surprised,' Lowery said.

'Just a freak accident,' Black said. 'One chance in a billion. Somebody printed up a list of good restaurants and stuck it in his hat, and then he got into one of the supply trucks and rode on in, and while he was unloading stuff from the truck the list fell out of his hat.' A notion struck him. 'Unloading cabbages, for instance. And when Vic Nielson started to carry the cabbages into the storage locker, he saw the list and said to himself, Just what I need; a list of good restaurants. So he picked it up, carried it home, and pasted it on the wall by the phone.'

Lowery smiled uncertainly.

'I wonder if anyone wrote down the numbers he called,' Black said. 'That might be important.'

'Seems to me that one of us will have to go over to the house,' Lowery said. 'I wasn't planning to go again until the end of the week. You could go this evening.'

'Do you suppose we could have been infiltrated by some traitor?'

'Successful approach,' Lowery said.

'Yes,' he said.

'Let's see if we can find out.'

'I'll drop over tonight,' Black said. 'After dinner. I'll take over something to show Ragle and Vic. By then I can whip up some sort of thing.' He started to leave and then he said, 'How'd he do on his entries for yesterday?'

'Seemed to be all right.'

'He's getting distraught again. The signs are all there. More empty beer cans on the back porch, a whole bagful of them. How can he guzzle beer and work at the same time? I've watched him at it for three years, and I don't understand it.'

Dead-pan, Lowery said, 'I'll bet that's the secret. It's not in Ragle; it's in the beer.'

Nodding good-bye, Black left the *Gazette* building.

On the drive back to the MUDO building, one thought kept returning to him. There was just that one possibility that he could not face. Everything else could be handled. Arrangements could be made. But –

Suppose Ragle was becoming sane again?

That evening, after he left the MUDO building, he stopped by a drugstore and searched for something to buy. At last his attention touched on a rack of ball-point pens. He tore several of the pens loose and started out of the store with them.

'Hey, mister!' the clerk said, with indignation.

'I'm sorry,' Black said. 'I forgot.' That certainly was true; it had slipped his mind, for a moment, that he had to go through the motions. From his wallet he took some bills, accepted change, and then hurried out to his car.

It was his scheme to show up at the house with the pens, telling Vic and Ragle that they had been mailed to the waterworks as free samples but that city employees weren't allowed to accept them. You fellows want them? He practised to himself as he drove home.

The best method was always the simple method.

Parking in the driveway he hopped up the steps to the porch and inside. Curled up on the couch, Junie was sewing a button on a blouse; she ceased working at once and looked up furtively, with such a flutter of guilt that he knew she had been out strolling with Ragle, holding hands and exchanging vows.

'Hi,' he said.

'Hi,' Junie said. 'How'd it go at work today?'

'About the same.'

'Guess what happened today.'

'What happened today?'

Junie said, 'I was down at the launderette picking up your

clothes and I ran into Bernice Wilks, and we got to talking about school – she and I went to Cortez High together – and we drove downtown in her car and had lunch, and then we took in a show. And I just got back. So dinner is four frozen beef pies.' She eyed him apprehensively.

'I love beef pies,' he said.

She got up from the couch. In her long quilted skirt and sandals and wide-collared blouse with the medal-sized buttons she looked quite charming. Her hair had been put up artfully, a coil tied at the back in a classical knot. 'You're real sterling,' she said, with relief. 'I thought you'd be mad and start yelling.'

'How's Ragle?' he said.

'I didn't see Ragle today.'

'Well,' he said reasonably, 'how was he last time you saw him?'

'I'm trying to remember when I last saw him.'

'You saw him yesterday,' he said.

She blinked. 'No,' she said.

'That's what you said last night.'

Doubtfully, she said, 'Are you sure?'

This was the part that annoyed him; not her slipping off into the hay with Ragle, but her making up sloppy tales that never hung together and which only served to create more confusion. Especially in view of the fact that he needed very badly to hear about Ragle's condition.

The folly of living with a woman picked for her affability. . . . She could be counted on to blunder about and do the right thing, but when it came time to ask her what had happened, her innate tendency to lie for her own protection slowed everything to a halt. What was needed was a woman who could commit an indiscretion and then talk about it. But too late to reshape it all, now.

'Tell me about old Ragle Gumm,' he said.

Junie said, 'I know you have your evil suspicions, but they only reflect projections of your own warped psyche. Freud showed how neurotic people do that all the time.'

'Just tell me, will you,' he said, 'how Ragle is feeling these days. I don't care what you've been up to.'

That did the trick.

'Look,' Junie said, in a thin, deranged voice that carried throughout the house. 'What do you want me to do, say I've been having an affair with Ragle, is that it? All day long I've been sitting here thinking; you know what about?'

'No,' he said.

'I possibly might leave you, Bill. Ragle and I may go somewhere together.'

'Just the two of you? Or along with the Little Green Man?'

'I suppose that's a slur on Ragle's earning capacity. You want to insinuate that he can't support both himself and I.'

'The hell with it,' Bill Black said, and went into the other room, by himself.

Instantly Junie materialized in front of him. 'You really have contempt because I don't have your educational background,' she said. Her face, stained with tears, seemed to blur and swell. She did not look so charming, now.

Before he could phrase an answer, the door chimes sounded.

'The door,' he said.

Junie stared at him and then she turned and left the room. He heard her open the front door and then he heard her voice, brisk and only partially under control, and another woman's voice.

Curiosity made him tag along after her.

On the porch stood a large, timid-looking, middle-aged woman in a cloth coat. The woman carried a clipboard, a leather binder, and on her arm was an armband with an insigne. The woman droned on to Junie in a monotone, and at the same time she fumbled in the binder.

Junie turned her head. 'Civil Defence,' she said.

Seeing that she was too upset to talk, Black stepped up to the door and took her place. 'What's this?' he said.

The timidity on the middle-aged woman's face increased; she cleared her throat and in a low voice said, 'I'm sorry to bother you during the dinner hour, but I'm a neighbour of yours, I live down the street, and I'm conducting a door-to-door campaign for CD, Civil Defence. We're badly in need of daytime volunteers, and we wondered if there might be anyone at home at your house during the day who could volunteer an hour or so during the week of his or her time. . . . '

Black said, 'I don't think so. My wife's home, but she has other commitments.'

'I see,' the middle-aged woman said. She recorded a few notes on a pad, and then smiled at him humbly. Evidently she took no for an answer the first time around. 'Thank you anyhow,' she said. Lingering, clearly not knowing how to make her exit, she said, 'My name is Mrs Keitelbein, Kay Keitelbein. I live in the house on the corner. The two-story older house.'

'Yes,' he said, closing the door slightly.

Returning, this time with a handkerchief to hold against her cheek, Junie said in a wavering voice, 'Maybe the people next door can volunteer. He's home during the day. Mr Gumm. Ragle Gumm.'

'Thank you, Mrs – ' the woman said, with gratitude.

'Black,' Bill Black said. 'Good night, Mrs Keitelbein.' He shut the door and switched on the porch light.

'All day,' Junie said. 'Siding salesmen, brush salesmen, home reducing systems.' She gazed at him bleakly, making first one shape and then another from her handkerchief.

'I'm sorry we quarrelled,' he said. But he still had not gotten any dope out of her. The ins and outs of residential daytime intrigues . . . wives were worse than politicians.

'I'll go look at the beef pies,' Junie said. She went off in the direction of the kitchen.

Hands in his pockets he trailed after her, still determined to pick up what information he could.

Stepping from the sidewalk on to the path of the next house, Kay Keitelbein felt her way to the porch and rang the bell.

The door opened and a plump, good-natured man in a white shirt and dark, unpressed slacks greeted her.

She said, 'Are . . . you Mr Gumm?'

'No,' he said. 'I'm Victor Nielson. Ragle is here, though. Come on inside.' He held the door open for her and she entered the house. 'Sit down,' he said, 'if you want. I'll go get him.'

'Thank you very much, Mr Nielson,' she said. She seated herself near the door, on a straight-backed chair, her binder and literature on her lap. The house, warm and pleasant, smelled of dinner. Not such a good time to drop by, she told herself. Too close to the dinner hour. But she could see the table in the dining room; they had not sat down yet. An attractive woman with brown hair was setting the table. The woman glanced at her questioningly. Mrs Keitelbein nodded back.

And then Ragle Gumm came along the hall toward her.

A charity drive, he decided as soon as he saw her. 'Yes?' he said, steeling himself.

The drab, earnest-faced woman arose from the chair. 'Mr Gumm,' she said, 'I'm sorry to bother you, but I'm here for CD. Civil Defence.'

'I see,' he said.

She explained that she lived down the street. Listening, he wondered why she had selected him, not Vic. Probably because of his fame. He had got a number of proposals in the mail, proposals that he contribute his winnings to causes that would survive him.

'I am at home during the day,' he admitted, when she had finished. 'But I'm working. I'm self-employed.'

'Just an hour or two a week,' Mrs Keitelbein said.

That didn't seem like much. 'Doing what?' he said. 'I don't have a car, if you're thinking of drivers.' Once the Red Cross had come by appealing for volunteer drivers.

Mrs Keitelbein said, 'No, Mr Gumm, it's a class in instruction for disaster.'

That struck him as being apt. 'What a good idea,' he said.

'Pardon me?'

He said, 'Instruction for disaster. Sounds fine. Any special kind of disaster?'

'CD works whenever there's a disaster from floods or windstorms. Of course, it's the hydrogen bomb that we're all so concerned about, especially now that the Soviet Union has those new ICBM missiles. What we want to do is train individuals in each part of the city to know what to do when disaster strikes. Administer first aid, speed the evacuation, know what food is probably contaminated and what food isn't. For instance, Mr Gumm, each family should lay in a seven-day store of food, including a seven-day store of fresh water.'

Dubious still, he said, 'Well, leave me your number and I'll give it some thought.'

With her pencil Mrs Keitelbein wrote out her name, address,

and phone number at the bottom of a pamphlet. 'Mrs Black next door suggested your name,' she said.

'Oh,' he said. And it occurred to him instantly that Junie saw it as a means by which they could meet. 'A number of individuals from this neighbourhood will be attending instruction, I take it,' he said.

'Yes,' Mrs Keitelbein said. 'At least we hope they will.'

'Put me down,' he said. 'I'm sure I can make it to class one or two hours a week.'

Thanking him, Mrs Keitelbein departed. The door closed after her.

Good for Junie, he said to himself.

And now dinner.

'You mean you signed up?' Margo demanded, as they seated themselves at the table.

'Why not?' he said. 'It's common sense and patriotic.'

'But you're over your head in your contest.'

'Couple hours a week won't make any difference,' he said.

'You make me feel guilty,' Margo sighed. 'I've got nothing to do all day, and you have. I should go. Maybe I will.'

'No,' he said, not wanting her along. Not if it was going to work out as a means of seeing Junie. 'You're not invited. Just me.'

'That seems unfair,' Vic said. 'Can't women be patriots?'

Sammy spoke up, 'I'm a patriot. Back in the clubhouse we've got the best atomic cannon in the United States, and it's trained to Moscow.' He created explosion-noises in the back of his mouth.

'How's the crystal set coming?' Ragle said.

'Swell,' Sammy said. 'It's finished.'

'What have you picked up?'

'Nothing so far,' Sammy said, 'but I'm just about to.'

'You let us know when you do,' Vic said.

'I just have a few adjustments to complete,' Sammy said.

After Margo had cleared the dinner dishes away and brought in the dessert, Vic said to Ragle, 'Make any progress today?'

'I got it off at six,' he answered. 'As usual.'

'I mean the other business,' Vic said.

Actually he had done very little. The contest work had tied him up. 'I started listing the separate facts in the magazines,' he said. 'Under different categories. Until I get it broken down and listed there's not much I can say.' He had set up twelve categories: politics, economics, movies, art, crime, fashions, science, etc. 'I got to looking up the different auto dealers in the white section, under their brand names. Chevrolet, Plymouth, DeSoto. They're all listed except one.'

'Which one?' Vic said.

'Tucker.'

'That's strange,' Vic said.

'Maybe the dealer has some personal title,' Ragle said. 'Such as "Norman G. Selkirk, Tucker Dealer". But anyhow, I pass it along to you for what it's worth.'

Margo said, 'Why do you use the name "Selkirk"?'

'I don't know,' he said. 'Just selected at random.'

'There's no random,' Margo said. 'Freud has shown that there's always a psychological reason. Think about the name "Selkirk". What does it suggest to you?'

Ragle thought about it. 'Maybe I saw the name when I was going through the phone book.' These damn associations, he thought. As in the puzzle clues. No matter how hard a person tried, he never got them under control. They continued to run him. 'I have it,' he said finally. 'The man that the book *Robinson Crusoe* was based on. Alexander Selkirk.'

'I didn't know it was based on anything,' Vic said.

'Yes,' he said. 'There was a real castaway.'

'I wonder why you thought of that,' Margo said. 'A man living alone on a tiny island, creating his own society around him, his own world. All his utensils, clothes – '

'Because,' Ragle said, 'I spent a couple of years on such an island during World War Two.'

Vic said, 'Do you have any theory yet?'

'About what's wrong?' Ragle inclined his head toward Sammy, who was listening.

'It's okay,' Vic said. 'He's been following the whole thing. Haven't you McBoy?'

'Yes,' Sammy said.

With a wink to Ragle, Vic said to his son, 'Tell us what's wrong, then.'

Sammy said, 'They're trying to dupe us.'

'He heard me say that,' Margo said.

'Who's trying to dupe us?' Vic said.

'The – enemy,' Sammy said, after hesitating.

'What enemy?' Ragle said.

Sammy considered and finally said, 'The enemy that's every-where around us. I don't know their names. But they're every-where. I guess they're the Reds.'

To the boy, Ragle said, 'And how are they duping us?'

With confidence, Sammy said, 'They've got their dupe-guns trained on us dead centre.'

They all laughed. Sammy coloured and began playing with his empty dessert dish.

'Their atomic dupe-guns?' Vic said.

Sammy muttered, 'I forget if they're atomic or not.'

'He's way ahead of us,' Ragle said.

After dinner Sammy went off to his room. Margo did the dishes in the kitchen, and the two men adjourned to the living room. Almost at once the doorbell rang.

'Maybe it's your pal Mrs Keitelbein back,' Vic said, going to the door.

Standing on the porch was Bill Black. 'Hi,' he said, entering the house. 'I've got something for you fellows.' He tossed Ragle a couple of objects, which Ragle caught. Ball-point pens, and good ones by their look. 'Couple for you, too,' Black said to Vic. 'Some firm up north mailed them to us, but we can't keep them. Against a city ruling involving gifts. You have to either eat it up, smoke it up, or drink it up the day you got it, or you can't keep it.'

'But it's all right to give them to us,' Vic said, examining the pens. 'Well thanks, Black. I can use these down at the store.'

I wonder, Ragle wondered. Should we say anything to Black? He managed to catch his brother-in-law's eye. There seemed to be a nod of approval there, so he said, 'You got a minute?'

'I guess so,' Black said.

'There's something we want to show you,' Vic said.

'Sure,' Black said. 'Let's see it.'

Vic started off to get the magazines, but Ragle suddenly said, 'Wait a minute.' To Black he said, 'Have you ever heard of some-body named Marilyn Monroe?'

Black, at that, got an odd, secretive look on his face. 'What is this?' he drawled.

'Have you or haven't you?'

'Sure I have,' he said.

'He's a phony,' Vic said. 'He thinks it's some gag and he doesn't want to bite.'

'Give us an honest answer,' Ragle said. 'There's no gag.'

'Of course I've heard of her,' Black said.

'Who is she?'

'She –' Black glanced into the other room to see if either Margo or Sammy could hear. 'She has about the biggest build there is.' He added, 'She's a Hollywood actress.'

I'll be darned, Ragle thought.

'Stay here,' Vic said. He went off and returned with the picture magazine. Holding it so Black couldn't see it, he said, 'What picture has she made that's supposed to be her best?'

'That's a matter of opinion,' Black said.

'Just name one, then.'

Black said, '*The Taming of the Shrew*.'

Both Ragle and Vic examined the article, but there was no mention of her having done the Shakespeare comedy.

'Name another,' Vic said. 'That one isn't listed.'

Black gestured irritably. 'What is this? I don't get to the movies very much.'

Ragle said, 'According to this article, she's married to an important playwright. What's his name?'

Without hesitation, Black said, 'Arthur Miller.'

Well, Ragle decided, there goes all of that.

'Why haven't we heard of her, then?' he asked Black.

Snorting with derision, Black said, 'Don't blame me.'

'Has she been famous long?'

'No. Not particularly. You remember Jane Russell. That big build-up about *The Outlaw*.'

'No,' Vic said. Ragle also shook his head.

'Anyhow,' Black said, clearly perturbed but trying not to show it, 'they've got the machinery going. Making a star out of her overnight.' He stopped talking and came over to see the magazine. 'What is this?' he asked. 'Can I look at it, or is it secret?'

'Let him see it,' Ragle said.

After he had studied the magazine Black said, 'Well, it's been a few years. Maybe she's dropped out of sight already. But when

Junie and I were going together, before we were married, we used to go to the drive-in movies, and I remember seeing this *Gentlemen Prefer Blondes* that the article mentions.'

In the direction of the kitchen, Vic shouted, 'Hey honey – Bill Black's heard of her.'

Margo appeared, drying a blue willow plate. 'Has he? Well then I guess that clears that up.'

'Clears what up?' Black asked.

'We had a theory we were experimenting with,' Margo said.

'What theory?'

Ragle said, 'It seemed to the three of us that something had gone wrong.'

'Where?' Black said. 'I don't get what you mean.'

None of them said anything, then.

'What else have you got to show me?' Black said.

'Nothing,' Ragle said.

'They found a phone book,' Margo said. 'Along with the magazines. Part of a phone book.'

'Where did you find all these?'

Ragle said, 'What the hell do you care?'

'I don't care,' Black said. 'I just think you're out of your mind.' He sounded more and more angry. 'Let's have a look at the phone book.'

Vic got the book and handed it to him. Black sat down and leafed through it, with the same frenetic expression on his face. 'What's there about this?' he said. 'It's from upstate. They don't use these numbers any more.' He slapped the book shut and tossed it on the table; it started to slide off, to the floor, and Vic rescued it. 'I'm surprised at the three of you,' Black said. 'Especially you, Margo.' Reaching out his hand he grabbed the phone book away from Vic, got to his feet, and started to the front door. 'I'll bring this back to you in a day or so. I want to go through it and see if I can track down some kids Junie went to Cortez High with. There's a whole flock of them she can't find; they're probably married by now. Mostly girls.' The front door closed after him and he was gone.

'He certainly got upset,' Margo said after a pause.

'Hard to know what to make of that,' Vic said.

Ragle wondered if he ought to go after Bill Black and get the telephone book back. But apparently it was worthless. So he did not.

Hopping mad, Bill Black flung open the front door of his house and ran past his wife to the phone.

'What's wrong?' Junie asked. 'Did you have a fight with them? With Ragle?' She came up close beside him as he dialled Lowery's number. 'Tell me what happened. Did you have it out with Ragle? I want to know what he said. If he said there had ever been anything between us, he's a liar.'

'Beat it,' he said to her. 'Please, Junie. For Christ's sake. This is business.' He glared at her until she gave up and went off.

'Hello,' Lowery's voice sounded in his ear.

Black squatted on his haunches, holding the receiver close to his mouth so that Junie couldn't hear. 'I was over there,' he said. 'They got their hands on a phone book, a current or nearly current one. I've got it, now. I managed to wangle it away from them; I still don't know how.'

'Did you find out where they got it?'

'No,' he admitted, 'I got sore and left. It really threw me, walking in there and having them say, "Hey Black – you ever heard of a woman named Marilyn Monroe?" and then trotting out a couple of battered, weather-beaten old magazines and flashing them in my face. That was a miserable few minutes.' He was still trembling and perspiring; holding the phone with his shoulder he succeeded in getting his cigarettes and lighter from his pocket. The lighter slipped from his hand and rolled out of reach; he gazed after it resignedly.

'Oh I see,' Lowry said. 'They don't have Marilyn Monroe. It didn't get fitted in.'

'No,' he said.

'You say the magazines and phone book were weather-beaten.'

'Yes,' he said. 'Very.'

'Then they must have found them in a garage or outdoors. I think probably in that old bombed-out armoury the county used to maintain. The rubble is still there; you people never cleared it.'

'We can't!' Black said. 'It's county property; it's up to them.

And anyhow there's nothing there. Just cement blocks and the drainage system that carried off the r.a. wastes.'

'You better get a city work truck and a few men and pave those lots. Put a fence up.'

'We've been trying to get permission from the county,' he said. 'Anyhow I don't think they found the stuff there. If they did – and I say *if* – it's because somebody salted the ground, there.'

'Enriched, you mean,' Lowery said.

'Yes, a few nuggets.'

'Maybe so.'

'So if we pave over the lots, whoever they are will just enrich a little closer home. And why would Vic or Margo or Ragle be poking around those lots? They're half a mile across town, and – ' Then he recalled Margo's petition. That possibly explained it. 'Maybe you're right,' he said. 'Forget it.' Or the boy Sammy. Well, it didn't matter. He had the phone book back.

'You don't think they looked up anything in it while they had it, do you?' Lowry said. 'Besides the numbers they tried to call.'

Black knew what he meant. 'Nobody looks themselves up,' he said. 'That's the one thing nobody ever turns to, his own number.'

'You have the book there?'

'Yes.'

'Read me what he would have found.'

Balancing the phone, Bill Black turned the tattered, water-crumbled pages of the phone book until he got to the Rs. There it was, all right.

Ragle Gumm Inc., Branch 25	Kentwood 6 0457
Betweeen 5 p.m. and 8 a.m.	Walnut 4 3965
Shipping dept.	Roosevelt 2 1181
Floor One	Bridgefield 8 4290
Floor Two	Bridgefield 8 4291
Floor Three	Bridgefield 8 4292
Receiving dept.	Walnut 4 3882
Emergency	Sherman 1 9000

'I wonder what he would have done if he had happened to turn to it,' Black said.

'God only knows. Gone into a catatonic coma, most likely.'

Black tried to imagine the conversation, if Ragle Gumm had found the number and called it – any of the numbers listed under

Ragle Gumm Inc. Branch 25. What a weird conversation that would be, he thought. Almost impossible to imagine.

6

The next day, after he arrived home from school, Sammy Nielson carried his still-malfunctioning crystal set from the house, through the back yard, to the locked clubhouse.

Over the door of the clubhouse was a sign his dad had got for him down at the store. The man who did the lettering for the store had made it.

NO FASCISTS, NAZIS, COMMUNISTS,
FALANGISTS, PERONISTS, FOLLOWERS
OF HLINKA AND/OR BELA KUN ALLOWED

Both his father and his uncle insisted that it was the best sign to have, so he had nailed it up.

With his key he unlocked the padlock on the door and carried the crystal set inside. After he was in he bolted the door after him, and, with a match, lit the kerosene lantern. Then he removed the plugs from the peep-slots in the walls and watched for a time to see if any of the enemy was sneaking up on him.

Nobody could be seen. Only the empty back yard. Washing hanging from the line next door. Dull grey smoke from an incinerator.

He placed himself at the table, strapped the set of earphones over his head, and began dipping the cat's whisker against the crystal. Each time, he heard static. Again and again he dipped it, and at last he heard – or imagined he heard – faint tinny scratchy voices. So he left the cat's whisker where it was and began slowly running the bead along the tuning coil. One voice separated itself from the others, a man's voice, but too faint for the words to be made out.

Maybe I need more antenna, he thought.

More wire.

Leaving the clubhouse – locked – he roamed about the yard,

searching for wire. He poked his head into the garage. At the far end was his dad's workbench. He started at one end of the bench, and by the time he reached the other he had found a great roll of uninsulated steelish-looking wire that probably was for hanging up pictures or for a wire clothesline if his dad ever got around to putting it up.

They won't mind, he decided.

He carried the picture wire to the clubhouse, climbed the side of the clubhouse to the roof, and attached the wire to the antenna that came up from the crystal set. Out of the two wires he made one vast antenna which trailed the length of the yard.

Maybe it ought to be high, he decided.

Finding a heavy spike he tied the free end of the antenna to it, got his throwing arm limbered up, and then heaved the spike up on the roof of the house. The antenna drooped. That won't do, he thought. It should be tight.

Returning to the house he climbed the stairs to the top floor. One window opened on to the flat part of the roof; he unlatched that window and in a moment he was scrambling out on to the roof.

From downstairs his mother called, 'Sammy, you're not going out on the roof, are you?'

'No,' he yelled back. I *am* out, he told himself, making in his mind a fine distinction. The spike with the antenna dangling from it lay on the sloping part of the roof, but by lying flat and inching along he was able to grab hold of it. Where to tie it?

Only place was the TV antenna.

He tied the end of his antenna to the metal pipe of the TV mast, and that was that. Quickly he crawled back inside the house, through the window, and ran downstairs and out into the yard to the clubhouse.

Shortly he had seated himself at the table, before the crystal set, and was running the bead along the tuning coil.

This time, in his earphones, the man's voice could be heard clearly. And a whole raft of other voices babbled in; his hands shook with excitement as he tuned them apart. From them he picked the loudest.

A conversation of some kind was in progress. He had got it part way through.

'. . . those long kind that look like sticks of bread. Practically break your front teeth when you bite on them. I don't know what they're for. Weddings maybe, where there's a lot of people you don't know and you want the refreshments to last . . . '

The man talked leisurely, the words spaced far apart.

'. . . not the hardness but the anise. It's in everything, even in the chocolate ones. There's one kind, white, with walnuts. Always makes me think of those bleached skulls you find out on the desert . . . rattlesnake skulls, jackrabbit skulls . . . small mammals. What a picture, right? Sink your teeth into a fifty-year-old rattlesnake skull . . . ' The man laughed, still leisurely, almost an actual ha-ha-ha-ha. 'Well, that's about all, Leon. Oh, one more thing. You know that thing your brother Jim said about ants going faster on hot days? I looked that up and I can't find anything about that. You ask him if he's sure, because I went out back and looked at ants for a couple of hours since I talked to you last, and when it got good and hot they looked to be walking around at about the same speed.'

I don't get it, Sammy thought.

He tuned the coil to another voice. This one talked briskly.

'. . . CQ, calling CQ; this is W3840-Y calling CQ; calling CQ; this is W3840-Y asking is there a CQ; is there a CQ anybody; W3840-Y asking for a CQ; CQ; CQ; this is W3840-Y calling CQ; CQ; come in CQ; is there a CQ; this is W3840-Y calling CQ; CQ . . . ' It continued on and on. So he tuned further.

The next voice droned so slowly that he gave up almost at once.

'. . . no . . . no . . . again . . . what? . . to . . . the . . . no, I don't believe so . . . '

This is just crud, he thought in disappointment. But anyhow he had gotten it to work.

He tried further.

Squeaks and hissing made him wince. Then frantic dot-dot noises. Code, he knew. Morse code. Probably from a sinking ship in the Atlantic, with the crew trying to row through the flaming oil.

The next one was better.

'. . . at 3.36 exactly. I'll track it for you.' A long silence. 'Yes, I'll track it from this end. You just sit tight.' Silence. 'Yes, you sit tight. Got me?' Silence. 'Okay, wait for it. What?' Long, long silence. 'No more like 2.8. 2.8. You got that? North East. Okay, Okay. Right.'

He looked at his Mickey Mouse wristwatch. The time was just about 3.36; his watch ran a little off, so he couldn't be sure.

Just then, in the sky above the clubhouse, a remote rumble made him shudder. And at the same time the voice in his earphones said.

'Did you get it? Yes, I see it changing direction. Okay, that's all for this afternoon. Up to full, now. Yes. Okay. Signing off.'

The voice ceased.

Hot dog, Sammy said to himself. Wait'll Dad and Uncle Ragle hear this.

Removing his earphones he ran from the clubhouse, across the yard, into the house.

'Mom!' he shouted, 'where's Uncle Ragle? Is he in the living room working?'

His mother was in the kitchen scrubbing the drainboard. 'Ragle went to mail off his entry,' she said. 'He finished up early.'

'Oh stunk!' Sammy shouted, devastated.

'All right, young man,' his mother said.

'Aw,' he muttered. 'I got a rocket ship or something on my crystal set; I wanted him to hear it.' He whirled about in a circle, not knowing what to do.

'Do you want me to listen?' his mother said.

'Okay,' he said grudgingly. He started from the house and his mother followed along with him.

'I can only listen for a couple of minutes,' she said. 'And then I have to get back in the house; I have a lot to do before dinner.'

At four o'clock Ragle Gumm mailed his registered package of entries at the main post office. Two hours ahead of the deadline, he told himself. Shows what I can do when I have to.

He took a cab back to the block in which he lived, but he did not get off in front of the house; he got off at the corner, by the rather old two-story house, painted grey, with a leaning front porch.

No chance of Margo stumbling in on us, he realized. It's all she can do to run next door.

Climbing the steep flight of steps to the porch he rang one of the three brass doorbells. Far off, past the lace curtains on the door, down the long, high-ceiling corridor, a chime rang.

A shape approached. The door opened.

'Oh, Mr Gumm,' Mrs Keitelbein said. 'I forgot to tell you what day the class meets.'

'That's right,' he said. 'I was walking by and I thought I'd go up the steps and ask you.'

Mrs Keitelbein said, 'The class meets twice a week. At two on Tuesday and three on Thursday. That's easy to remember.'

With caution, he said, 'Have you had good luck signing people up?'

'Not too awfully good,' she said, with a wry smile. Today she did not seem so tired; she wore a blue-grey smock, flat heels, and she lacked the frailness, the aura of the aging spinster lady who kept an altered cat and read detective novels. Today she reminded him more of active churchwomen who put on charity bazaars. The size of the house, the number of doorbells and mailboxes, suggested that she earned at least part of her livelihood as a landlady. Apparently she had divided up her old house into separate apartments.

'Offhand,' he said, 'can you recall anybody I might know who's signed up? It would give me confidence if I knew somebody in the class.'

'I'd have to look in my book,' she said. 'Do you want to step inside and wait while I look?'

'Surely,' he said.

Mrs Keitelbein passed down the corridor, into the room at the end. When she did not reappear he followed.

The size of the room surprised him; it was a great draughty empty auditorium-like place, with a fireplace that had been converted to a gas heater, an overhead chandelier, chairs pushed together in a group at one end, and a number of yellow-painted doors on one side and high wide windows on the other. At a bookshelf, Mrs Keitelbein stood holding a ledger, the kind bookkeepers usually used.

'I can't find it,' she said disarmingly, closing the ledger. 'I have it written down, but in all the confusion – ' She gestured at the disorderly room. 'We're trying to get it set up for the first meeting.

Chairs, for instance. We're short on chairs. And we need a black-board ... but the grammar school has promised us one.' Suddenly she caught hold of his arm. 'Listen, Mr Gumm,' she said. 'There's a heavy oak desk I want to get upstairs from the basement. I've been trying to get somebody all day long to come in and help Walter – my son – get it upstairs. Do you think you could take one end? Walter thinks that two men could get it up here in a few minutes. I tried to lift one end, but I couldn't.'

'I'd be glad to,' he said. He took off his coat and laid it over the back of a chair.

A gangling, grinning teen-ager ambled into the room; he wore a white cheer-leader sweater, blue jeans, and shiny black oxfords. 'Hi,' he said shyly.

After she had introduced them, Mrs Keitelbein herded them down a flight of dishearteningly steep, narrow stairs, to a base-ment of damp concrete and exposed wiring, empty fruit jars matted with cobwebs, discarded furniture and mattresses, and an old-fashioned washtub.

The oak desk had been dragged almost to the stairs.

'It's a wonderful old desk,' Mrs Keitelbein said, hovering critically about. 'I want to sit at it when I'm not at the blackboard. This was my father's desk – Walter's grandfather.'

Walter said, in a croaking tenor voice, 'It weighs around one-fifty. Pretty evenly distributed, except the back's heavier, I think. We can probably tip it, so we can clear the overhead. We can get our hands under it okay; I'll get hold first with my back to it, and then when I get my end up, you can get your hands under it. Okay?' He already had knelt down at his end, reaching behind him to take hold. 'Then when it's up, I'll get my grip.'

From his years of active military life, Ragle prided himself on his physical agility. But by the time he had raised his end of the desk waist-high, he was red-faced and panting. The desk swayed as Walter got his grip. At once Walter set off for the stairs; the desk twisted in Ragle's hands as Walter climbed the stairs.

Three times they had to set the desk down on the stairs, once for Ragle to rest, twice because the desk failed to clear the top and had to be taken in a different grip. At last they had it up and into the big draughty room; with a thump the desk dropped from their stiff fingers, and that was that.

'I certainly do appreciate your kindness,' Mrs Keitelbein said, emerging from the basement and switching off the stairlight. 'I hope you didn't hurt yourself or anything. It's heavier than I thought.'

Her son was contemplating him with the same shyness as before. 'You're the Mr Gumm who's the contest winner?' he asked.

'Yes,' Ragle said.

The boy's kindly face clouded over with embarrassment. 'Maybe I shouldn't ask you this, but I always wanted to ask some guy who wins a lot of money in a contest . . . do you think of it as luck, or do you think of it like earning a big fee, the way a lawyer gets a big fee if he's got something on the ball no other lawyer has? Or like some old painters whose paintings are worth millions.'

'It's a lot of hard work,' Ragle said. 'That's how I think of it. I put in eight to ten hours a day.'

The boy nodded. 'Oh yeah. I see what you mean.'

'How did you get started?' Mrs Keitelbein asked him.

Ragle said, 'I don't know. I saw it in the paper and I sent in an entry. That was close to three years ago. I just drifted into it. My entries won right from the start.'

'Mine didn't,' Walter said. 'I never won once; I entered around fifteen times.'

Mrs Keitelbein said, 'Mr Gumm, before you go I have something I want to give you. You wait here.' She hurried off into a side room. 'For helping.'

He thought, Probably a cookie or two.

But when she returned she had a brightly-coloured decal. 'For your car,' she said, holding it out to him. 'It goes on the back window. A CD sticker; you dip it in warm water, and then the paper slides off and you slide the emblem on the car window.' She beamed at him.

'I don't currently have a car,' he said.

Her face showed dismay. 'Oh,' she said.

With a braying, but good-natured, laugh, Walter said, 'Hey, maybe he could paste it on to the back of his coat.'

'I'm so sorry,' Mrs Keitelbein said, in confusion. 'Well, thank you anyhow; I wish I could reward you, but I can't think how. I'll try to make the classes as interesting as I can; how's that?'

'Swell,' he said. Picking up his coat he moved toward the hall. 'I have to be going,' he said. 'I'll see you Tuesday, then. At two.'

In a corner of the room, on a window seat, somebody had built a model of some sort. Ragle stopped to inspect it.

'We'll be using that,' Mrs Keitelbein said.

'What is it?' he said. It appeared to be a representation of a military fort: a hollow square in which tiny soldiers could be viewed at their duties. The colours were greenish brown and grey. Touching the miniature gun-barrel that stuck up from the top of it, he discovered that it was carved wood. 'Quite real,' he said.

Walter said, 'We built a bunch of those. The earlier classes, I mean. CD classes last year, when we lived in Cleveland. Mom brought them along; I guess nobody else wanted them.' He laughed his braying laugh again. It was more nervous than unkind.

'That's a replica of a Mormon fort,' Mrs Keitelbein said.

'I'll be darned,' Ragle said. 'I'm interested in this. You know, I was in World War Two; I was over in the Pacific.'

'I dimly remember reading that about you,' Mrs Keitelbein said. 'You being such a celebrity . . . every once in a while I come across a little article about you in one of the magazines. Don't you hold some sort of record as the longest contest winner of any of the newspaper or TV contests?'

'I suppose so,' he said.

Walter said, 'Did you see heavy fighting in the Pacific?'

'No,' he said candidly. 'Another fellow and I were stuck on a hunk of dirt with a few palm trees and a corrugated-iron shack and a radio transmitter and weather-measuring instruments. He measured the weather and I transmitted the information to a Navy installation a couple hundred miles to the south of us. That took about an hour a day. The rest of the day I lay around trying to figure out the weather. I used to try to predict what it would be like. That wasn't our job; all we did was send them the readings and they did the predicting. But I got pretty good. I could look up at the sky and that plus the readings gave me enough to go on, so my guesses worked out more times than not.'

'I imagine weather conditions were of prime importance to the Navy and Army,' Mrs Keitelbein said.

He answered, 'A storm could wreck a landing operation, scatter a convoy of supply carriers. Change the course of the war.'

'Maybe that's where you got your practice,' Walter said. 'For the contest. Making book on the weather.'

At that, Ragle laughed. 'Yes,' he said. 'That's what he and I did; we made book on it. I'd say it was going to rain at ten o'clock and he'd bet me it wouldn't. We managed to fritter away a couple of years doing that. That, and drinking beer. When they brought in our supplies once a month they left off a standard ration of beer – standard, we figured, for a platoon. Only trouble was, we had no way to cool it. Warm beer, day after day.' How it took him back to remember all that. Twelve, thirteen years ago . . . He had been thirty-three years old. An employee in a steam laundry when the draft-notice showed up in the mailbox.

'Hey, Mom,' Walter said excitedly. 'I got a real good idea; what about Mr Gumm talking to the class about his military experiences? He could give them a sense of participation; you know, the immediacy of the danger and all that. He probably remembers a whole bunch of training they gave the GIs about safety and what to do under fire and emergency situations.'

Ragle said, 'That's about all there is; what I Q told you.'

'But you remember stories the other guys swapped, about air-raids and bombing,' Walter persisted. 'They don't have to actually have happened to you.'

Kids are all about the same, Ragle thought. This boy talked along the lines Sammy talked. Sammy was ten; this boy was say, sixteen. But he liked both of them. And he took it as a compliment.

Fame, he thought. This is my reward for being the greatest – or longest – winner in the history of puzzle contests. Boys between the ages of ten and sixteen think I'm somebody.

It amused him. And he said, 'I'll wear my full general's uniform when I show up Tuesday.'

The boy's eyes widened; then he tried to stiffen and appear blasé. 'No kidding?' he said. 'A full general? Four star?'

'Absolutely,' he said, as solemnly as possible. Mrs Keitelbein smiled, and he smiled across at her.

At five-thirty, when the store had been closed and locked up, Vic Nielson called the three or four checkers over together.

'Listen,' he said. All day he had been planning this out. The window shades were down; the customers had left. At the registers

76

one of the store's assistant managers had started counting the money and setting the tapes for tomorrow. 'I want you people to do me a favour. It's a psychological experiment. It'll only take thirty seconds. Okay?' Especially he appealed to Liz; she was the power among the checkers, and if she said okay the others probably would.

'Can't it be done tomorrow!' Liz said. She already had her coat on, and she had changed from low heels to high heels. In them she seemed like some majestic three-dimensional pineapple juice display poster.

Vic said, 'My wife's parked out in the lot waiting. If I don't get out there in a minute or so, she'll start honking. So you know this won't take long.'

The other checkers, male, small, watched Liz for her reaction. They still had on their white aprons, and their pencils behind their ears.

'All right,' she said. Waggling her finger at him she said, 'But you better be telling the truth; we better be right out of here.'

He walked over to the produce department, shook a paper bag loose from one of the bins, and began blowing it up. Liz and the other checkers gazed at him dully.

'What I want you to do is this,' he said, throttling the full bag of air. 'I'm going to pop this bag and then I'm going to yell a command at you. I want you to do exactly what I say; don't think about it – just do it when you hear me yell it. I want you to react without giving it any time. You understand what I mean?'

Chewing on a piece of gum that she had pilfered from the candy and gum rack, Liz said, 'Yeah, we understand. Go on, pop and yell.'

'Face me,' he said. The four of them stood with their backs to the wide glass exit door. It was the only door through which any of them passed to get into and out of the store. 'Okay,' he said, and, lifting up the bag, yelled, 'Run!' And then he popped it. As he yelled, the four of them jumped slightly, startled. When the bag popped – its noise in the empty store was terrific – the four of them bolted like hares.

None of them ran toward the door. As a group they ran directly left, toward an upright support pillar. Six, seven, eight steps at it . . . and then they halted, wheezing and disconcerted.

'Now what's this?' Liz demanded. 'What's this about? You said you were going to pop the bag first, and then you went ahead and you yelled first.'

'Thanks, Liz,' he said. 'That's fine. You can go meet your boy friend.'

As they filed out of the store, the checkers gave him a look of scorn.

The assistant manager, counting money and setting tape, said to him, 'Did you mean for me to run, too?'

'No,' he said, only half-hearing him; his mind was on his experiment.

'I tried to duck down under the register,' the assistant manager said.

'Thanks,' he said. Going out of the store, he locked the door after him, and then he crossed the lot toward the Volkswagen.

But in the Volkswagen was a heavy-set black German shepherd which eyed him as he approached. And the front bumper of the car had a deep dent in it. And the car needed a wash.

Talk about psychological experiments, he said to himself. It wasn't his car. It wasn't Margo. He had glimpsed the VW drive on to the lot at about the time she usually came for him. The rest had been supplied by his mind.

He started back in the direction of the store. As he got near, the glass door opened and the assistant manager stuck his head out and said, 'Victor, your wife's on the phone. She wants you.'

'Thanks,' he said, catching the door and passing on inside and over to the wall phone.

'Honey,' Margo said, when he said hello, 'I'm sorry I didn't get down to pick you up; do you still want me to come, or do you want to go ahead on the bus? If you're tired I can get you, but probably it would be faster just to catch the bus.'

'I'll catch the bus,' he said.

Margo said, 'I've been out in Sammy's clubhouse, listening on his crystal set. It's fascinating!'

'Fine,' he said, starting to hang up. 'I'll see you later.'

'We listened to all sorts of broadcasts.'

After saying good night to the assistant manager he walked down to the corner and caught a bus. Soon he was riding home, along with shoppers and employees, old ladies and school children.

A city ordinance forbade smoking in a public conveyance, but he felt disturbed enough to light a cigarette. By opening the window next to him he managed to get the smoke to go out, and not into the face of the woman next to him.

My experiment was a whizzer, he said to himself. It worked better than I wanted.

He had assumed that the checkers would scatter in various directions, one toward the door, one toward the wall, one away from the door. That would have supported his theory that this situation, in which they found themselves, was in some manner episodic. That a good part of their lives had been spent elsewhere, and in an elsewhere that none of them remembered.

But – each should have had his own reflexes. Not the same for all four of them. They had all bolted in the same direction. It had been the wrong direction, but it had been uniform. They had acted as a group, not as individuals.

That meant, simply, that the prior and substantial experiences of the four had been similar.

How could that be?

His theory didn't cover that.

And, smoking his cigarette and manoeuvring the smoke out the bus window, he could not immediately concoct another theory.

Except, he realized, some mediocre explanation; for instance, that the four checkers had attended some sort of function together. They might have lived in a boarding house together, or eaten in the same café over a period of years, been in school together. . . .

We have a hodge-podge of leaks in our reality, he said to himself. A drop here, a couple of drops over in that corner. A moist spot forming on the ceiling. But where's it getting in? What's it mean?

He put his mind into rational order. Let's see how I came across it, he said to himself. I ate too much lasagne, and I hurried away from a poker game, in which I held a medium-fair hand, to take a pill in a dark bathroom.

Is there anything previous to that?

No, he decided. Previous to that it's a sunny universe. Kids

79

romping, cows mooing, dogs wagging. Men clipping lawns on Sunday afternoon, while listening to the ball game on TV. We could have gone on forever. Noticed nothing.

Except, he realized, Ragle's hallucination.

And what, he wondered, is the hallucination? Ragle had never quite got around to telling him.

But it goes something along the lines of my experience, he said to himself. Somehow, in some manner, Ragle found himself poking through reality. Enlarging the hole. Or been faced with its enlargement, perhaps a splitting rent opening up, a great gash.

We can put everything we know together, he realized, but it doesn't tell us anything, except that something is wrong. And we knew that to start with. The clues we are getting don't give us a solution; they only show us how far-reaching the wrongness is.

I think, though, he thought, we made a mistake in letting Bill Black walk off with that phone book.

And what should we do now? he asked himself. Conduct more psychological experiments?

No. One told him enough. The one he had conducted involuntarily in his bathroom. Even this last one had done more harm than good, had introduced confusion rather than verification.

Don't confuse me any more, he thought. I'm bewildered enough now to last me the rest of my life. What do I know for sure? Maybe Ragle is right; we ought to pull out the big philosophy books and start boning up on Bishop Berkeley and whoever the rest of them are – he did not remember any philosophy well enough even to know the names.

Maybe, he thought, if I squeeze my eyes darn near shut, so just a crack of light shows, and I concentrate like hell on this bus, on the weary, hefty old women shoppers with their bulging shopping bags, and the chattering schoolgirls, and the clerks reading the evening paper, and the red-necked driver, maybe they'll all go away. The squeaking seat under me. The smelly fumes every time the bus starts up. The jolting. The swaying. The ads over the windows. Maybe it'll just fade away. . . .

Squeezing his eyes together he tried to dislodge the presence of the bus and passengers. For ten minutes he tried. His mind fell into a stupor. The navel, he thought blearily. Concentration on one point. He picked out the buzzer on the side of the bus opposite him. The round, white buzzer. Go, he thought. Fade away.

Fade away.

Fade

Fa

F

. . .

With a start, he awoke. He had drifted off.

Self-hypnosis, he declared. Nodding off into a doze, like the other passengers around him. Heads lolling together, in time to the motion of the bus. Left, right. Forward. Sideways. Right. Left. The bus stopped at a light. The heads remained on an even angle.

Back, as the bus started.

Forward, as the bus stopped.

Fade away.

Fade

Fa

And then, through his half-closed eyes, he saw the passengers fade away.

Lo and behold! he thought. How pleasant it was.

No. It wasn't fading at all.

The bus and its passengers hadn't faded a bit. Throughout the bus a deep change had begun taking place, and like his experiment in the store it did not fit; it was not what he wanted.

Damn you, he thought. Fade away!

The sides of the bus became transparent. He saw out into the street, the sidewalk and stores. Thin support struts, the skeleton of the bus. Metal girders, an empty hollow box. No other seats. Only a strip, a length of planking, on which upright featureless shapes like scarecrows had been propped. They were not alive. The scarecrows lolled forward, back, forward, back. Ahead of him he saw the driver; the driver had not changed. The red neck. Strong, wide back. Driving a hollow bus.

The hollow men, he thought. We should have looked up poetry.

He was the only person on the bus, outside of the driver.

The bus actually moved. It moved through town, from the

business section to the residential section. The driver was driving him home.

When he opened his eyes wide again, all the nodding people had returned. The shoppers. The clerks. The school children. The noise and smells and chatter.

Nothing works right, he thought to himself.

The bus honked at a car pulling from a parking slot. All had become normal.

Experiments, he thought. Suppose I had fallen through to the street? With fear he thought, Suppose I had ceased to exist, too?

Is this what Ragle saw?

7

When he got home, there was not a soul in the house.

For an instant he was overcome by panic. *No*, he thought.

'Margo!' he called.

All the rooms were deserted. He wandered about, trying to keep control of himself.

And then he noticed that the back door was open.

Going out into the back yard he looked around. Still no sign of them. Ragle or Margo or Sammy; none of them.

He walked down the path, past the clothesline, past the rose arbour, to Sammy's clubhouse built against the back fence.

As soon as he rapped on the door a peep-slot slid open and his son's eye appeared. 'Oh, hello, Dad,' Sammy said. At once the door was unbolted and held open for him.

Inside the clubhouse, Ragle sat at the table, the earphones on his head. Margo sat beside him, at a great sheaf of paper. Both of them had been writing; sheet after sheet was covered with rapid jottings.

'What's going on?' Vic said.

Margo said, 'We're monitoring.'

'So I see,' he said. 'But what are you bringing in?'

Ragle, with the earphones still on his head, turned and with a gleam in his eye said, 'We're picking them up.'

'Who?' Vic said. 'Who's "them"?'

'Ragle says it may take years to find out,' Margo said, her face animated, her eyes bright. Sammy stood stock-still, in a trance of ecstasy; the three of them were in a state he had never witnessed before. 'But we have a way of overhearing them,' she said. 'And we've already started keeping notes. Look.' She pushed the sheaf of paper at him. 'Everything they say; we're writing it all down.'

'Ham operators?' Vic said.

'That,' Ragle said. 'And communication between ships and their field; evidently there's a field very close to here.'

'Ships,' Vic echoed. 'You mean ocean ships?'

Ragle pointed up.

Christ, Vic thought. And he felt then, the same tension and wildness. The frenzy.

'When they go over,' Margo said, 'they come in strong and clear. For about a minute. Then they fade out. We can hear them talking, not just signals but conversation. They kid a lot.'

'Great kidders,' Ragle said. 'Jokes all the time.'

'Let me listen,' Vic said.

When he had seated himself at the table, Ragle passed the earphones to him and fitted them over his head. 'You want me to tune it?' Ragle said. 'I'll tune, and you just listen. When a signal comes in good and clear, tell me. I'll leave the bead at that point."

A signal came in presently. Some man giving information about some industrial process. He listened, and then he said, 'Tell me what you've figured out.' He felt too impatient to listen; the voice droned on. 'What can you tell?'

'Nothing yet,' Ragle said, with no loss of satisfaction. 'But don't you see? We *know they're there.*'

'We knew that already,' Vic said. 'Every time they flew over.'

Both Ragle and Margo – and Sammy, too – seemed a little taken aback. After a pause, Margo glanced at her brother. Ragle said, 'It's a hard concept to explain.'

From outside the clubhouse a voice called, ' . . . hayfeloz. Whirya.'

Margo raised her hand warningly. They listened.

Someone, in the yard, was looking for them. Vic heard footsteps on the path. And then the voice again, this time closer:

'People?'

Softly, Margo said, 'It's Bill Black.'

Sammy slid back a peep-slot. 'Yeah,' he whispered. 'It's Mr Black.'

Lifting his son aside, Vic got down and peeped through the peep-slot. Bill Black stood in the centre of the walk, obviously searching for them. On his face was an expression of aggravation and puzzlement. No doubt he had gone inside the house, finding it unlocked and nobody there.

'I wonder what he wants,' Margo said. 'Maybe if we keep quiet he'll go away. Probably wants us all to have dinner with them, or go out somewhere.

They waited.

Bill Black strolled about aimlessly, kicking at the grass. 'Hey fellows!' he called. 'Where the heck are you?'

Silence.

'I'd sure feel silly if he caught us hiding in here,' Margo said with a nervous laugh. 'It's as if we were children or something. He certainly looks funny, craning his neck like that, trying to spot us. As if he thought we were hiding in the tall grass.'

Mounted on the wall of the clubhouse was a toy gun that Vic had given his son one Christmas. It had fins and coils sticking up from it, and the box had described it as a 'Robot Rocket Blaster from the 23rd Century, Capable of Destroying Mountains.' Sammy had scampered about clicking it for a few weeks, and then the spring had broken and the gun had gone up on the wall, trophy-like, to scare by its presence alone.

Vic lifted the gun down. He unlocked the clubhouse door, pushed it open, and stepped out.

Standing with his back to him, Bill Black called, 'Hey, people! Where are you?'

Vic crouched down and held the gun up, pointed at Black. 'You're a dead man,' he said.

Spinning to face him, Black saw the gun. He blanched and half-raised his arms. Then he noticed the clubhouse, Ragle and Margo and Sammy peeping out, and the fins and coils and bright enamel of the gun. His hands dropped and he said, 'Ha-ha.'

'Ha-ha,' Vic said.

'What are you doing?' Black said. From inside the Nielsons' house, Junie Black appeared. She descended the porch steps, slowly, to join her husband; both she and Bill frowned and drew together. She put her arm around his waist. Black said nothing, then.

'Hi,' Junie said.

Margo stepped from the clubhouse. 'What were you doing?' she asked Junie in a voice that any woman would shrink at. 'Just making yourself at home in our house?'

The Blacks gazed at them.

'Oh come on,' Margo said, standing with her arms folded. 'Just make yourself at home.'

'Take it easy,' Vic said.

To him, his wife said, 'Yes, they just walked right in. Into every room, I imagine. How did you find it?' she asked Junie. 'Beds made properly? Any dust on the curtains? Find anything you liked?'

Ragle and Sammy came out of the clubhouse and joined Vic and his wife. The four of them faced Bill and Junie Black.

At last Black said, 'I apologize for trespassing on your property. We wondered if you'd like to go bowling with us tonight.'

Beside her husband, Junie smiled idiotically. Vic felt a little sorry for her. She had clearly no idea that she would offend any-one; probably she had not even been conscious of transgression. In her sweater and blue cotton trousers, her hair tied up with a ribbon, she looked very cute and childlike.

'I'm sorry,' Margo said. 'But you shouldn't barge into other people's houses, you know that, Junie.'

Junie drew back, flinching and unhinged. 'I – ' she murmured.

'I said I apologize,' Black said. 'What do you want, for Christ's sake?' He seemed equally perturbed.

Vic put out his hand and they shook hands. All was over.

'You stay if you want,' Vic said to Ragle, indicating the club-house. 'We'll go on inside and see about dinner.'

'What do you have in there?' Black said. 'I mean if it's none of my business, tell me. But you're sure in a serious mood.'

Sammy spoke up, 'You can't come in the clubhouse.'

'Why not?' Junie said.

'You're not members,' Sammy said.

'Can we join?' Junie asked.

'No,' Sammy said.

'Why not?'

'You just can't,' Sammy said, glancing at his father.

'That's right,' Vic said. 'I'm sorry.'

He and Margo and the Blacks walked up the steps, on to the back porch of the house. 'We haven't had dinner,' Margo said, still tense with hostility.

'We didn't mean go bowling now,' Junie protested. 'We just wanted to catch you before you made plans. Look, kids, if you haven't started dinner, why don't you come over and eat with us? We've got a leg of lamb, and there's plenty of frozen peas and Bill picked up a quart of ice cream on the way home from work.' She appealed to Margo with tremulous urgency. 'What say?'

'Thanks,' Margo said, 'but maybe some other time.'

Bill Black did not seem to have quite calmed down; he kept aloof from them, dignified and somewhat cool. 'You know you're always welcome in our house,' he said. He led his wife in the direction of the front door. 'If you feel like going bowling with us, drop over about eight. If not – ' He shrugged. 'Well, no harm done.'

'We'll see you,' Junie called, as Bill led her out of the house. 'I hope you'll come.' She smiled yearningly at them, and then the door shut after them.

'What a pill,' Margo said. Opening the hot-water tap she ran water into a kettle.

Vic said. 'A whole psychological technique could be erected on how people act when they're startled, before they have time to think.'

As she fixed dinner, Margo said, 'Bill Black just seems rational. He put up his hands until he saw it was only a toy gun and then he put them down again.'

Vic said, 'What are the chances of his wandering over at that particular moment?'

'One of them is always over here. You know how they are.'

'True,' he said.

In the locked clubhouse, Ragle Gumm sat with the earphones on, monitoring a strong signal and making occasional notes. Over the years, in his contest work he had learned excellent systems of quick notation, all his own; as he listened he not only made a permanent record of what he heard but he also jotted down comments and the ideas and reactions of his own. His ball-point pen – one that Bill Black had given him – flew.

Watching him, Sammy said, 'You sure write fast, Uncle Ragle. Can you read it when you get finished?'

'Yes,' he said.

The signal, beyond a doubt, emanated from the nearby landing field. He had got so he recognized the voice of the operator. What he wanted to find out was the nature of the traffic coming into and leaving the field. Where did they go? They shot overhead at terrific speed. How fast? Why did nobody in town know about the flights? Was it a secret military installation, some new experimental ships that the public was ignorant of? Reconnaissance missiles . . . tracking devices . . .

Sammy said, 'I'll bet you helped crack the Japanese code during World War Two.'

Hearing the boy say that, Ragle once again had a sudden and complete sensation of futility. Shut up in a child's clubhouse, an earphone pressed to his head, listening for hours to a crystal set built by a grammar-school child . . . listening to ham operators and traffic instructions like a school child himself.

I must be crazy, he said to himself.

I'm the man who's supposed to have fought in a war. I'm forty-six years old, supposedly an adult.

Yes, he thought. And I'm a man who lies around the house scrounging a living by filling out *Where Will the Little Green Man Be Next?* Puzzles in a newspaper contest. While other adults have jobs, wives, homes of their own.

I'm a retarded – psychotic. Hallucinations. Yes, he thought. Insane. Infantile and lunatic. What am I doing, sitting here? Daydreams, at best. Fantasies about rocket ships shooting by overhead, armies and conspiracies. Paranoia.

A paranoiac psychosis. Imagining that I'm the centre of a vast effort by millions of men and women, involving billions of dollars and infinite work . . . a universe revolving around me. Every molecule acting with me in mind. An outward radiation of importance . . . to the stars. Ragle Gumm the object of the whole cosmic process, from the inception to final entropy. All matter and spirit, in order to wheel about me.

Sammy said, 'Uncle Ragle, do you think you can crack their code, like the Japanese code?'

Rousing himself he said, 'There's no code. They're just talking like anybody. It's some man sitting in a control tower watching military aircraft land.' He turned toward the boy, who was watching him with fixed intensity. 'Some fellow in his thirties who shoots pool once a week and enjoys TV. Like we do.'

'One of the enemy,' Sammy said.

With anger, Ragle said, 'Forget that kind of talk. Why do you say that? It's all in your mind.' My fault, he realized. I put it there.

In his earphones the voice said, '. . . all right, LF-3488. I have it down in corrected form. You can go ahead. Yes, you should be practically overhead.'

The clubhouse shook.

'There one goes,' Sammy said excitedly.

The voice continued, '. . . entirely clear. No, it's fine. You're passing over him now.'

Him, Ragle thought.

'. . . down there,' the voice said. 'Yes, you're looking down at Ragle Gumm himself. Okay, we have you. Let go.'

The vibrations subsided.

'It's gone,' Sammy said. 'Maybe it landed.'

Setting down the earphones, Ragle Gumm got to his feet. 'You listen for a while,' he said.

'Where are you going?' Sammy asked.

'For a walk,' Ragle said. He unlocked the door of the club-house and stepped outside, into the fresh, brisk, evening air.

The kitchen light of the house . . . his sister and brother-in-law in the kitchen. Fixing dinner.

I'm leaving, Ragle said to himself. I'm getting out of here. I meant to before. Now I can't wait.

Walking carefully down the path around the side of the house, he reached the front porch; he entered the house and got into his room without either Vic or Margo hearing him. There, he gathered up all the money he could find in his assorted dresser drawers, clothes, unopened envelopes, change from a jar. Putting on a coat he left the house by the front door and walked rapidly off down the sidewalk.

A block or so away, a cab approached. He waved his arms and the cab stopped.

'Take me to the Greyhound bus station,' he told the driver.

'Yes, Mr Gumm,' the driver said.

'You recognize me?' Here it was again, the projection of the paranoiac infantile personality: the infinite ego. Everyone aware of me, thinking about me.

'Sure,' the driver said, as he started up his cab. 'You're that contest winner. I saw your picture in the paper and I remarked, Why, that guy lives right here in town. Maybe one day I'll pick him up in my cab.'

So it was legitimate, Ragle thought. The odd blurring of reality and his insanity. Genuine fame, plus the fantasy fame.

When cab drivers recognize me, he decided, it's probably not in my mind. But when the heavens open and God speaks to me by name . . . that's when the psychosis takes over.

It would be hard to distinguish.

The cab moved along the dark streets, past houses and stores. At last, in the downtown business section, it drew up before a five-story building and stopped at the curb.

'Here you are, Mr Gumm,' the driver said, starting to leap out to open the door.

Reaching into his coat for his wallet, Ragle stepped from the cab. He glanced up at the building as the driver reached for the bill.

In the street light the building was familiar. Even at night he recognized it.

It was the *Gazette* building.

Getting back into the cab he said, 'I want to go to the Greyhound bus station.'

'What?' the driver said, thunderstruck. 'Is that what you told me? I'll be darned – of course it was.' He jumped back in and started up the engine. 'Sure, I remember. But we got to talking about that contest of yours, and I got to thinking about the newspaper.' As he drove he swung his head around, grinning back at Ragle. 'I've got you so tied in with the *Gazette* in my mind – what a sap I am.'

'It's okay,' Ragle said.

They drove on and on. Eventually he lost track of the streets.

He had no idea where they were; the nocturnal shapes of closed-up factories lay off to the right, and what appeared to be railroad tracks. Several times the cab bucked and floundered as it passed over tracks. He saw vacant lots . . . an industrial district, with no lights showing.

I wonder, Ragle thought. What would the cab driver say if I asked him to drive me out of town?

Leaning forward he tapped the driver on the shoulder. 'Hey,' he said.

'Yes, Mr Gumm,' the driver said.

'What about driving me out of town? Let's forget the bus.'

'I'm sorry, sir,' the driver said. 'I can't get out on the road between towns. There's a rule against it. We're city carriers; we can't compete with the bus line. It's an ordinance.'

'You ought to be able to make a few extra bucks on the side. Forty-mile trip with your meter running – I'll bet you've done it, ordinance or no ordinance.'

'No, I never done that,' the driver said. 'Some other drivers maybe, but not me. I don't want to lose my permit. If the highway patrol catches a city cab out on the highway, they haul it right down, and if it's got a fare in it, bam, there goes the driver's permit. A fifty-buck permit. And his livelihood.'

To himself, Ragle thought, Are they out to keep me from leaving the town? Is this a plot on their part?

My lunacy again, he thought.

Or is it?

How can I tell? What proof do I have?

A blue neon glow hung in the centre of a limitless flat field. The cab approached it and stopped at a curb. 'Here we are,' the driver said. 'This is the bus station.'

Opening the door, Ragle got out on to the sidewalk. The sign did not read Greyhound; it read NONPAREIL COACH LINES.

'Hey,' he said, jolted. 'I said Greyhound.'

'This is Greyhound,' the cab driver said. 'The same as. It's the bus line. There isn't any Greyhound here. The state only allows one bus line to be franchised for a town this size. Nonpareil got in here years ago, before Greyhound. Greyhound tried to buy them out, but they wouldn't sell. Then Greyhound tried – '

'Okay,' Ragle said. He paid the fare, tipped the driver, and walked across the sidewalk to the square brick building, the only building for miles around. On each side of it weeds grew. Weeds and broken bottles . . . litter of paper. Deserted region, he thought. At the edge of town. Far off he could see the sign of a gas station, and beyond that street lights. Nothing else. The night air made him shiver as he opened the wooden door and stepped into the waiting room.

A great blast of rackety, distorted sound and tired blue air rolled out over him. The waiting room, packed with people, confronted him. The benches had already been taken over by sleeping sailors and despondent, exhausted-looking pregnant women, by old men in overcoats, salesmen with their sample cases, children dressed up and fretting and squirming. A long line stood between him and the ticket window. He could see, without going any farther, that the line was not moving.

He closed the door after him and joined the line. Nobody paid any attention to him. This is one time I wish my psychosis would come true, he thought to himself. I'd like to have all this revolve around me, at least to the extent of making the ticket window available to me.

How often, he wondered, does Nonpareil Lines run its buses?

He lit a cigarette and tried to make himself comfortable. By leaning against the wall he could take some weight off his legs. But it did not help much. How long will I be tied up here? he asked himself.

A half hour later he had moved forward only a few inches. And no one had left the window. Craning his neck, he tried to see the clerk behind the window. He could not. A wide, elderly woman in a black coat held the first place in line; her back was to him and he assumed that she was involved in buying her ticket. But she did not finish. The transaction did not end. Behind her a thin middle-aged man in a double-breasted suit gnawed on a toothpick and looked bored. After him a young couple murmured together, intent on their own conversation. And after that the line merged into itself, and he could make out nothing but the back of the man ahead of him.

After forty-five minutes he still stood in the same spot. Can a lunatic go out of his mind? he wondered. What does it take to get a ticket on the Nonpareil Lines? Will I be here forever?

A growing fright began to settle over him. Maybe he would stand in this line until he died. Unchanging reality . . . the same man ahead of him, the same young soldier behind him, the same unhappy, empty-eyed woman seated on the bench across from him.

Behind him, the young soldier stirred fitfully, bumped against him and muttered, 'Sorry, buddy.'

He grunted back.

The soldier locked his hands together and cracked his knuckles. He licked his lips and then he said to Ragle, 'Hey, buddy, can I ask you a favour? Will you hold my place in line?' Before Ragle could answer, the soldier turned to the woman standing behind him. 'Lady, I got to go make sure my buddy's okay; can I get back in line here without losing my place?'

The woman nodded.

'Thanks,' the soldier said, and pushed a passage through the people, over to the corner of the waiting room.

In the corner another soldier sat with his legs apart, his face resting on his knee, his arms hanging down. His compatriot dropped down next to him, shook him, and began talking urgently to him. The bent-over soldier raised his head, and Ragle saw the bleary eyes and twisted, slack mouth of the drunk.

Poor guy, he thought to himself. Out on a toot. During his own days in the service he had several times wound up in a dismal bus station with a hangover, trying to get back to the base.

The soldier sprinted back to his place in line. Agitated, he plucked at his lip, glanced up at Ragle and said, 'This here line; it isn't moving one bit. I think I must have been standing here since five this afternoon.' He had a smooth young face, tormented now by anxiety. 'I have to get back to my base,' he said. 'Phil and I have to be in by eight o'clock or we're AWOL.'

To Ragle, he appeared to be eighteen or nineteen. Blond, somewhat thin. Clearly, he of the two of them did the problem-solving.

'Too bad,' Ragle said. 'How far's your base?'

'It's the airfield up the highway,' the soldier said. 'The missile base, actually. Used to be an airfield.'

Ragle thought, By god. Where those things take off and land. 'You've been hitting the bars down here?' he said, in as conversational a voice as he could manage.

The soldier said, 'Hell no, not in this jerkwater dump.' His disgust was enormous. 'No, we come all the way in from the Coast; we had a week furlough. Driving.'

'Driving,' Ragle repeated. 'Well, why are you in here?'

The young soldier said, 'Phil's the driver; I can't drive. And he hasn't sobered up. It's just a crummy old jalopy. We dumped it. We can't wait around for him to sober up. Anyhow, it needs a new tyre. It's back along the road with a flat. It's only worth about fifty bucks; it's a '36 Dodge.'

'If you had somebody who could drive,' Ragle said, 'would you go on by car?' I can drive, he was thinking.

The soldier, staring at him, said, 'What about the tyre?'

'I'll chip in on it,' he said. Taking hold of the soldier by the arm he led him out of the line and across the waiting room to his hunched-over buddy. 'Maybe he better stay here until we get the car going,' he said. The soldier, Phil, didn't look as if he could walk very far or very well. He appeared to understand only vaguely where he was.

To him, the soldier said, 'Hey, Phil, this guy's going to drive. Give me the keys.'

'Is that you, Wade?' Phil groaned from his coma.

Wade crouched down and rooted in his buddy's pockets. 'Here,' he said, finding the keys and handing them to Ragle. 'Listen,' he said to Phil. 'You stay here. We're going to walk back to the car and get it running; we'll drive by and pick you up. Okay? You got that?'

Phil nodded.

'Let's go,' Wade said to Ragle. As they pushed open the door and stepped out of the waiting room, on to the dark, cold street, Wade said, 'I sure hope the son of a bitch don't get into a panic and run out of there; we'd never find him.'

How dark everything was. Ragle could barely see the cracked, weed-ridden pavement under his shoes as he and Wade started off.

'Isn't this to hell and gone?' Wade said. 'They always stick these bus stations in the slums if it's a big enough town to have slums, and if it don't, then it's out to hell and gone like this.' He strode along, crunching the miscellaneous debris that neither of them could see. 'Sure dark,' he said. 'What have they got, a street light every two miles?'

From behind them a hoarse shout caused both of them to stop. Ragle turned around and saw, standing in the blue neon light of the Nonpareil Coach Lines sign, the other soldier. He had staggered out of the waiting room after them; now he leaned first one way and then the other, yelling after them, walking a few steps, stopping, setting down the two suitcases that he lugged.

'Oh Jesus,' Wade said. 'We got to go back. Otherwise he'll fall on his face and we'll never find him.' He started back and Ragle had no choice but to go along. 'He'll sleep all night in the vacant lot here.'

When they reached the soldier he caught hold of Wade, rested against him and said, 'You guys walked off and left me.'

'You got to stay here,' Wade said. 'Stay here with the luggage while we go hunt up the car.'

'I got to drive,' Phil said.

At great length, Wade again explained the situation to him. Ragle, wandering about helplessly, wondered if he could stand it. Finally Wade picked up one of the suitcases and started off. To Ragle he said, 'Let's get going. Take the other suitcase or he'll leave it off and we'll never see it again.'

'Somebody must have rolled me,' Phil muttered.

They stumbled on and on. Ragle lost track of time and space; one street light grew, passed overhead flooding them temporarily with brilliant yellow light, and then died away behind them. The next one grew in its turn. They passed the vacant lot, and square inert factory buildings appeared instead. He and his two companions laboured across multiple tracks, one after another. To his right, concrete loading docks at shoulder-level hove close. Phil stumbled against one and came to rest against it, his head buried on his arm, evidently sound asleep.

Ahead, at the curb, a car attracted Ragle's attention.

'Is that it?' he said.

The two soldiers regarded the car. 'I think so,' Wade said excitedly. 'Hey, Phil – ain't that the car?'

'Sure,' Phil said.

The car sagged on one side. It had a flat. So they had found it.

'Now we got to get a tyre,' Wade said, throwing the two suitcases into the back of the car. 'Let's get the jack under it and get the wheel off and see what size tyre it takes.'

In the trunk compartment he and Ragle found a jack. Phil had meanwhile wandered off; they saw him standing a few yards away, his head back, staring up at the sky.

'He'll stand like that for an hour,' Wade said, as they jacked up the car. 'There's a Texaco Station back aways; we passed it just before the flat.' Showing skill and experience, he got the wheel off and rolled it on to the sidewalk. Ragle followed. 'Where's Phil?' Wade said, looking around.

Phil was nowhere to be seen.

'God damn him,' Wade said. 'He must have rambled off.'

Ragle said, 'Let's get to the gas station. I don't have all night and neither do you.'

'That's a fact,' Wade said. 'Well,' he said philosophically, 'maybe he'll come back and flop in the car and we'll find him there when we get back.' He began rolling the tyre and wheel, at a good speed.

The gas station, when they got to it, was dark. The proprietor had closed up and gone home.

'I'll be a bug-eared frag,' Wade said.

'Maybe there's another station nearby,' Ragle said.

'I don't remember another one,' Wade said. 'How do you like that.' He seemed stunned, unable to act any further.

'Come on,' Ragle said. 'Let's go.'

After a long hard interval of tramping along, they saw ahead of them the white and red and blue square of a Standard Station.

'Amen,' Wade said. 'You know,' he said happily to Ragle, 'I been walking along here praying like a bastard. And there it is.' He rolled his tyre and wheel faster and faster, squalling a cry of triumph. 'Come on!' he yelled back to Ragle.

In the station a clean-cut boy in the starched white uniform of the company watched them without interest.

'Hey, there, man,' Wade said, shoving open the station house door. 'You want to sell us a tyre? Let's move it.'

The boy put down a chart he had been working on, picked up a cigarette from an ash tray, and came over to see the tyre.

'What's this for?' he asked Wade.

' 'Thirty-six Dodge sedan,' Wade said.

The boy flashed a light on the tyre, trying to read the size. Then he got out a heavy ringed note-binder and leafed through the printed pages. It seemed to Ragle that he examined each page at least four different times, turning them first one way and then another. Finally he closed the note-binder and said, 'Can't do you any good.'

'What do you suggest, then?' Ragle said patiently. 'This soldier and his buddy have to be back at their base or they're AWOL.'

The gas station attendant scratched his nose with his pencil and then he said, 'There's a recap place up on the highway, about five miles.'

'We can't walk five miles,' Ragle said.

The attendant said, 'I've got my Ford pick-up truck parked over there.' He pointed with his pencil. 'One of you stay here, and leave your wheel here. And the other of you can drive the pick-up over to the highway. It's a Seaside Station. At the first light. Bring the tyre back and I'll put it on here for you. It'll cost you six bits for me to put it on.' He took down a set of car keys from the register and handed them to Ragle. 'And,' he said, 'while you're up there, there's an all-night restaurant across the highway. You want to bring me back a fried ham and cheese sandwich and a malt.'

'Any special kind of malt?' Ragle said.

'Pineapple, I guess.' He handed Ragle a dollar bill.

'I'll stay here,' Wade said. 'Hurry back,' he yelled after him.

'Okay,' Ragle said.

A few minutes later he had backed the pick-up truck out on to the deserted street. Then he was driving in the direction the attendant had pointed. At last he saw the lights of the highway.

What a situation, he thought to himself.

8

The young man wearing shorts and undershirt placed the end of a reel of tape, looped, into the slot of the reel-hub. He revolved the reel until the tape had caught, and then he pressed the key that started the transport. On the sixteen-inch screen a picture appeared. The young man seated himself on the edge of the bed to watch.

First, the picture showed a six-lane divided highway with white concrete pavement. In the centre strip bushes and grass grew. On each side of the highway billboards advertising retail products could be seen. Cars moved along the highway. One changed lanes. Another slowed to take advantage of a cut-off.

A yellow Ford pick-up truck appeared.

From the speaker of the tape machine a voice said, 'That is a 1952 Ford pick-up truck.'

'Yes,' the young man said.

The truck, seen now from the side, showed its profile. Then it came at the screen. The young man noted it from the front.

Darkness descended. The truck switched on its headlights. The young man observed it from the front, side, and rear, its tail lights in particular.

Daylight returned to the screen. The truck moved along under sunlight. It changed lanes.

'The vehicle code requires a driver to make a hand-signal when he changes lanes,' the voice said.

'Right,' the young man said.

The truck stopped off on the gravel shoulder.

'The vehicle code requires that when a vehicle stops, the driver make a hand-signal,' the voice said.

The young man got up and went over to rewind the tape.

'I've got that down pat,' he said to himself. He rewound the tape and put on another reel. While he was threading it, the telephone rang. From where he stood he called, 'Hello.'

The ringing stopped and from the wall a muted voice that he did not recognize said, 'He's still standing in line.'

'Okay,' the young man said.

The phone clicked off. The young man finished threading the tape and started up the transport.

On the screen appeared the image of a man in uniform. Boots, brown pants stuffed into the boots, leather belt, pistol in holster, brown canvas shirt, necktie poking out at his collar, heavy brown jacket, visored cap, sun-glasses. The man in uniform turned around, showing himself from several sides. Then he climbed on to a motorcycle, kicked the motor into life, and roared off.

The screen showed him riding along.

'Fine,' the young man wearing shorts and undershirt said. He got out his electric shaver, snapped it on, and, watching the screen, finished shaving.

The highway patrolman on the screen began pursuing a car. After a while he caught up with the car and waved it to a stop at the side of the road. The young man, shaving reflexively, studied the expression on the highway patrolman's face.

The highway patrolman said, 'All right, may I see your driver's licence please?'

The young man said, 'All right, may I see your driver's licence please.'

The door of the trapped car opened and a middle-aged man wearing a white shirt and unpressed slacks got out, reaching into his pocket. 'What's the matter, officer?' he said.

The highway patrolman said, 'Are you aware that this is a limited speed zone, sir?'

The young man said, 'Are you aware that this is a limited speed zone, sir?'

The driver said, 'Sure, I was only doing forty-five, like it said back there on the sign.' He passed his wallet to the highway patrolman, who took it and studied the licence. On the screen a blow-up of the licence appeared. It remained until the young man had finished shaving, dabbed after-shave lotion in his face, rinsed out his mouth with antibax, squirted deodorant under his arms, and started to find his shirt. Then the licence vanished.

'Your licence has expired, mister,' the highway patrolman said.

As he slid his shirt from the hanger the young man said, 'Your licence has expired, mister.'

The telephone rang. He leaped over to the tape-transport, struck the idle-key, and called, 'Hello.'

From the wall the muted voice said, 'He is now talking to Wade Schulmann.'

'Okay,' the young man said.

The phone clicked off. He started up the tape again, this time at fast forward wind. When he stopped it and returned it to the play position, the highway patrolman was walking around a car and saying to the lady driver,

'Would you please press down with your foot on the brake pedal.'

'I don't see what this is all about,' the lady driver said. 'I'm in a

98

hurry and this is a ridiculous inconvenience. I know a little about law, furthermore.'

The young man tied his tie, looped his heavy leather belt, strapped on his pistol and holster. 'I'm sorry, mister,' he said as he stuck on his visored cap. 'Your tail light isn't showing. You're not permitted to drive without a proper tail light. You'll have to park your car. Could I see your licence?'

As he was putting on his coat, the telephone rang again.

'Hello,' he said, peering at himself in the mirror.

'He's walking to the car with Wade Schulmann and Philip Burns,' the muted voice said.

'Okay,' the young man said. Going to the tape-transport he halted an inch of tape that showed the highway patrolman, close-up, front-view, and then, at the mirror, he compared himself with him. Darn good, he decided.

'Now they're entering the Standard Station,' the muted voice said. 'Get ready to leave.'

'I'm on my way,' he said. He closed the door after him, walked up the dark concrete ramp to the parked motorcycle. Getting on to the seat he jumped with his full weight on the starter-pedal. The motor started. Hopping along he glided the motorcycle out on to the street, switched on the headlight, pressed the clutch down, put it in gear, let the clutch out as he gave the motor gas. With a loud noise the motorcycle moved forward; he hung on inexpertly until it had gained speed, and then he relaxed and sat back. At the first inter-section he turned right, toward the highway.

He had got on to the highway before he realized that he had forgotten something. What was it? Some part of his uniform.

His sun-glasses.

Did he wear them at night? As he rode along the highway, past the cars and trucks, he tried to remember. Maybe to cut down the glare from oncoming headlights. Holding on to the handlebar with one hand he reached into his coat pocket. There they were. He lifted them out and fitted them on to his nose.

How dark, with the sun-glasses in place. For a moment he saw nothing, only blackness.

Maybe it was a mistake.

Taking off the sun-glasses he experimented, watching the road through them and then not through them. On his left, a big vehicle of some kind moved up abreast with him. He paid little attention to it. A trailer with a car pulling it; he speeded up his motorcycle to pass it. The trailer speeded up, too.

Damn, he said to himself. He had forgotten something, all right. His gloves. His bare hands, one gripping the handlebar, the other holding the sun-glasses, began to become numb with cold.

Time enough to go back? No, he decided.

Squinting, he peered for a sight of the yellow Ford pick-up truck. It would enter the highway at the signal light.

On his left, the trailer had got up so that it was ahead of him. He became aware that gradually it was pulling into his lane. Christ, he thought. Putting away the sun-glasses, he steered his motor-cycle into the lane to his right. A horn sounded; there was a car directly on his right. He swerved back. At the same time, the trailer came sweeping at him. His hand flew to the horn. What horn? Did motorcycles have horns? Sirens. He bent to switch on the siren.

When the siren wailed on, the trailer ceased to press at him. It returned to its own lane. And the car on his right gave him more clearance.

Noticing that, he felt more confidence.

By the time he spotted the yellow Ford pick-up truck, he had begun to enjoy his job.

As soon as he heard the siren behind him, Ragle knew that they had made up their minds to get him. He did not slow down. But he did not speed up. He waited until he could tell for certain that it was a cycle, not a car, that had got on his tail. And he saw only one of them.

Now I've got to use my sense of time and space, he said to him-self. My masterful talent.

He sized up the traffic-pattern around him, the positions and speeds of the cars. Then, when he had it fixed in mind, he cut sharply into the lane to his left, between two cars. The one behind slowed; it had no choice. Without any fuss he had wedged the pick-up truck into a dense pack of traffic. Then, in rapid suc-cession, he lane-hopped until he had got ahead of a massive two-section rig that hid him from anything following. Meanwhile, the siren continued to wail. Now he could not tell exactly where the cycle was. And, he thought, he's undoubtedly lost sight of me.

Between the rig and the sedan ahead of him, his tail lights could not be seen. And, at night, the cop had only the tail lights to go on.

All at once the motorcycle shot by in the lane to his left. The cop turned his head and identified him. But he could not get near the pick-up truck; he had to go on. Traffic had not stopped. The drivers could not tell who was being pursued; they thought the motorcycle meant to go farther on.

Now he'll wait for me, Ragle guessed. At once he changed lanes, cutting over to the left-hand lane, so that there were two lanes of traffic between him and the motorcycle. He'll be off on the shoulder. Ragle slowed down so that cars behind him felt forced to pass on the right. The traffic to his right became heavy.

Momentarily he glimpsed the motorcycle parked off on the gravel shoulder. The cop, in his uniform, peered back. He did not see the pick-up truck, and a moment later Ragle was safe. Well past. Now he speeded up; for the first time he shot ahead of the other traffic.

Soon he saw the signal light that he wanted.

But he did not see the Seaside Station that he had been told to look for.

Odd, he thought.

I had better get off the highway, he said to himself. So that I don't get flagged down again. No doubt there is something I've violated; this truck doesn't have the proper-coloured reflector strips on its rear bumper or some such device. Anything for an excuse, so that the machinery can go into motion, and all the forces can close in around me.

I know it's my psychosis, he said to himself, but I still don't want to get caught.

Making a hand-signal, he left the highway. The truck bumped off on to a rutted dirt pasture. As soon as it had stopped moving he shut off the lights and the motor. Nobody will notice me, he said to himself. But where the hell am I? And what do I do next?

Craning his neck, he searched in vain for any sign of the Seaside Station. The cross street, at the light, vanished off into the darkness, lit up for only a few hundred yards. Nothing there. A minor route. This is the big road out of town.

Far off, up the highway, a single coloured neon sign could be made out.

I'll drive down there, he decided. Or can I take the risk of getting back on the highway?

He waited until, looking back, he saw dense traffic. And then, gunning the motor, he shot out on to the road a split-second ahead of it. If any cop was coming, he wouldn't see one more tail light among all the others.

A moment later, Ragle identified the neon sign as that of a roadside tavern. A brief flash as it swept into view: the parking lot, gravel. Tall upright sign, FRANK'S BAR-B-Q AND DRINKS. Illuminated windows of a pentagonal stucco one-story building, somewhat modern. Few cars parked. He signalled and hurtled off the highway, into the parking lot. The truck barely halted in time. A foot from the wall of the bar-b-q. Trembling, he shifted into low and drove the truck around the side of the building, out of sight, back among the garbage cans and stacks of boxes at the service entrance. Where the delivery trucks no doubt came.

After he had gotten out of the pick-up truck he walked back to see if it could be seen. No, not from the highway. Not by a passing car. And if anyone did ask, he had only to deny any relationship to the truck. How could they prove he had arrived in it? I walked, he would say. Or I hitch-hiked and got a lift this far with somebody who turned off at the cross street.

Pushing open the door of the bar-b-q, he entered. Maybe they'll know where the Seaside Station is, he said to himself. This is probably the place where I'm supposed to pick up the fried ham sandwich and the malted milk.

In fact, he thought, I'm positive. There are just too many people in it. Like the bus depot. The same pattern.

Most of the booths were filled with couples. And at the doughnut-shaped counter in the centre a number of men sat eating dinner or drinking. The place smelled of frying hamburgers; a jukebox roared off in the corner.

Not enough cars in the lot to explain so many people.

As yet they hadn't noticed him. He drew the door shut without entering, and then he walked rapidly off, across the lot and around the side of the place, to the parked pick-up truck.

Too large. Too modern. Too lit-up. Too full of people. Is this the last stage of my mental difficulty. Suspicion of people . . . of groups and human activity, colour and life and noise. I shun them, he thought. Perversely. Seeking the dark.

Back in the darkness he felt his way up into the truck, switched on the engine, and then, with the lights still off, backed around until the truck faced the highway. During a break in the traffic he drove out into the first lane. Again he found himself in motion, heading away from town, in somebody else's truck. A gas station attendant whom he had never seen before in his life. I'm stealing his truck, he realized. But what else can I do?

I know they are conspiring against me. The two soldiers, the attendant. Plotting against me. The bus depot, too. The cab driver. Everybody. I can't trust anyone. They sent me off in this truck to get picked up by the first highway cop that came cruising by. Probably the back end of the truck lights up and reads RUSSIAN SPY. A sort of paranoiac 'kick me,' he thought.

Yes, he thought. I'm the man with the KICK ME sign pinned on him. No matter how hard he tries he can't whirl around fast enough to see it. But his intuition tells him it's there. He watches other people and gauges their actions. He infers from what they do. He infers that the sign is there because he sees them lining up to kick him.

I'm not entering any brightly lit places. I'm not starting conversations with people I don't know. There are no genuine strangers when it comes to me; everybody knows me. They're either a friend or an enemy. . . .

A friend, he thought. Who? Where? My sister? My brother-in-law? Neighbours? I trust them as much as I do anybody. But not enough.

So here I am.

He continued driving. No more neon lights came into view. The land, on both sides of the highway, lay dark and lifeless. Traffic had thinned out. Only an occasional headlight flashed at him from the oncoming traffic beyond the dividing strip.

Lonely.

Glancing down, he noticed that the truck had a radio mounted on the dashboard. He recognized the slide-rule dial. The two knobs.

If I turn it on, I'll hear them talking about me.

He reached out his hand, hesitated, and then turned the radio on. The radio began to hum. Gradually the tubes warmed; sounds, mostly static, faded in. He fiddled with the volume as he drove.

' . . . afterwards,' a voice said squeakily.

' . . . not,' another voice said.

' . . . my best.'

' . . . okay.' A series of pops.

They're calling back and forth, Ragle said to himself. The airwaves filled with alarm. Ragle Gumm eluded us! Ragle Gumm escaped!

The voice squeaked, ' . . . more experienced.'

Ragle thought, Next time send a more experienced team. Bunch of amateurs.

' . . . might as well . . . no further . . . '

Might as well give up, Ragle filled in. No further use in tracking him. He's too shrewd. Too wily.

The voice squeaked, ' . . . Schulmann says.'

That would be Commander Schulmann, Ragle said to himself. The Supreme Commander with headquarters in Geneva. Mapping the top-level secret strategy to synchronize world-wide military movements so they converge on this pick-up truck. Fleets of warships steaming toward me. Atomic cannon. The usual works.

The squeaking voice became too nerve-racking; he shut the radio off. Like mice. Yammering mice squeaking back and forth . . . it made his flesh crawl.

According to the odometer he had gone about twenty miles. A long distance. No town. No lights. Not even traffic, now. Only the road ahead, the dividing strip to his left. The pavement showing in his headlights.

Darkness, a flatness of fields. Up above, stars.

Not even farmhouses? Signs?

God, he thought. What would happen if I broke down out here? Where am I? *Anywhere?*

Maybe I'm not moving. Caught in a between-place. Wheels of the pick-up truck spinning in gravel . . . spinning uselessly, forever. The illusion of motion. Motor noise, wheel noise, headlights on pavement. But immobility.

And yet, he felt too uneasy to stop the truck. To get out and search around. The hell with that, he thought. At least he was safe here in the truck. Something around him. Shell of metal. Dashboard before him, seat under him. Dials, wheel, foot-pedals, knobs.

Better than the emptiness outside.

And then, far off to the right, he saw a light. And, a little later, a sign flashed in his headlights. The marker indicating an inter-section. Road travelling off right and left.

Slowing, he made a right turn on to the road.

Broken, narrow pavement loomed up in his lights. The truck bounced and swayed; he slowed down. An abandoned road. Unmaintained. The front wheels of the truck dropped into a trough; he shifted into second gear and came almost to a stop. Almost broke an axle. With care he drove forward. The road twisted and began to rise.

Hills and dense growth around him, now. A tree branch under his wheels; he heard it splinter. Once a white furred creature scuttled frantically. He swerved to avoid it and the truck-wheels spun in dirt. Terrified, he wrenched the wheel. Nightmare of a few moments before . . . stuck and spinning, sinking down in the loose, crumbly soil.

Shifting into low gear, he let the truck climb the awfully steep hill. Now the pavement had turned to packed dirt. Deep troughs, from previous vehicles. Something brushed the top of the truck; he ducked involuntarily. His headlights flashed into foliage, streaming off the road as the truck pointed toward the edge of a descent. Then the road veered sharply to the left; he forced the wheel to turn. Again the road appeared, hemmed in by shrubbery that had crept out on to it. The road became narrower; he pushed down on the brake as the truck lurched over a pothole.

On the next turn the truck missed the edge of the road. Both right wheels spun into the underbrush; the truck spun about and he slammed down on the brakes, killing the motor. The truck leaned. He felt himself sliding away from the wheel; clutching with his hands he managed to grasp the door handle. The truck lifted, groaned, and then came to rest, half turned over.

That's all of that, he thought to himself.

After a few moments he was able to open the door and step out.

The headlights glared from the trees and bushes. Sky above. The road almost lost as it climbed still farther up. Turning, Ragle looked back down. Far below he could see the line of lights, the highway. But no town. No settlement. The edge of the hill cut the lights off, sheared them away.

He began to walk up the road, going more by touch than sight. When his right foot struck foliage he directed himself left. The radar beam, he said to himself. Keep on course, or go off headfirst.

In the foliage various things rustled. He heard them depart at the sound of his approach. Harmless, he thought. Or they wouldn't be getting away as fast as possible.

Suddenly he missed his footing; stumbling, he managed to right himself. The road had levelled out. Wheezing, he halted. He had reached the top of the hill.

To his right, the light glowed. A house, set back from the road. A ranch house. Evidently occupied. Light coming from windows.

He walked toward it, up a dirt trail to a fence. Feeling with his hands he discovered a gate. At great length he slid the gate back. The trail, two deep ruts, led on toward the house. At last, after falling a number of times, he crashed against stone steps.

The house. He had got to it.

Arms extended, he climbed the steps to the porch. His hands groped about until his fingers closed over an old-fashioned bell.

He rang the bell and stood waiting, gasping for breath, shivering in the night cold.

The door opened and a drab, brown-haired, middle-aged woman looked out at him. She wore tan slacks and a checkered red and brown shirt and work shoes with high, buttoned tops. *Mrs Keitelbein*, his mind said. It's she. But it wasn't. He stared at her and she stared back.

'Yes?' she said. Behind her, in the living room, someone else, a man, peered past her at him. 'What do you want?' she said.

Ragle said, 'My car broke down.'

'Oh, come in,' the woman said. She held the door wide for him. 'Are you injured? You're alone?' She stepped out on to the porch to see if there was anyone else.

'Just me,' he said. Bird's-eye maple furniture . . . a low chair, table, long bench with a portable typewriter on it. A fireplace.

Wide boards, beams overhead. 'Nice,' he said, going toward the fireplace.

A man, holding an open book. 'You can use our phone,' the man said. 'How far did you have to walk?'

'Not too far,' he said. The man had a bland, ample face, as smooth as a boy's. He appeared to be much younger than the woman, her son perhaps. *Like Walter Keitelbein*, he thought. Striking resemblance. For a moment . . .

'You're lucky to find us,' the woman said. 'We're the only house up on the hill that's occupied. Everyone else is away until summer.'

'I see,' he said.

'We're year-round,' the young man said.

The woman said, 'I'm Mrs Kesselman. And this is my son.'

Ragle stared at the two of them.

'What's the matter?' Mrs Kesselman said.

'I—thought I recognized the name,' Ragle said. What did it imply? But the woman definitely was not Mrs Keitelbein. And the young man was not Walter. So the fact that they resembled one another meant nothing.

'What are you doing out this way?' Mrs Kesselman asked. 'This is such a godforsaken mound of earth when everyone's away. I know it may sound paradoxical for me to say that since we live up here.'

Ragle said, 'I was looking for a friend.'

That seemed to satisfy the Kesselmans. They both nodded.

'My car left the road and turned over on one of those spiral curves,' Ragle said.

'Oh dear,' Mrs Kesselman said. 'How distressing. Did it slide off the road? Down into the gully?'

'No,' he said. 'But it'll have to be towed back up. I'd be afraid to get back into it. It might slip and go further down.'

'By all means stay out of it,' Mrs Kesselman said. 'There have been instances of cars sliding off the edge and going all the way to the bottom. Do you want to telephone your friend and tell him you're all right?'

Ragle said, 'I don't know his number.'

'Can't you look it up in the book?' the young Mr Kesselman asked.

'I don't know his name,' Ragle said. 'Or even if it's a man.' Or, he thought, even if he or she exists.

The Kesselmans smiled at him trustingly. Supposing, of course, that what he meant was not as cryptic as it sounded.

'Would you like to call a tow truck?' Mrs Kesselman said. But her son spoke up.

'Nobody'll send a tow truck up here at night,' he said. 'We've had that out with the different garages. They won't budge.'

'That's true,' Mrs Kesselman said. 'Oh dear. This is a problem. We've always dreaded this happening to us. But it never has. Of course we know the road so well, after so many years.'

The younger Kesselman said, 'I'd be glad to drive you to your friend's place, if you have any idea where it is. Or I could drive you back down to the highway, or into town.' He glanced at his mother and she nodded in agreement.

'That's very kind of you,' Ragle said. But he did not want to leave; he placed himself at the fireplace, warming himself and enjoying the peacefulness of the room. It seemed to him to be in some respects the most civilized house he had been in that he could remember. The prints on the walls. The lack of clutter. No useless bric-a-brac. And everything arranged with taste, the books, the furniture, the drapes ... it satisfied his strong innate sense of order. His awareness of pattern. There exists a real æsthetic balance here, he decided. That's why it's so restful.

Mrs Kesselman waited for him to do or say something. When he continued to stand at the fireplace she said, 'Would you like something to drink?'

'Yes,' he said. 'Thanks.'

'I'll see what there is,' Mrs Kesselman said. 'Excuse me.' She departed from the room. Her son remained.

'Kind of cold out,' her son said.

'Yes,' Ragle said.

Awkwardly, the young man stuck out his hand. 'My name's Garret,' he said. They shook hands. 'I'm in the interior decorating field.'

That explained the taste shown in the room. 'This looks very nice,' Ragle said.

'What line are you in?' Garret Kesselman asked.

'I'm involved in newspaper work,' Ragle said.

'Oh, I'll be darned,' Garret said. 'No kidding. That must be a fascinating business. When I was in school I took a couple of years of journalism.'

Mrs Kesselman returned with a tray on which were three small glasses and an unusual-shaped bottle. 'Tennessee sour mash whisky,' she said, setting the tray down on the glass-topped coffee table. 'From the oldest distillery in the country. Jack Daniel's black label.'

'I never heard of it,' Ragle said, 'but it sounds wonderful.'

'It's excellent whiskey,' Garret said, handing Ragle a glass of the stuff. 'Something like Canadian whisky.'

'I'm a beer drinker, usually,' Ragle said. He tasted the sour-mash whiskey and it seemed all right. 'Fine,' he said.

The three of them said nothing, then.

'It seems a bad time to be driving around looking for someone,' Mrs Kesselman said, when Ragle had finished his glass of whisky and was pouring himself a second. 'Most people tackle this hill during the daylight hours.' She seated herself facing him. Her son perched on the arm of the couch.

Ragle said, 'I had a quarrel with my wife and I couldn't stand it any more. I had to get out.'

'How unfortunate,' Mrs Kesselman said.

'I didn't even stop to pack my clothes,' Ragle said. 'No objective in mind, just getting away. Then I remembered this friend and I thought I might be able to hole up with him for a while, until I got my bearings. Haven't seen him in years. He probably moved away a long time ago. It's lousy when a marriage breaks up. Like the end of the world.'

'Yes,' Mrs Kesselman agreed.

Ragle said, 'How about letting me stay here tonight?'

They glanced at each other. Embarrassed, they both started to answer at once. The gist of it was no.

'I have to stay somewhere,' Ragle said. He reached into his coat pocket and rooted about for his wallet. Getting it out he opened it up and counted his money. 'I've got a couple hundred dollars on me,' he said. 'I can pay you according to the inconvenience it causes you. Money for inconvenience.'

Mrs Kesselman said, 'Let us have a chance to talk it over.'

Arising, she motioned to her son. The two of them disappeared into the other room; the door shut after them.

I've got to stay here, Ragle said to himself. He poured himself another glass of the sour-mash whisky and walked back to the fireplace with it, to stand in the warmth.

That pick-up truck, he thought to himself. With its radio. It must have belonged to *them;* otherwise it wouldn't have had a radio. The boy at the Standard Station . . . he represented them.

Proof, Ragle said to himself. The radio is proof. It's not in my mind. It's a fact.

By their fruits, ye shall know them, he thought. And their fruits are that they communicate by radio.

The door opened. Mrs Kesselman and her son returned. 'We've talked it over,' she said, sitting down on the couch across from Ragle. Her son stood by her, looking grave. 'It's obvious to us that you're in distress. We'll allow you to stay, seeing that you are clearly in some unfortunate situation. But we want you to be honest with us, and we don't feel you have. There's more to your situation than you've told us so far.'

Ragle said, 'You're right.'

The Kesselmans exchanged glances.

'I was driving around intending to commit suicide,' Ragle said. 'I meant to get up speed and leave the road. Crack up in a ditch. But I lost my nerve.'

The Kesselmans stared at him in horror. 'Oh no,' Mrs Kesselman said. She got up and started toward him. 'Mr Gumm – '

'My name's not Gumm,' Ragle said. But obviously they recognized him. Had recognized him from the start.

Everybody in the universe knows me. I shouldn't be surprised. In fact I'm not surprised.

'I knew who you were,' Mrs Kesselman said, 'but I didn't want to embarrass you if you didn't feel inclined to tell us.'

Garret said, 'If you don't mind my asking, who is Mr Gumm? I guess I should know, but I don't.'

His mother said, 'Dear, this is the Mr Gumm who keeps winning the contest in the *Gazette.* Remember last week on TV we saw that film about him.' To Ragle, she said, 'Oh, I know all about you. In 1937 I entered the Old Gold contest. I got all the way up to the top; I got every single puzzle right.'

'She cheated, though,' her son said.

'Yes,' Mrs Kesselman said. 'A girl friend and I used to slip out on our lunch hour with five dollars we pooled together, and buy a dope-sheet from a little old news vendor who slipped it to us from under the counter.'

Garret said, 'I hope you don't mind sleeping down in the basement. It's not really a basement; we made it into a rumpus room a few years back. There's a bathroom and a bed down there . . . we've been using it for guests who couldn't make it back down the hill.'

'You don't still intend to – do away with yourself, do you?' Mrs Kesselman asked. 'Hasn't that left your mind?'

'Yes,' Ragle said.

With relief, she said, 'I'm so glad. As a fellow contest enterer I'd take it very hard. We're all looking to you to keep winning.'

'Just think,' Garret said. 'We'll go down in history as the persons who kept – ' he stumbled over the name – 'Mr Gumm from yielding to the impulse toward self-destruction. Our names will be linked with his. Fame.'

'Fame,' Ragle agreed.

Another round of Tennessee sour-mash whisky was poured. The three of them sat about the living room, drinking it and watching one another.

9

The door chimes rang. Junie Black dropped her magazine and got up to answer it.

'Telegram for Mr William Black,' the uniformed Western Union boy said. 'Sign here, please.' He handed her a pencil and pad; she signed and received the telegram.

Closing the door she carried the telegram to her husband. 'For you,' she said.

Bill Black opened the telegram, turned away so that his wife couldn't read it over his shoulder, and saw what it had to say.

CYCLE MISSED TRUCK. GUMM PASSED
BAR-B-Q. YOUR GUESS.

Never send a boy to do a man's job, Bill Black said to himself. Your guess is as good as mine. He glanced at his wristwatch. Nine-thirty p.m. Later and later. It was too late now.

'What's it say?' Junie asked.

'Nothing,' he said. I wonder if they'll find him, he wondered. I hope so. Because if they don't some of us will be dead by this time tomorrow. God knows how many thousands of dead people. Our lives depend on Ragle Gumm. Him and his contest.

'It's a catastrophe,' Junie said. 'Isn't it? I can tell by the expression on your face.'

'Business,' he said. 'City business.'

'Oh indeed?' she said. 'Don't lie to me. I'll bet it has something to do with Ragle.' Suddenly she snatched the telegram away from him and rushed out of the room with it. 'It is!' she cried, standing off by herself and reading the telegram. 'What did you do – hire somebody to kill him? I know he's disappeared; I was talking to Margo on the phone and she says – '

He managed to get the telegram back from her. 'You haven't got any idea what this means,' he said with mighty control.

'I can tell what it means. As soon as Margo told me Ragle had disappeared – '

'Ragle didn't disappear,' he said, almost at the end of his mighty control. 'He walked off.'

'How do you know?'

'I know,' he said.

'You know because you're responsible for his disappearance.'

In a sense, Bill Black thought, she's right. I'm responsible because, when he and Vic popped out of that clubhouse, I thought they were kidding. 'Okay,' he said. 'I'm responsible.'

Her eyes changed colour. The pupils became tiny. 'Oh I hate you,' she said, shaking her head. 'I wish I could slit your throat.'

'Go ahead,' he said. 'Maybe it would be a good idea.'

'I'm going next door,' Junie said.

'Why?'

'I'm going to tell Vic and Margo that you're responsible.' She hurried to the front door; he went after her and caught hold of her. 'Let me go,' she said, yanking away from him. 'I'm going to tell them that Ragle and I are in love with each other, and if he survives your vicious – '

'Sit down,' he said. 'Be quiet.' And then he thought again of Ragle not being around to work tomorrow's puzzle. Panic got started in him, then, and began to control him. 'I feel like getting into the closet,' he told his wife. 'No,' he said, 'I feel like burrowing down into the floor. Down into the ground.'

'Infantile guilt,' Junie said, with derision.

Bill Black said, 'Fear. Plain fear.'

'You're ashamed.'

'No,' he said. 'Infantile fear. Adult fear.'

' "Adult fear", ' Junie snorted. 'There's no such thing.'

'Yes there is,' he said.

Garret laid a folded, fresh bath towel on the arm of the chair, and, with it, a washrag and a bar of soap in its wrapper. 'You'll have to get along without pyjamas,' he said. 'The bathroom is through this door.' He opened a door, and Ragle saw down a narrow corridor, like a ship's passage, to a cramped, closet-like bathroom at the far end.

'Fine,' Ragle said. The liquor had made him sleepy. 'Thanks,' he said. 'I'll see you tomorrow.'

'There's plenty of books and magazines in the rumpus room itself,' Garret said. 'If you can't sleep and want to read. And there's a chess set and other games. None for one person, though.'

He departed. Ragle heard his footsteps as he climbed the stairs to the first floor. The door at the top of the flight of stairs closed.

Sitting down on the bed, Ragle tugged his shoes off and let them drop to the floor. Then he caught hold of them with a finger in each, hoisted them high, and searched for a place to put them. He noticed a shelf running along the wall; on the shelf was a lamp, a wind-up clock, and a small white plastic radio.

As soon as he saw the radio he put his shoes back on, buttoned up his shirt, and dashed out of the room to the stairs.

They almost fooled me. But they gave themselves away. He ascended two steps at a time and pushed open the door at the top. Only a minute or so had passed since Garret Kesselman had preceded him. Ragle stood in the hallway, listening. From a distance came the sounds of Mrs Kesselman's voice.

She's getting in touch with them. Calling them on the phone or broadcasting to them. One way or another. With as little noise as possible he moved along the hall, in the direction of her voice. The hall, dark, ended at a half-open door. Light streamed out into the hall, and as he got near he saw into a dining room.

Wearing a robe and slippers, her hair up in a turban, Mrs Kesselman was feeding a small black dog from a dish on the floor. Both she and the dog started with surprise as Ragle pushed the door open. The dog backed away and began to bark in a rapid staccato.

'Oh,' Mrs Kesselman said. 'You scared me.' In her hands she held a box of dog biscuits. 'Did you need something?'

Ragle said, 'There's a radio downstairs in my room.'

'Yes,' she said.

'That's how they communicate,' Ragle said.

'Who?'

'They,' he said. 'I don't know who they are, but they're all around me. They're the ones who are after me.' And, he thought, you and your son are two of them. You almost had me. Too bad you forgot to hide the radio. But probably you didn't have time.

From the hallway Garret appeared. 'Everything okay?' he asked, in a worried voice.

To him his mother said, 'Dear, close the door so I can talk to Mr Gumm alone. Will you?'

'I want him in here,' Ragle said. He moved toward Garret, who blinked and backed away, his arms flapping helplessly. Closing the door Ragle said, 'There's no way I can tell if you've called to say I'm here. I'll have to take the chance that you haven't had time.'

I don't know where else to go, he thought. Certainly not tonight.

'Now what's this about?' Mrs Kesselman said. Stooping down, she resumed the feeding of the dog. The dog, after a few more barks at Ragle, returned to his food. 'You're being pursued by a group of people and you say we're part of that group. Then that business about your "committing suicide" is something you made up.'

'I made it up,' he agreed.

'Why are they pursuing you?' Garret said.

Ragle said, 'Because I'm the centre of the universe. At least, that's what I've inferred from their actions. They act as if I am. I only have that to go on. They've gone to a great deal of trouble to

114

construct a sham world around me to keep me pacified. Buildings, cars, an entire town. Natural looking, but completely unreal. The part I don't understand is the contest.'

'Oh,' Mrs Kesselman said. 'Your contest.'

'Evidently it plays a vital role with them,' Ragle said. 'But I'm baffled. Do you know?'

'I don't know any more than you do,' Mrs Kesselman said. 'Of course, we always hear that these big contests are rigged . . . but except for the usual rumours – '

'I mean,' Ragle said, 'do you know what the contest really is?'

Neither of them spoke. Mrs Kesselman, her back to him, continued feeding the dog. Garret sat down on a chair and crossed his legs, leaning back with his hands wrapped behind his head, trying to appear calm.

'Do you know what I'm really doing every day?' Ragle said. 'When I'm supposedly plotting where the little green man will show up next? I must be doing something else. They know, but I don't.'

Both the Kesselmans were silent.

'Had you called?' Ragle asked them.

Garret quivered with embarrassment. Mrs Kesselman seemed shaken, but she continued to feed the dog.

'Can I look through the house?' Ragle said.

'Surely,' Mrs Kesselman said, straightening up. 'Look, Mr Gumm. We're doing the best we can to accommodate you. But – ' With a wild gesture she burst out, 'Honestly, you've got us both so upset we hardly know what we're doing. We never saw you before in our lives. Are you crazy – is that it? Maybe you are: you certainly are acting as if you are. I wish now you hadn't come here; I wish – ' She hesitated. 'Well, I started to say I wished you'd gone off the road with your car. It isn't fair to us to cause us all this trouble.'

'That's right,' Garret murmured.

Am I making a mistake? Ragle asked himself.

'Explain the radio,' he said aloud.

'There's nothing to explain,' Mrs Kesselman said. 'It's an ordinary five-tube radio that we got right after World War Two. It's been down there for years. I don't even know if it works.'

Now she seemed angry. Her hands trembled and her face had become strained, pinched with fatigue. 'Everybody owns a radio. Two or three of them.'

Ragle opened each of the doors that led off the dining room. One of them opened on to a storage closet, with shelves and bins. He said, 'I want to look around the house. Get in here, so I won't have to worry about what you're doing while I look.' In the lock there was a key.

'Please,' Mrs Kesselman began, glaring at him and almost inarticulate.

'Just for a few minutes,' he said.

They glanced at each other. Mrs Kesselman made a sign of resignation, and then they walked wordlessly into the closet. Ragle closed it and threw the bolt. He put the key in his pocket.

Now he felt better.

At its dish, the black dog watched him intently. Why is it watching me? he wondered. And then he noticed that the dog had finished its food and was hoping that he would give it more. The package remained on the long dinner table where Mrs Kesselman had left it; he sprinkled a few more dog biscuits into the dish and the dog fell to eating again.

From within the closet Garret's voice was distinctly audible. '. . . face it – he's a nut.'

Ragle said, 'I'm not a nut. I've watched this thing grow step by step. At least, I've become aware of it step by step.'

Mrs Kesselman said to him through the closet door, 'Look, Mr Gumm. It's clear to us that you believe what you say. But don't you see what you're doing? Because you believe everyone's against you, you force everyone to be against you.'

'Like ourselves,' Garret said.

There was a lot in what they said. Ragle, uncertainly, said, 'I can't take any chances.'

'You have to take a chance with someone,' Mrs Kesselman said. 'Or you can't live.'

Ragle said, 'I'll look through the house and then I'll make up my mind.'

The woman's voice, controlled and civilized, went on, 'At least call your family and tell them you're all right. So they won't worry about you. They're probably quite upset.'

'You should let us call them,' Garret said. 'So they wouldn't phone the police or something.'

Ragle left the dining room. First he inspected the living room. Nothing seemed out of order. What did he intend to find? The same old problem . . . he wouldn't know until he found it. And perhaps even then he wouldn't be sure.

On the wall, beyond a small spinet piano, hung a telephone, a bright pink plastic phone with a curly plastic cord. And upright, in the book case, the phone book. He lifted the book out.

It was the same phone book as the one Sammy had found in the vacant lot. He opened it. Written, in pencil, red crayon, ball-point pen and fountain pen, were numbers and names on the blank first page. Addresses, jotted notations of dates, times, events . . . the current phone book, in use in this house by these people. Walnut, Sherman, Kentfield, Devonshire numbers.

The number on the wall phone itself was a Kentfield number. So that settled that.

Carrying the book he strode back through the house, into the dining room. He got out the key and unlocked the closet door, swinging it wide.

The closet was empty. A large hole had been neatly cut in the rear wall, a still-warm rim of wood and plaster through which showed one of the bedrooms. They had cut a passage out in a matter of minutes. On the floor, by the hole, lay two tiny drill-like points; one had been bent, damaged and scored. The wrong size. Too small. And the other, probably not tried; they had found the right size and finished the job, scrambled out in such haste that they had forgotten these parts of the cutting-tool.

Holding the drill-like points in the palm of his hand he saw that they were like nothing he had ever seen before. In all his life.

While they had talked reasonably and rationally, they had been cutting through the back wall.

I'm hopelessly outclassed, he said to himself. I might as well give up.

He made a cursory tour of the house. No sign of them. The back door banged open and shut in the late-evening wind. They had gone outside. Left the house entirely. He sensed the empti-ness of the house. Only he and the dog. Not even the dog; there was no sign of it, now. The dog had gone with them.

He could plunge out on to the road; possibly somewhere in the house was a flashlight he could take. There might even be a heavy coat he could wear. With luck, he could march a good distance before the Kesselmans had time to return with support. He could hide in the woods, wait until daylight. Try to reach the highway . . . try to hike all the way to the bottom of the hill, however many miles it was.

What a dismal prospect. He shrank from it; he needed rest and sleep, not more walking.

Or – he could stay in the house, and in the time left to him explore it as fully as possible. Learn as much as he could before they got him in tow again.

The latter appealed to him, if it had to be one or the other.

He returned to the living room. This time he opened drawers and cupboards and poked into the ordinary objects, such as the television set in the corner.

On top of the television set, mounted in a mahogany frame, was a tape recorder. He snapped the switch, and a reel of tape, already on the mechanism, began to move. After a moment or so the screen of the television set lit up. The tape, he realized, was for video use, as well as audio. Standing back, he watched the screen.

On the television screen appeared Ragle Gumm, first a front view and then a side view. Ragle Gumm strolled along a tree-lined residential street, past parked cars, lawns. Then a close-up of him, full-face.

From the speaker of the TV set a voice said, 'This is Ragle Gumm.'

On the screen Ragle Gumm now sat in a deck-chair in the back yard of a house, wearing a Hawaiian sports shirt and shorts.

'You will hear an excerpt of his conversational manner,' the voice from the speaker said. And then Ragle heard his own voice. ' . . . *get home ahead of you I'll do it*,' Ragle Gumm said. '*Otherwise you can do it tomorrow. Is that okay?*'

They have me down in black and white, Ragle thought. In colour, as a matter of fact.

He stopped the tape. The image remained, inert. Then he clicked the switch off, and the image dwindled to a spot of brightness and at last vanished entirely.

No wonder everybody recognizes me. They've been trained.

When I start to imagine I'm crazy I'll remember this tape machine. This training-programme of identification with me as the topic.

I wonder how many tapes like this are sitting in how many machines in how many homes. Over how large an area. Every house that I ever passed. Every street. Every town, perhaps.

The entire earth?

He heard, from far off, the noise of an engine. It started him into motion.

Not long, he realized. He opened the front door, and the noise increased. In the darkness below him, twin lights flashed and then were temporarily broken off.

But what is it for? he wondered. Who are they?

What are things really like? I've got to see. . . .

Running through the house he passed one object after another, from one room to the next. Furnishings, books, food in the kitchen, personal articles in drawers, clothes hanging in closets . . . what would tell him the most?

At the back porch he stopped. He had reached the end of the house. A washing machine, mop hanging from a rack, package of Dash soap, a stack of magazines and newspapers.

Reaching into the stack he dragged out a handful, dropping them, opening them at random.

The date on a newspaper made him stop searching; he stood holding it.

May 10, 1997.

Almost forty years in the future.

His eyes took in the headlines. Meaningless jumble of isolated trivia: a murder, bond issue to raise funds for parking lots, death of famous scientist, revolt in Argentina.

And, near the bottom, the headline:

VENUSIAN ORE DEPOSITS OBJECT OF DISPUTE

Litigation in the International system of courts concerning the ownership of property on Venus . . . he read as rapidly as he could, and then he tossed the newspaper down and pawed through the magazines.

A copy of *Time*, dated April 7, 1997. Rolling it up he stuck it in his trouser pocket. More copies of *Time ;* he rooted through them, opening them and trying to devour the articles all at once, trying to grasp and retain something. Fashions, bridges, paintings, medicine, ice hockey – everything, the world of the future laid out in careful prose. Concise summaries of each branch of the society that had not yet come into existence. . . .

That *had* come into existence. That existed now.

This was a current magazine. This *was* the year 1997. Not 1959.

From the road outside, the noise of a vehicle stopping caused him to grab up the rest of the magazines. An arm-load . . . he started to open the back door, to the yard outside.

Voices. In the yard men moved; a light flashed. His arm-load of magazines struck the door and most of them tumbled to the porch. Kneeling down, he gathered them up.

'There he is,' a voice said, and the light flicked in his direction, dazzling him. He swung so that his back was to it; lifting up one of the copies of *Time* he stared at the cover.

On the cover of *Time*, dated January 14, 1996, was his picture. A painting, in colour. With the words underneath it:

RAGLE GUMM – MAN OF THE YEAR

Sitting down on the porch he opened the magazine and found the article. Photographs of him as a baby. His mother and father. Him as a child in grammar school. He turned the pages frantic-ally. Him as he was now, after World War Two or whatever war it had been that he had fought in . . . military uniform, himself smiling back at the camera.

A woman who was his first wife.

And then a scenic sprawl, the sharp city-like spires and minarets of an industrial installation.

The magazine was plucked from his hands. He looked up and saw, to his amazement, that the men lifting him up and away from the porch had on familiar drab coveralls.

'Watch out for that gate,' one of them said.

He glimpsed dark trees, men stepping on flower beds, crushing plants under their shoes, flashlights swinging across the stone path out of the yard, to the road. And, in the road, trucks parked with their motors noisily running, headlights on. Olive-green service trucks, ton and a half. Familiar, too. Like the drab coveralls.

City trucks. City maintenance men.

And then one of the men held something to his face, a bubble of plastic that the man compressed with his fingers. The bubble split apart and became fumes.

Held between four of the men, Ragle Gumm could do nothing but breathe in the fumes. A flashlight poured yellow fumes and glare into his face; he shut his eyes.

'Don't hurt him,' a voice murmured. 'Be careful with him.'

Under him the metal of the truck had a cold, damp quality. As if, he thought, he had been loaded in a refrigerator tank. Produce, from the countryside, to be hauled into town. To be ready for the next day's market.

10

Hearty morning sunlight filled his bedroom with a white glare. He put his hand over his eyes, feeling sick.

'I'll pull down the shades,' a voice said. Recognizing the voice he opened his eyes. Victor Nielson stood at the windows, pulling down the shades.

'I'm back,' Ragle said. 'I didn't get anywhere. Not a step.' He remembered the running, the scrambling uphill, through shrubbery. 'I got up high,' he said. 'Almost to the top. But then they rolled me back.' Who? he wondered. He said aloud, 'Who brought me back here?'

Vic said, 'A burly taxi driver who must have weighed three hundred pounds. He carried you right in the front door and set you down on the couch.' After a moment he added, 'It cost you or me, depending on who foots the bill, eleven dollars.'

'Where did they find me?'

'In a bar,' Vic said.

'What bar?'

'I never heard of it. Out at the end of town. The north end. The industrial end, by the tracks and the freight yards.'

'See if you can remember the name of the bar,' Ragle said. It seemed important to him; he did not know why.

'I can ask Margo,' Vic said. 'She was up; we both were up. Just a minute.' He left the room. After a moment or so, Margo appeared at the end of his bed.

'It was a bar called Frank's Bar-B-Q,' she said.

'Thanks,' Ragle said.

'How do you feel?' she asked.

'Better.'

'Can I fix you something bland to eat?'

'No,' he said. 'Thanks.'

Vic said, 'You really tanked up. Not on beer. Your pockets were full of shoestring potatoes.'

'Anything else?' Ragle said. There was supposed to be something else; he had a memory of stuffing something valuable into them; something that he wanted vitally to keep and bring back.

'Just a paper napkin from Frank's Bar-B-Q,' Margo said.

'And a lot of change. Quarters and dimes.'

'Maybe you were making phone calls,' Vic said.

'I was,' he said. 'I think.' Something about a phone. A phone book. 'I remember a name,' he said. 'Jack Daniels.'

Vic said, 'That was the cab driver's name.'

'How do you know?' Margo asked him.

'Ragle kept calling the cab driver that,' Vic said.

'What about city maintenance trucks?' Ragle said.

'You didn't say anything about them,' Margo said. 'But it's easy to see why you might have them on your mind.'

'Why?' he said.

She raised the window shade. 'They've been out there since sunup, since before seven o'clock. The din probably affected your subconscious and got into your thoughts.'

Lifting himself up, Ragle looked out of the window. Parked at the far curb were two olive-green maintenance trucks. A crew of city workmen in their drab coveralls had started digging up the street; the racket of their trip hammers jarred him, and he realized that he had been hearing the sound for some time.

'It looks like they're there to stay,' Vic said. 'Must be a break in the pipe.'

'It always makes me nervous when they start digging up the street,' Margo said. 'I'm always afraid they'll just walk off and leave it dug up. Not finish it.'

'They know what they're doing,' Vic said. Waving goodbye to Margo and Ragle, he set off for work.

Later, after he had got shakily out of bed, washed and shaved and dressed, Ragle Gumm wandered into the kitchen and fixed himself a glass of tomato juice and a soft-boiled egg on unbuttered toast.

Seated at the table he sipped some of the coffee that Margo had left on the stove. He did not feel like eating. From a distance he could hear the drapapapapapa of the trip hammers. I wonder how long that'll be going on, he asked himself.

He lit a cigarette and then picked up the morning paper. Vic or Margo had brought it in and laid it on the chair by the table where he would find it.

The texture of the paper repelled him. He could hardly bear to hold it in his hands.

Folding the first sheets back he glanced over the puzzle page. There, as usual, the names of the winners. His name, in its special box. In all its glory.

'How does the contest look today?' Margo asked, from the other room. Wearing toreador pants, and a white cotton shirt of Vic's, she had started to polish the television set.

'About the same,' he said. The sight of his name on the newspaper page made him restless and uncomfortable, and his first nausea of the morning returned. 'Funny business,' he said to his sister. 'Seeing your name in print. All of a sudden it can be nerve-racking. A shock.'

'I've never seen my name in print,' she said. 'Except in some of those articles about you.'

Yes, he thought. Articles about me. 'I'm pretty important,' he said, putting the paper down.

'Oh you are,' Margo agreed.

'I have the feeling,' he said, 'that what I do affects the human race.'

She straightened up and stopped polishing. 'What a peculiar thing to say. I don't really see – ' She broke off. 'After all, a contest is only a contest.'

Going into his room, he began setting up his charts, graphs, tables and machines. An hour or so later he had gotten deep into the order of solving the day's puzzle.

At noon, Margo rapped on the closed door. 'Ragle,' she said, 'can you be interrupted? Just say you can't if you can't.'

He opened the door, glad of a break.

'Junie Black wants to talk to you,' Margo said. 'She swears she'll stay only a minute; I told her you hadn't finished.' She made a motion, and Junie Black appeared from the living room. 'All dressed up,' Margo said, eyeing her.

'I'm going downtown shopping,' Junie explained. She had on a red knit wool suit, stockings and heels, and a shorty coat over her shoulders; her hair was done up and she had on make-up, a good deal of it. Her eyes seemed extra dark, and her lashes long, dramatic. 'Close the door,' she said to Ragle, stepping into his room. 'I want to talk to you.'

He shut the door.

'Listen,' Junie said. 'Are you okay?'

'Yes,' he said.

'I know what happened to you.' She put her hands on his shoulders and then she drew away from him with a quake of anguish. 'Damn him!' she said. 'I told him I'd leave him if he did anything to you.'

'Bill?' he asked.

'He's responsible. He had you followed and spied on; he hired some private detectives.' She paced about the room, tense and smouldering. 'They beat you up, didn't they?'

'No,' he said. 'I don't think so.'

She pondered that. 'Maybe they just wanted to scare you.'

'I don't think this has anything to do with your husband,' Ragle said hesitantly. 'Or with you.'

Shaking her head, Junie said, 'I know it does. I saw the telegram he got. When you were missing he got this telegram – he didn't want me to see it, but I grabbed it away from him. I remember exactly what it said. It was about you. A report on you.'

Ragle said, 'What did it say?'

For a moment she squeezed together her faculties. Then, fervently, she said, 'It said, "Sighted missing truck. Gumm passed barbecue. Your move next".'

'You're sure?' he said, aware of her vagaries.

'Yes,' she said. 'I memorized it before he got it back.'

City trucks, he thought. Outside, in the street, the olive-drab

124

trucks had not left. The men still worked away at the pavement; they had gotten quite a stretch of it dug up, by now.

'Bill has no contact with maintenance, does he?' he asked. 'He doesn't dispatch the service trucks, does he?'

'I don't know what he does down at the water company,' Junie said. 'And I don't care, Ragle. Do you hear that? I don't care. I wash my hands of him.' Suddenly she ran toward him and put her arms around him; hugging him she said loudly in his ear, 'Ragle, I've made up my mind. This thing, this awful criminal vengeance business of his, finishes it forever. Bill and I are through. Look.' She tugged off the glove of her left hand and waved her hand before his face. 'Do you see?'

'No,' he said.

'My wedding ring. I'm not wearing it.' She put her glove back on. 'I came over here to tell you that, Ragle. Do you remember when you and I lay out on the grass together, and you read poetry to me and told me you loved me?'

'Yes,' he said.

'I don't care what Margo says or anybody says,' Junie said. 'I have an appointment at two-thirty this afternoon with an attorney. I'm going to see about leaving Bill. And then you and I can be together for the rest of our lives, and nobody can interfere. And if he tries any more of his strong-arm criminal tactics, I'll call the police.'

Gathering up her purse, she opened the door to the hall.

'You're leaving?' he asked, somewhat dazed to find himself now in the ebb of the whirlwind.

'I have to get downtown,' she said. She glanced up and down the hall and then she made a pantomine, in his direction, of ardent kissing. 'I'll try to phone you later today,' she whispered, leaning toward him. 'And tell you what the lawyer said.' The door snapped shut after her, and he heard her heels against the floor as she rushed off. Then, outside, a car started up. She had gone.

'What was all that?' Margo said, from the kitchen.

'She's upset,' he said vaguely. 'Fight with Bill.'

Margo said, 'If you're important to the whole human race you ought to be able to do better than her.'

'Did you tell Bill Black I had gone off?' he said.

'No,' she said. 'But I told her. She showed up here, after you had gone. I told her I was too worried about where you were to give a darn what she had to say. Anyhow, I think it was just an excuse on her part to see you; she didn't really want to talk to me.' Drying her hands on a paper towel she said, 'She looked quite nice, just now. She really is physically attractive. But she's so juvenile. Like some of the little girls Sammy has for his playmates.'

He barely heard what she was telling him. His head ached and he felt more sick and confused than before. Echoes of the night . . .

Outside, the city maintenance crew leaned on their shovels, smoked cigarettes, and seemed to be keeping in the vicinity of the house.

Are they there to spy on me? Ragle wondered.

He felt a strong, reflexive aversion to them; it bordered on fear. And he did not know why. He tried to think back, to remember what had happened to him, what he had done and what had been done to him. The olive-green trucks . . the running and crawling. An attempt, somewhere along the line, to hide. And something valuable that he had found, but which had slipped or been taken away . . .

II

The following morning, Junie Black called him on the phone.

'Were you working?' she asked.

'I'm always working,' Ragle said.

Junie said, 'Well, I talked to Mr Hempkin, my attorney.' Her tone of voice informed him that she intended to go into the details. 'What a cumbersome business,' she said, sighing.

'Let me know how it comes out,' he said, wanting to get back to his puzzle solving. But, as always, he was snared by her. Involved in her elaborate, histrionic problems. 'What did he say?' he asked. After all, he had to take it seriously; if she took it to court, he might be hailed in as the correspondent.

'Oh Ragle,' she said. 'I want to see you so badly. I want to have you with me. Close to me. This is such a grind.'

'Tell me what he said.'

'He said it all depends on how Bill feels. What a mess. When can I see you? I'm scared to come around your place. Margo gave me the worst look I've ever gotten from anybody in my life. Does she think I'm after you for your money, or what? Or is it just her naturally morbid mind?'

'Tell me what he said.'

'I hate to talk to you over the phone. Why don't you drop over here for a while? Or would Margo be suspicious? You know, Ragle, I feel so much better now that I've decided. I can be myself with you, not held back artificially by doubts. This is the most important moment in my life, Ragle. It's really solemn. Like a church. When I woke up this morning I felt as if I had awakened in a church, and all around me was this sacred spirit. And I asked myself what the spirit was, and pretty soon I identified it as you.' She became silent, then, waiting for him to contribute something.

'What about this Civil Defence business?' he said.

'What about it? I think it's a good idea.'

'Are you going to be there?'

'No,' she said. 'What do you mean?'

'I thought that was the idea.'

'Ragle,' she said with exasperation, 'you know, sometimes you're so mysterious I just can't follow you.'

He gathered, at that point, that he had made a mistake. Nothing remained but to drop the business about the Civil Defence classes. It was hopeless to try to explain to her what he meant and what he had thought when Mrs Keitelbein approached him. 'Look, June,' he said. 'I want very much to see you, as much as you want to see me. More, very possibly. But I have this goddamn puzzle to finish.'

'I know,' she said. 'You have your responsibility.' She said it resignedly. 'What about tonight, after you mail off your entry?'

'I'll try to call you,' he said. But her husband would be home, so nothing could come of it. 'Maybe later today,' he said. 'Late this afternoon. I think I can get my entry off early, today.' He had had fair luck with it so far.

'No,' she said. 'I won't be home this afternoon. I'm having lunch with an old friend. A girl friend. I'm sorry, Ragle. I've got so much I want to say to you and do with you. A whole lifetime ahead of us.' She talked on; he listened. At last she said good-bye and he hung up, feeling let-down.

How hard it was to communicate with her.

As he started back to his room, the phone rang again.

'Want me to get it?' Margo called from the other room.

'No,' he said. 'It's probably for me.' He lifted the receiver, expecting to hear June's voice. But instead an unfamiliar older female voice said haltingly,

'Is – Mr Gumm there?'

'Speaking,' he said. His disappointment made him gruff.

'Oh Mr Gumm. I wonder if you remembered the Civil Defence class. This is Mrs Keitelbein.'

'I remembered,' he lied. 'Hello, Mrs Keitelbein.' Making himself hard, he said, 'Mrs Keitelbein, I'm sorry to have to – '

She interrupted, 'It's this afternoon. This is Tuesday. At two o'clock.'

'I can't come,' he said. 'I'm bogged down in my contest work. Some other time.'

'Oh dear,' she said. 'But Mr Gumm, I went ahead and told them all about you. They're expecting to hear you speak about World War Two. I phoned every one of them up, and they're all enthusiastic.'

'I'm sorry,' he said.

'This is a calamity,' she said, plainly overcome. 'Maybe you could come and not speak; if you could be at the class and just answer questions – I know that would please them so. Don't you think you could find time for that? Walter can drop by and pick you up in his car; and I know he can drive you back home afterward. The class is only about an hour at the longest, so it wouldn't be more than an hour and fifteen minutes at the very most.'

'He doesn't have to give me a ride,' Ragle said. 'You're only half a block away.'

'Oh that's so,' she said. 'You're just up the street from us. Then you surely ought to be able to make it; please, Mr Gumm – as a favour to me.'

'Okay,' he said. It wasn't that important. An hour or so.

'Thank you so much.' Her relief and gratitude flooded through her voice. 'I really appreciate it.'

After he had hung up he got immediately to work on his entries.

128

He had only a couple of hours to get them in the mail, and the sense that they had to be posted was, as always, dominant in him.

At two o'clock he climbed the flight of unpainted, sloping steps to the porch of the Keitelbein house and rang the bell.

Opening the door, Mrs Keitelbein said, 'Welcome, Mr Gumm.'

Past her he could see a shadowy collection of ladies in flowery dresses and a few ill-defined thin-looking men; they all peered at him, and he understood that they had been standing around expecting him. Now the class could begin. Even here, he realized. My importance. But it brought him no satisfaction. The one person important to him was missing. His claim on Junie Black was slight indeed.

Mrs Keitelbein led him up beside her desk, the massive old wooden desk that he and Walter had lugged up from the basement. She had arranged a chair for him so that he would face the class. 'Here,' she said, pointing to the chair. 'You sit there.' For the class she had dressed up; her long silk robe-like skirt and blouse, with billows and lace, made him think of school graduations and musical recitals.

'Okay,' he said.

'Before they ask you anything,' she said, 'I think I'll discuss a few aspects of Civil Defence with them, just to get it out of the way.' She patted him on the arm. 'This is the first time we've had a celebrity at our meetings.' Smiling, she seated herself at her desk and rapped for order.

The indistinct ladies and gentlemen became quiet. The murmur stilled. They had seated themselves in the first rows of the folding chairs that Walter had set up. Walter himself had taken a chair in the back of the room, near the door. He wore a sweater, slacks, and necktie, and he nodded formally to Ragle.

I should have worn my coat, Ragle decided. He had sauntered down in his shirt-sleeves; now he felt ill-at-ease.

'At our last class,' Mrs Keitelbein said, folding her hands before her on the desk, 'somebody raised a question concerning the impossibility of our intercepting all the enemy missiles in the event of a full-scale surprise attack on America. That is quite true. We know that we could not possibly shoot down all the missiles. A percentage of them will get through. This is the dreadful truth, and we have to face it and deal with it accordingly.'

The men and women – they responded as a body, images of one another – put on sombre expressions.

'If war should break out,' Mrs Keitelbein said, 'we would be faced, at best with terrible ruin. Dead and dying in the tens of millions. Cities into rubble, radioactive fallout, contaminated crops, germ-plasm of future generations irretrievably damaged. At best, we would have disaster on a scale never before seen on earth. The funds appropriated by our government for defence, which seem such a burden and drain on us, would be a drop in the bucket compared with this catastrophe.'

What she says is true, Ragle thought to himself. As he listened to her, he began to imagine the death and suffering . . . dark weeds growing in the ruins of towns, corroded metal and bones scattered across a plain of ash without contour. No life, no sounds . . .

And then he experienced, without warning, an awful sense of danger. The near presence of it, the reality, crushed him. As it fell on to him he let out a croak and half-jumped from his chair. Mrs Keitelbein paused. Simultaneously all of them turned toward him.

Wasting my time, he thought. Newspaper puzzles. How could I escape so far from reality?

'Are you feeling unwell?' Mrs Keitelbein asked.

'I'm – okay,' he said.

One of the class raised her hand.

'Yes, Mrs F.,' Mrs Keitelbein said.

'If the Soviets send over their missiles in one large group, won't our anti-missile missiles, by the use of thermonuclear warheads, be able to get a higher percentage than if they are sent over in small successive waves? From what you said last week – '

'Your point is well made,' Mrs Keitelbein said. 'In fact, we might exhaust our anti-missile missiles in the first few hours of the war, and then find that the enemy did not plan to win on the basis of one vast single attack analogous to the Japanese attack on Pearl Harbour, but planned rather to win by a sort of hydrogen "nibbling away", over a period of years if necessary.'

A hand came up.

'Yes, Miss P.,' Mrs Keitelbein said.

A blurred portion detached itself, a woman saying, 'But could the Soviets afford such a prolonged attack? In World War Two, didn't the Nazis find that their economy wouldn't support the daily losses of heavy bombers incurred in their round-the-clock raids on London?'

Mrs Keiltelbein turned to Ragle. 'Perhaps Mr Gumm could answer that,' she said.

For a moment Ragle did not grasp that she had addressed him. All at once he saw her nodding at him. 'What?' he said.

'Tell us the effect losses of heavy bombers had on the Nazis,' she said. 'From the raids on England.'

'I was in the Pacific,' he said. 'I'm sorry,' he said. 'I don't know anything about the European Theatre.' He could not remember anything about the war in Europe; in his mind nothing but the sense of immediate menace remained. It had driven everything else out, emptied him. Why am I sitting here? he asked himself. I should be – where?

Tripping across a country pasture with Junie Black . . . spreading out a blanket on the hot, dry hillside, among the smells of grass and afternoon sun. No, not there. Is that gone, too? Hollow outward form instead of substance; the sun not actually shining, the day not actually warm at all but cold, grey and quietly raining, raining, the god-awful ash filtering down on everything. No grass except charred stumps, broken off. Pools of contaminated water . . .

In his mind he chased after her, across a hollow, barren hillside. She dwindled, disappeared. The skeleton of life, white brittle scarecrow support in the shape of a cross. Grinning. Space instead of eyes. The whole world, he thought, can be seen through. I am on the inside looking out. Peeking through a crack and seeing – emptiness. Seeing into its eyes.

'It's my understanding,' Mrs Keitelbein said, in answer to Miss P., 'that the German losses of experienced pilots were more serious than the losses in planes. They could build planes to replace those shot down, but it took months to train a pilot. This illustrates one change in store for us in the next war, the first Hydrogen War; missiles will not be manned, so there will be no experienced pilots to be depleted. Missiles won't stop coming

131

over simply because nobody exists to fly them. As long as factories exist, the missiles will keep coming.'

On her desk, before her, lay a mimeographed sheet. Ragle understood that she had been reading from it. A prepared programme made up by the government.

It's the government that's talking, he thought to himself. Not simply a middle-aged woman who wants to be doing something useful. These are facts, not the opinions of a single person.

This is reality.

And, he thought, I am in it.

'We have some models to show you,' Mrs Keitelbein said. 'My son Walter made them up . . . they show various vital installations.' She motioned to her son, and he got to his feet and came toward her.

'If this country is to survive the next war,' Walter said in his youthful tenor, 'it will have to learn a new way to produce. The factory as we know it now will be wiped off the face of the globe. An underground industrial network will have to be brought into being.'

For a moment he disappeared from sight; he had gone off into a side room. Everyone watched expectantly. When he returned he carried a large model which he set down before them all, on his mother's desk.

'This shows a projected factory system,' he said. 'To be built a mile or so underground, safe from attack.'

Everyone stood up to see. Ragle turned his head and saw, on the desk, a square of turrets and spires, replicas of buildings, the minarets of an industrial enterprise. How familiar, he thought. And the two of them, Mrs Keitelbein and Walter, bending over it . . . the scene had occurred before, somewhere in the past.

Getting up he moved closer to look.

A magazine page. Photograph, but not of a model; photograph of the original, of which this was a model.

Did such a factory exist?

Seeing his intensity, Mrs Keitelbein said, 'It's a very convincing replica, isn't it, Mr Gumm?'

'Yes,' he said.

'Have you ever seen anything like it before?'

The room became silent. The shapes of people listened.

'Yes,' he said.

'Where?' Mrs Keitelbein said.

He almost knew. He almost had an answer.

'What do you suppose a factory like that would turn out?' Miss P. said.

'What do you think, Mr Gumm?' Mrs Keitelbein said.

He said, 'Possibly – aluminium ingots.' It sounded right. 'Almost any basic mineral, metal, plastic or fibre,' he said.

'I'm proud of that model,' Walter said.

'You should be,' Mrs F. said.

Ragle thought, I know every inch of that. Every building and hall. Every office.

I've been inside that, he said to himself. Many times.

After the Civil Defence class he did not go home. Instead, he caught a bus and got off downtown, in the main shopping district.

For a time he walked. And then, across from him, he saw a wide parking lot and building with a sign reading: LUCKY PENNY SUPERMARKET. What an immense place, he thought to himself. Everything for sale except ocean-going tugs. He crossed the street and stepped up on to the concrete wall that surrounded the parking lot. Holding his arms out to balance himself, he followed the wall to the rear of the building, to the high steel-plated loading dock.

Four interstate trucks had backed up to the dock. Men wearing cloth aprons loaded up dollies with cardboard cartons of canned goods, mayonnaise bottles, crates of fresh fruits and vegetables, sacks of flour and sugar. A ramp composed of free-spinning rollers permitted smaller cartons, such as cartons of beer cans, to be slid from the truck to the warehouse.

Must be fun, he thought. Tossing cartons on that ramp and seeing them shoot down, across the dock and into the open door. Where somebody no doubt takes them off and stacks them up. Invisible process at the far end . . . the receiver, unseen, labouring away.

Lighting a cigarette, he strolled over.

The wheels of the trucks had a diameter equal to his own height, or nearly so. Must give a man a sense of power to drive one of those interstate rigs. He studied the licence plates tacked to the rear door of the first truck. Ten plates from ten states. Across the

Rockies, the Utah Salt Flat, into the Nevada Desert . . . snow in the mountains, hot glaring air in the flatlands. Bugs splattering on the windshield. A thousand drive-ins, motels, gas stations, signboards. Hills constantly in the distance. The dry monotony of the road.

But satisfying to be in motion. The sense of getting somewhere. Physical change of place. A different town each night.

Adventure. Romance with some lonely waitress in a roadside café, some pretty woman yearning to see a big city, have a big time. A blue-eyed lady with nice teeth, nice hair, fed by and created by a stable country scene.

I have my own waitress. Junie Black. My own adventure into the shady deals of wife-stealing romance. In the cramped environment of little houses, with the car parked under the kitchen window, clothes hanging in the yard, countless skimpy errands keeping her involved until nothing else is left, only a preoccupation with things to get done, things to have ready.

Isn't that enough for me? Aren't I satisfied?

Maybe that's why I feel this apprehension. Anxiety that Bill Black will show up with a pistol and plug me for frolicking with his wife. Catch me entwined in the middle of the afternoon, among the washing and the lawn and the shopping. My guilt transformed . . . fantasy of doom as a just payment for my transgressions. Trifling as they are.

At least, he thought, that's what the psychiatrist would say. That's what all the wives, having read Harry Stack Sullivan and Karen Horney and Karl Menninger, would declare. Or maybe it's my hostility toward Black. Anxiety is supposed to be a transformation of repressed hostility. My domestic problems projected outward on to a world screen. And Walter's model. I must want to live in the future. Because the model is a model of a thing in the future. And when I saw it, it looked perfectly natural to me.

Walking around to the front of the supermarket he passed through the electric eye, causing the door to swing wide for him. Past the check-out stands, in the produce department, Vic Nielson could be seen at the onion bin; he busily separated the unsavoury onions from the rest and tossed them into a round zinc tub.

'Hi,' Ragle said, walking up to him.

'Oh hi,' Vic said. He continued with the onions. 'Finished with your puzzle for today?'

'Yes,' he said. 'It's in the mail.'

'How are you feeling today?'

'Better,' Ragle said. The store had few customers at the moment so he said, 'Can you get off?'

'For a few minutes,' Vic said.

'Let's go somewhere we can talk,' Ragle said.

Vic took off his apron and left it with the zinc tub. He and Ragle passed by the check-out stands and Vic told the checkers that he would be back in ten or fifteen minutes. Then the two of them left the store and crossed the parking lot to the sidewalk.

'How about the American Diner Café?' Vic said.

'Fine,' Ragle said. He followed Vic out into the street, into the aggressive late-afternoon traffic; as always, Vic showed no hesitation at competing with the two-ton cars for the right-of-way. 'Don't you ever get hit?' he asked, as a Chrysler passed them so close that its tail pipes warmed the calves of his legs.

'Not yet,' Vic said, his hands in his pockets.

As they entered the café, Ragle saw an olive-green city service truck parking in one of the slots nearby.

'What's the matter?' Vic said, as he halted.

Ragle said, 'Look.' He pointed.

'So what?' Vic said.

'I hate those things,' he said. 'Those city trucks.' Probably the city work crew digging up the street in front of the house had seen him go down to the Keitelbeins'. 'Forget the coffee,' he said. 'Let's talk in the store.'

'Whatever you want,' Vic said. 'I have to go back there anyhow, sooner or later.' As they recrossed the street he said, 'What have you got against the city? Anything to do with Bill Black?'

'Possibly,' he said.

'Margo says that Junie showed up yesterday after I left for work. All dressed up. And saying something about an attorney.'

Without answering, Ragle entered the store. Vic followed him. 'Where can we go?' Ragle said.

'In here.' With a key, Vic unlocked the check-cashing booth at the far end of the store, by the liquor department. In the booth Ragle found a pair of stools, nothing more. Vic shut the door after them and dropped down on one of the stools. 'The window's shut,' he said, indicating the window at which the checks were cashed. 'Nobody can hear us. What did you want to say?'

'It has nothing to do with June,' Ragle said, on the stool across from his brother-in-law. 'I have no sordid tale to tell you.'

'That's good,' Vic said. 'I don't feel much in the mood anyhow. You've been different since the taxi driver carried you in the door. It's hard to pin down, but Margo and I talked about it after we went to bed last night.'

'What did you decide?'

Vic said, 'You seem more subdued.'

'I guess so,' he said.

'Or calmer.'

'No,' he said. 'I'm not calmer.'

'You didn't get beaten up, did you? In that bar.'

'No,' he said.

'That was the first thing that occurred to me when Daniels – the taxi driver – dumped you on the couch. But you didn't have any marks on you. And you'd know it if you had; you'd feel it and you'd see it. I got beaten up, once, years ago. It was months before I got over it. A thing like that lasts.'

Ragle said, 'I know that I almost got away.'

'From what?'

'From here. From them.'

Vic raised his head.

'I almost got over the edge and saw things the way they are. Not the way they've been arranged to look, for our benefit. But then I was grabbed and now I'm back. And it's been arranged that I don't remember enough clearly for it to have done me any good. But – '

'But what?' Vic said. Through the check-cashing window he kept his eyes fixed on the store, the stands and registers and door.

'I know I didn't spend nine hours in Frank's Bar-B-Q. I think I was there . . . I have an image of the place. But for a long time first I was somewhere else, and afterward I was somewhere up high, in a house. Doing something, with some people. It was in the house that I got my hands on whatever it was. And that's as well as I can detail it. The rest is lost forever. Today somebody showed me a replica of something, and I think that in the house I saw a photograph of the thing, the same thing. Then the city brought its trucks around – '

He broke off.

Neither of them said anything, then.

Vic said, at last, 'Are you sure it's not just fear of Bill Black finding out about you and Junie?'

'No,' he said. 'That's not it.'

'Okay,' Vic said.

'Those big interstate rigs out back,' Ragle said. 'They go a long distance, don't they? Farther than almost any other kind of vehicle.'

'Not as far as a commercial jet or a steamship or a major train,' Vic said. 'But sometimes a couple thousand miles.'

'That's far enough,' Ragle said. 'A lot farther than I got, the other night.'

'Would that get you out?'

'I think so,' Ragle said.

'What about your contest?'

'I don't know.'

'Shouldn't you keep it going?'

'Yes,' he said.

Vic said, 'You have problems.'

'Yes,' he said. 'But I want to try again. Only this time I know that I can't simply start walking until I walk out. They won't let me walk out; they'll turn me back every time.'

'What would you do, wrap yourself up in a barrel and have yourself packed with the broken stuff going back to the manufacturer?'

Ragle said, 'Maybe you can make a suggestion. You see them loaded and unloaded all the time; I never set eyes on them before today.'

'All I know is that they truck the stuff from where it's made or produced or grown; I don't know how well it's inspected or how many times the doors are opened or how long you might be sealed up. You might find yourself parked off somewhere for a month. Or they may clean the trucks out as soon as they leave here.'

'Do you know any of the drivers?'

Vic considered. 'No,' he said finally. 'Actually I don't. I see them, but they're just names. Bob, Mike, Pete, Joe.'

'I can't think of anything else to do,' Ragle said. And I am going to try again, he said to himself. I want to see that factory; not the photograph or the model, but the thing itself. The *Ding an sich*, as Kant said. 'It's too bad you're not interested in philosophy,' he said to Vic.

'Sometimes I am,' Vic said. 'Not right now, though. You mean problems such as What are things really like? The other night coming home on the bus I got a look at how things really are. I saw through the illusion. The other people in the bus were nothing but scarecrows propped up in their seats. The bus itself –' He made a sweeping motion with his hands. 'A hollow shell, nothing but a few upright supports, plus my seat and the driver's seat. A real driver, though. Really driving me home. Just me.'

Ragle reached into his pocket and brought out the small metal box that he carried with him. Opening it he presented it to Vic.

'What's this?' Vic said.

'Reality,' Ragle said. 'I give you the real.'

Vic took one of the slips of paper out and read it. 'This says "drinking fountain",' he said. 'What's it mean?'

'Under everything else,' Ragle said. 'The word. Maybe it's the word of God. The logos. "In the beginning was the Word." I can't figure it out. All I know is what I see and what happens to me. I think we're living in some other world than what we see, and I think for a while I knew exactly what that other world is. But I've lost it since then. Since that night. The future, maybe.'

Handing him back the box of words, Vic said, 'I want you to look at something.' He pointed out the check-cashing window, and Ragle looked. 'At the check-out stands,' Vic said. 'The big tall girl in the black sweater. The girl with the chest.'

'I've seen her before,' Ragle said. 'She's a knockout.' He watched as the girl rang up items on the register; as she worked she smiled merrily, a wide beaming smile of smooth white teeth. 'I think you even introduced me to her, once.'

Vic said, 'Very seriously, I want to ask you something. This may sound like a nasty remark, but I mean it in the most important sense. Don't you think you could solve your problems better in that direction than by anything else? Liz is intelligent – at least she's got more on the ball than Junie Black. She's certainly attractive. And she's not married. You've got enough money and

138

you're famous enough to interest her. The rest is up to you. Take her out a couple of times and then we'll talk about all this business again.'

'I don't think it would help,' Ragle said.

'You're seriously giving it a tumble, though, aren't you?'

'I always give it a tumble,' he said. 'That particular thing.'

'Okay,' Vic said. 'If you're sure, I guess that's that. What do you want to do, try to get hold of one of the trucks?'

'Could we?'

'We could try.'

'You want to come along?' Ragle said.

'All right,' Vic said. 'I'd like to see; sure, I'd like to have a look outside.'

'You tell me then,' Ragle said, 'how we should go about getting one of the trucks. This is your store; I'll leave it up to you.'

At five o'clock Bill Black heard the service trucks parking in the lot outside his office window. Presently his intercom buzzed and his secretary said,

'Mr Neroni to see you, Mr Black.'

'I want to talk to him,' he said. He opened the door of his office. After a moment a large muscular dark-haired man appeared, still in his drab coveralls and work shoes. 'Come on in,' Black said to him. 'Tell me what happened today.'

'I made notes,' Neroni said, setting down a reel of tape on the desk. 'For a permanent record. And there's some video tape, but it hasn't come through. The phone crew says he got a call from your wife at about ten o'clock. Nothing in it, except that he apparently thought he'd run into her at his Civil Defence class. She told him she had a date to meet a girl friend downtown. Then the woman who runs the Civil Defence class called to remind him that it was at two o'clock this afternoon. Mrs Keitelbein.'

'No,' Black said. 'Mrs Kesselman.'

'A middle-aged woman with a teen-age son.'

'That's right,' Black said. He remembered meeting the Kesselmans several years ago, when the whole situation had been dreamed up. And Mrs Kesselman had dropped by recently with her Civil Defence clipboard and literature. 'Did he go for his Civil Defence class?'

'Yes. He mailed off his entries and then he dropped by their house.'

Black had not been told about the Civil Defence class; he had no idea what its purpose was. But the Kesselmans did not get their instructions from anyone in his department.

'Did somebody cover the Civil Defence class?' Black asked.

'Not to my knowledge,' Neroni said.

'It doesn't matter,' he said. 'She gives it herself, doesn't she?'

'As far as I know. When he rang the bell she opened the door herself.' Neroni, at that point, frowned and said, 'You're sure we're talking about the same person? Mrs Kesselbein?'

'Something like that.' He felt on edge. Ragle Gumm's actions of the last several days had permanently upset him; the sense of the shaky, day-to-day balance that they had achieved had not left him with Ragle's return.

We know now that he can get away, Black thought to himself. In spite of everything, we can lose him. He can revert gradually to sanity, make plans and carry them out; we won't know until it's too late or almost too late.

The next time, we probably won't manage to find him. Or if not the next time, then the time after that. Eventually.

Hiding deep in the closet won't save me, Black said to himself. Burying myself under the clothes, in the darkness, out of sight . . . it won't do me any good.

12

When Margo arrived at the parking lot she saw no sign of her husband. Shutting off the engine of the Volkswagen, she sat for a time, watching the glass doors of the store.

Usually he's ready to go by now, she said to herself.

She got out of the car and started across the parking lot toward the store.

'Margo,' Vic called. He came from the rear of the store, from the loading docks. His pace, and the tension on his face, made her aware that something had happened.

'Are you all right?' she asked. 'You didn't agree to work Sunday, did you?' That had been in contention between them for years.

Vic caught hold of her arm and led her back to the car. 'I'm not driving home with you.' Opening the car door he nudged her inside; he got in after her, shut the door and rolled up the windows.

Behind the store, at the dock, a giant two-section truck had started to move in the direction of the Volkswagen. Is that monster going to sideswipe us? Margo wondered. One touch of that front bumper, and nothing would remain of this car and us.

'What's he doing?' she asked Vic. 'I don't think he knows how to handle that. And trucks aren't supposed to use this exit, are they? I thought you told me – '

Interrupting her, Vic said, 'Listen. It's Ragle in the truck.'

She stared at him. And then she saw up into the cab of the truck. Ragle waved at her, a slight flip of his hand. 'What do you mean, you won't be driving home with me?' she demanded. 'Do you mean you're going to take that big thing to the house and park it?' In her mind she envisioned the truck parked in their driveway, advertising to the neighbours that her husband worked in a grocery store. 'Listen,' she said, 'I won't have you driving home in one of those; I mean it.'

'I'm not driving home in it,' he said. 'Your brother and I are going on a trip in it.' He put his arm around her and kissed her. 'I don't know when we'll be back. Don't worry about us. There're a couple of things I want you to do – '

She interrupted, 'You're both going?' It made no sense to her. 'Tell me what this is about,' she said.

'The main thing I want you to do,' Vic said, 'is tell Bill Black that Ragle and I are working here at the store. Don't tell him anything else; don't tell him we've left and don't tell him when or how we've left. Do you understand that? Whatever time the Blacks show up at the house and ask where Ragle is, say you just talked to him down at the store. Even if it's two in the morning. Say I've asked him to help me do an inventory for a surprise auditing.'

'Can I ask you one thing?' she said, hoping to get at least a trifle of information; it was obvious that he had no intention of telling her much more. 'Was Ragle with Junie Black the other night when the taxi driver carried him in the door?'

'God no,' Vic said.

'Are you getting him off somewhere so that Bill Black can't find him and murder him?'

Vic eyed her. 'You're on the wrong track, honey,' He kissed her again, squeezed her, and pushed open the car door. 'Say good-bye to Sammy for us.' Turning toward the truck he yelled, 'What?' Then leaning back in the Volkswagen he said, 'Ragle says to tell Lowery at the newspaper that he found a contest that pays better.' Grinning at her, he loped over to the truck and around to the far side; she heard him climb up into the cab beside her brother, and then his face appeared next to Ragle's.

'So long,' Ragle shouted down at her. Both he and Vic waved. Roaring and spluttering, sending up black exhaust from its stack, the truck started from the lot, on to the street. Cars slowed for it; the truck performed a laborious, awkward right turn, and then it had disappeared beyond the store. For a long time she heard the heavy vibrations of it as it gained speed and departed.

They're out of their minds, she thought wretchedly. In a reflexively purposeful fashion she put the ignition key back into the lock of the Volkswagen and switched on the motor. Behind her, its wheezing obscured the last noises of the truck.

Vic's trying to save Ragle, she said to herself. Trying to get him away where he's safe. I know Junie consulted an attorney. Do they intend to marry? Maybe Bill won't divorce her.

What a dreadful event, to have Junie Black as a sister-in-law. Meditating about that, she drove slowly home.

As the truck moved through the early-evening traffic, Vic said to his brother-in-law, 'You don't think these big rigs vanish a mile outside of town?'

Ragle said, 'Food has to be brought in from outside. The same thing we'd do if we wanted to keep a zoo going.' Very much the same, he thought. 'It seems to me that those men unloading cartons of pickles and shrimp and paper towels are the connexion between us and the real world. It makes sense, anyhow. What else can we go on?'

'I hope he can breathe back there,' Vic said, meaning the driver.

They had waited until the others had gone, leaving this one. While Ted, the driver, was inside stacking cartons on the hand truck, he and Ragle had closed and bolted the thick metal doors. It had taken perhaps one minute, then, to get up into the cab and begin warming the diesel motor. While they were doing that, Margo had arrived in the Volkswagen.

'As long as it's not a refrigerator truck,' Ragle said. Or so Vic had said while they waited for the other trucks to leave.

'You don't think it would have been better to leave him in the store? Nobody looks in some of the back storerooms.'

Ragle said, 'I just have the intuition that he'd get right out. Don't ask me why.'

Vic did not ask him why. He kept his eyes on the road. They had left the downtown business section. Traffic had thinned. Stores gave way to a residential section, small modern houses, one-story, with tall TV masts and washing hanging on lines, high redwood fences, cars parked in driveways.

'I wonder where they'll stop us,' Ragle said.

'Maybe they won't.'

'They will,' he said. 'But maybe we'll be across by that time.'

After a while Vic said, 'Just consider. If this doesn't work out, you and I will face a charge of felony kidnapping and I'll no longer be in the produce business and you probably will be asked to resign from the Where Will the Little Green Man Be Next? contest.'

The houses became fewer. The truck passed gas stations, tawdry cafés, ice cream stands and motels. The dreary parade of motels . . . as if, Ragle thought, we had already gone a thousand miles and were just now entering a strange town. Nothing is so alien, so bleak and unfriendly, as the strip of gas stations – cut-rate gas stations – and motels on the rim of your own city. You fail to recognize it. And at the same time, you have to clasp it to your bosom. Not just for one night, but as long as you intend to live where you live.

But we don't intend to live here any more. We're leaving. For good.

Did I get this far before? he wondered. They had got to open fields, now. A last intersection, a minor road serving industries that had been zoned out of the city proper. The railroad tracks . . .

he noticed an infinitely long freight train at rest. The suspended drums of chemicals on towers over factories.

'Nothing like it,' Vic said. 'Especially at sunset.'

The traffic, now, had become other trucks, with few sedans.

'There's your barbecue place,' Vic said.

On the right, Ragle saw the sign, Frank's Bar-B-Q and Drinks. Modern-looking enough. Clean, certainly. New cars in the lot. The truck rumbled on past it. The place fell behind.

'Well, you got farther this time,' Vic said.

Ahead of them, the highway led into a range of hills. Up high, Ragle thought. Maybe somehow I got up there, up to the top. Tried to *walk* across those peaks. Could I have been that tanked up?

No wonder I didn't make it.

On and on they drove. The countryside became monotonous. Fields, rolling hills, everything featureless, with advertising signs stuck at intervals. And then, without warning, the hills flattened and they found themselves rolling down a long, straight grade.

'This is what makes me sweat,' Ragle said. 'Driving a big rig down a really long grade.' He had already shifted into a gear low enough to hold back the mass of the truck. At least they carried no load; the mass was small enough for him, with his limited experience, to control. During the time that they had warmed the motor, he had learned the gear-box pattern. 'Anyhow,' he said to Vic, 'we've got a horn loud as hell.' He blew a couple of blasts on it, experimentally; it made both of them jump.

At the end of the grade a yellow and black official sign attracted their attention. They could make out a cluster of sheds or temporary buildings. It had a grim look.

'Here it is,' Vic said. 'This is what you meant.'

At the sheds, several trucks had lined up. And now, as they got closer, they saw uniformed men. Across the highway the sign flapped in the evening wind.

STATE LINE AGRICULTURAL INSPECTION STATION
TRUCKS USE SCALE IN RIGHT LANE ONLY

'That means us,' Vic said. 'The scale. They're going to weigh us. If they're inspecting, they'll open up the back.' He glanced at Ragle. 'Should we stop here and try to do something with Ted?'

Too late now, Ragle realized. The state inspectors could see the truck and them inside it; anything they did would be visible. At the first shed two black police cars had been parked so that they could get on to the highway at an instant's notice. We couldn't outrun them, either, he realized. Nothing to do but continue on to the scale.

An inspector, wearing sharply pressed dark blue trousers, a light blue shirt, badge and cap, sauntered toward them as they slowed to a stop. Without even glancing at them he waved them on.

'We don't have to stop,' Ragle said excitedly, with insight. 'It's a fake!' He waved back at the inspector, and Vic did the same. The man's back was already to them. 'They don't ever stop these big carriers – just passenger cars. We're out.'

The sheds and sign dropped back and disappeared. They had got out; already, they had done it. Any other kind of vehicle would not have got through. But the genuine carriers passed back and forth all day long . . . in his rear-view mirror Ragle saw three more trucks being waved on. The trucks parked in a line at the sheds were dummies, like the other equipment.

'None of them,' he said. 'None of the trucks have to stop.'

'You were right,' Vic said. He settled back against the seat. 'I suppose if we had tried to get by them in the Volkswagen they would have told us that we had some variety of insect infestation clinging to the upholstery. Japanese beetles . . . you have to drive back and get sprayed and apply for a one-month permit for re-inspection, subject to indefinite withdrawal.'

As he drove, Ragel noticed that the highway had undergone a change. Now that they had passed the inspection station the highway had separated into two distinct roads, each five lanes wide, absolutely straight and flat. And no longer concrete. He did not recognize the material over which they now drove.

This is the outside, he said to himself. The outside highway, which we were never supposed to see or know about.

Trucks behind them and ahead of them. Some carrying supplies in, some empty and leaving, as they were. The ant trails leading into and out of the town. Ceaseless movement. And not one passenger car. Only the rumble of diesel trucks.

And, he realized, the advertising signs had vanished.

'Better switch on your lights,' Vic said. Evening gloom had settled on to the hills and fields. One truck coming toward them along the other road had its lights on. 'We want to obey the laws. Whatever they are.'

Ragle switched on the lights. The evening seemed quiet and lonely. Far off, a bird skimmed along the surface of the earth, its wings rigid. The bird lighted on a fence.

'What about fuel?' Ragle said.

Leaning past him, Vic read the fuel gauge. 'Half full,' he said. 'I frankly have no idea how far a rig like this can go on a tank. Or if there's a reserve tank. Without a load we should go fairly far. Depends a great deal on what kind of grades we run across. A heavy vehicle loses a lot on grades; you've seen trucks stuck half-way up a grade, moving ten miles an hour in lowest gear.'

'Maybe we better let Ted out,' Ragle said. It had occurred to him that their money might be worthless. 'We'll have to buy fuel and food – we don't know where, or even if we can. He must have credit cards on him. And money that's good.'

Vic tossed a handful of papers into his lap. 'From the glove compartment,' he said. 'Credit cards, maps, meal tickets. No money, though. We'll see what we can do with the credit cards. They're usually good at – ' He broke off. 'Motels,' he said finally. 'If they have them. What do you think we'll find?'

'I don't know,' Ragle said. Darkness had obliterated the landscape around them; in the open spaces between towns there were no street lights to give them clues. Only the flat land, up to the sky, where lighter colours, a bluish-black, began. Stars had appeared.

'Do we have to wait until morning?' Vic said. 'Are we going to have to drive all night?'

'Maybe so,' Ragle said. On a curve, the headlights of the truck lit up a section of fence and scrub plants beyond it. I feel as if all this had happened before, he thought. Reliving it a second time ...

Beside him, Vic examined the papers that he had brought out of the glove compartment. 'What do you make of this?' He held up a long paper strip, brightly coloured; Ragle glanced at it and saw that it read:

ONE HAPPY WORLD

At each end, in luminous yellow, a snake coiled into an S-shape.

'Has glue on back,' Vic said. 'It must be for the bumper.'

'Like "make mine milk",' Ragle said.

After a pause Vic said in a low voice, 'Let me hold the wheel. I want you to look at it closer.' He caught hold of the steering wheel and passed the bumper strip to Ragle. 'At the bottom. In type.'

Holding the strip near the dome light, Ragle read the words: *Federal law requires that this be displayed at all times.*

He passed it back to Vic. 'We're going to run into a lot more we don't understand,' he said. But the strip had disturbed him, too. Mandatory . . . it had to be on the bumper, or else.

Vic said, 'There're more.' From the glove compartment he lifted out a stack of strips, ten or eleven of them, all alike. 'He must glue it on every time he makes a trip. Probably rips it off when he enters town.'

At the next stretch of empty highway, when no other trucks could be seen, Ragle drove from the road on to the gravel shoulder. He stopped the truck and put on the hand brake. 'I'm going to go around to the back,' he said. 'I'll see if he's getting enough air.' As he opened the cab door he said, 'And I'll ask him about the strip.'

Nervously, Vic slid over behind the wheel. 'I doubt if he'll give you a right answer,' he said.

Walking with care, Ragle made his way through the darkness along the side of the truck, past the great wheels, to the back. He climbed the iron ladder and rapped on the door. 'Ted,' he said. 'Or whatever your name is. Are you all right?'

From within the truck a voice said indistinctly, 'Yeah. I'm okay, Mr Gumm.'

Even here, Ragle thought. Parked on the shoulder of the highway, in a deserted region between towns. I'm recognized.

'Listen, Mr Gumm,' the driver said, his mouth close to the crack of the doors. 'You don't know what's out here, do you? You have no idea. Listen to me; there isn't a chance in the world you'll run into anything but harm – harm for you, harm for everybody else. You have to take my word for it. I'm telling you the truth. Someday you'll look back and know I was right. You'll thank me. Here.' A small white square of paper slid out from between the doors and fluttered down; Ragle caught it. A card, on the back of which the driver had written a phone number.

'What's this for?' Ragle said.

The driver said, 'When you get to the next town, pull off the road and go phone that number.'

'How far's the next town?'

A hesitation, and then the driver said, 'I'm not sure. Pretty soon now. It's hard to keep track of the miles stuck back here.'

'Can you get enough air?'

'Yeah.' The driver sounded resigned, but at the same time highly keyed up. 'Mr Gumm,' he said, in the same intense, beseeching voice, 'you just got to believe me. I don't care how long you keep me cooped up in this thing, but in the next hour or two you've just got to get in touch with somebody.'

'Why?' Ragle said.

'I can't say. Look, you apparently got it figured out enough to hijack this rig. So you must have some idea. If you have that much, you can figure out that it's important and not just somebody's smart idea, building all those houses and streets and those old cars back there.'

Talk on, Ragle thought to himself.

'You don't even know how to drive a two-section rig,' the driver said. 'Suppose you hit a steep grade? This clunk carries forty-five thousand pounds when it's loaded; of course it ain't loaded right now. But you might sideswipe something. And there're a couple of railroad trestles this thing won't clear. You probably don't have any idea what the clearance of this is. And you don't know how to gear down a grade or anything.' He lapsed into silence.

'What's the bumper strip for?' Ragle said. 'The motto and the snake.'

'Christ's sake!' the driver snarled.

'Does it have to go on?'

Cursing at him, the driver managed finally to say, 'Listen, Mr Gumm – if you don't have that on right, they'll blow you sky-high; so help me god, I'm telling you the truth.'

'How does it go on?' he said.

'Let me out and I'll show you. I'm not going to tell you.' The man's voice rose in hysteria. 'You better let me out so I can stick it on, or honest to god, you won't get by the first tank that spots you.'

Tank, Ragle thought. The notion appalled him.

Hopping down, he walked back to the cab. 'I think we're going to have to let him out,' he said to Vic.

'I heard him,' Vic said. 'I'd just as soon he was out of there, in any case.'

'He may be stringing us along,' Ragle said.

'We better not take the chance.'

Ragle walked back, climbed the ladder, and unfastened the door. It swung back, and the driver, still cursing sullenly, dropped down on to the gravel.

'Here's the strip,' Ragle said to him. He handed it over. 'What else do we have to know?'

'You have to know everything,' the driver said bitterly. Kneeling down he yanked a transparent covering from the back of the strip, pressed the strip to the rear bumper, and then rubbed it smooth with his fist. 'How are you going to buy fuel?'

'Credit card,' Ragle said.

'What a laugh,' the driver said, standing up. 'That credit card is for in – ' He ceased. 'In town,' he said. 'It's a fake. It's a regular old Standard Oil credit card; there haven't been any of them for twenty years.' Glaring at Ragle he continued, 'It's all rationed, kerosene for the truck – '

'Kerosene,' Ragle echoed. 'I thought it took diesel oil.'

'No,' the driver said, with massive reluctance. He spat into the gravel. 'It's not diesel. The stack is fake. It's turbine. Uses kerosene. But they won't sell you any. The first place you go, they'll know something isn't right. And out here – ' Again his voice rose to a screech. 'You can't take no risks! None at all!'

'Want to ride in front with us?' Ragle said. 'Or in the back? I'll leave it up to you.' He wanted to get the truck into motion again.

The driver said, 'Go to hell.' Turning his back, he started off down the gravel shoulder, hands in his pockets, body hunched forward.

As the shape of the driver disappeared into the darkness, Ragle thought, it's my own fault for unbolting the door. Nothing I can do; I can't run after him and hit him over the head. In a fight he'd take me apart. Take us both apart.

And anyhow, that isn't the answer. That isn't what we're looking for.

Returning to the cab, he said to Vic, 'He's gone. I guess we're lucky he didn't jump out of the back waving a tyre-iron.'

'We better start up,' Vic said, sliding away. 'Want me to drive? I could. Did he stick the bumper strip on?'

'Yes,' Ragle said.

'I wonder how long it'll be before he gets word to them about us.'

Ragle said, 'We would have had to let him out eventually.'

For another hour they passed no sign of activity or habitation. Then, suddenly, as the truck came out of a sharp descending curve, a group of bright bluish lights flashed ahead of them, far off down the highway.

'Here's something,' Vic said. 'It's hard to know what to do. If we slow down or stop –'

'We'll have to stop,' Ragle said. Already, he could make out the sight of cars, or vehicles of some sort, parked across the road.

As the truck slowed, men appeared, waving flashlights. One of them strode to the window of the cab and called up, 'Shut off your motor. Leave your lights on. Get down.'

They had no choice. Ragle opened the door and stepped down, Vic behind him. The man with the flashlight had on a uniform, but in the darkness Ragle could not make it out. The man's helmet had been painted so that it did not shine. He flashed his light into Ragle's face, then Vic's face, and then he said,

'Open up the back.'

Ragle did so. The man and two companions hopped into the truck and rummaged about. Then they reappeared and jumped down.

'Okay,' one of them said. He held something out to Ragle, a piece of paper. Accepting it, Ragle saw that it was some sort of punched form. 'You can go ahead.'

'Thanks,' Ragle said. Numbly, he and Vic returned to the cab, climbed in and started up the motor, and drove off.

Presently Vic said, 'Let's see what he gave you.'

Holding the wheel with his left hand, Ragle fished the form from his pocket.

'There's your date,' Ragle said. April third, 1998. The balance
of the form consisted of IBM-style punches.

'They seemed satisfied with us,' Vic said. 'Whatever it was they
were looking for, we didn't have it.'

'They had uniforms.'

'Yes, they looked like soldiers. One of them had a gun, but I
couldn't tell anything about it. There must be a war on, or
something.'

Or, Ragle thought, a military dictatorship.

'Did they see if we had the bumper strip on?' Vic said. 'In the
excitement I didn't notice.'

'Neither did I,' Ragle said.

A while later he saw what appeared to be a town ahead of them.
A variety of lights, the regular rows that might be street lights,
neon signs with words . . . somewhere in his coat he had the card
the driver had given him. This is where we're supposed to call
from, he decided.

'We got through the border clearance okay,' Vic said. 'If we can
do that, with them shining their lights right on us, we ought to
be able to walk into a beanery and order a plate of hotcakes. I
didn't have any dinner after work.' He rolled back his sleeve to
read his wristwatch. 'It's ten-thirty,' he said. 'I haven't had anything to eat since two.'

'We'll stop,' Ragle said. 'We'll try to get fuel while we're here.
If we can't get it, we'll leave the truck.' The gauge showed the
tank to be almost empty. The level had dropped surprisingly
fast. But they had gone quite a distance; they had been on the
road for hours.

It struck him, as they passed the first houses, that something
was missing.

Gas stations. Usually, on highway approaches to a town, even
a tiny unimportant town, a solid line of gas stations could be seen
on both sides. Before anything else. None here.

'It doesn't look good,' he said. But they had seen no traffic,
either. No traffic and no gas stations. Or kerosene stations, if that
was the equivalent. Suddenly he slowed the truck and turned

on to a side road. He brought the truck to a halt at the curb.

'I agree,' Vic said. 'We better try it on foot. We don't know enough to drive this thing around town.'

They got warily out and stood together, in the dull light of an overhead street lamp. The houses appeared ordinary. Small, square, one storey, with lawns that were black in the night darkness. Houses, Ragle thought, haven't changed much since the thirties anyhow. Especially if seen at night. One taller shape might have been a multiple unit.

'If they stop us,' Vic said, 'and ask for identification or some such, what should we do? We better agree on it now.'

Ragle said, 'How can we agree? We don't know what they'll ask for.' The driver's remarks still bothered him. 'Let's see,' he said, and started off in the direction of the highway.

The first lights resolved themselves into a roadside diner. Within, sitting at the counter, two boys ate sandwiches. High school boys, with blond hair.

Their hair had been wound up into topknots. Tall cones of hair, each with a sharp, colourful spike stuck into it. The boys wore identical clothes. Sandals, wrap-around bright blue toga-like gowns, metal bracelets on their arms. And when one of them twisted his head to drink from a cup, Ragle saw that the boy's cheeks had been tattooed. And, he saw with disbelief, the boy's teeth had been filed.

Beyond the counter, the middle-aged waitress wore a simple green blouse, and her hair had been trained in a familiar manner. But the two boys . . . both he and Vic stared at them, through the window, until at last the waitress noticed them.

'We had better go on in,' Ragle said.

The door opened for them by electric eye. Just like the supermarket, Ragle thought.

Both boys watched them as they self-consciously seated themselves in one of the booths. The interior of the diner, the fixtures and signs and lighting, seemed ordinary to him. Ads for a number of foods . . . but the prices made no sense. 4.5, 6.7, 2.0. Obviously not dollars and cents. Ragle stared around him, as if he were trying to decide what he wanted. The waitress began to gather up her order pad.

One of the boys, nodding his topknotted head toward Vic and

Ragle, said audibly, 'Necktie-fellows, them smell fright-fright.'

His companion laughed.

The waitress, stationing herself at their booth, said, 'Good evening.'

'Good evening,' Vic muttered.

'What would you like?' the waitress asked.

Ragle said, 'What do you recommend?'

'Oh, depends on how hungry you are,' the waitress said.

The money, Ragle thought. The damn money. He said, 'How about a ham and cheese sandwich and coffee.'

Vic said, 'The same for me. And some pie à la mode.'

'Pardon?' the waitress said, writing.

'Pie with ice cream,' Vic said.

'Oh,' she said. Nodding, she returned to the counter.

One of the boys said in a clear voice, 'Necktie-fellows, many old thing-sign. You s'pose – ' He stuck his thumbs in his ears. The other boy snickered.

When the sandwiches and coffee had been brought, and the waitress had gone off, one of the boys swivelled around in his chair to face them. The tattooing on his cheeks, Ragle noticed, had been carried out in design on his arm bracelets. He gazed at the intricate lines, and at last he identified the figures. The designs had been copied from Attic vases. Athena and her owl. Kore rising from the Earth.

The boy said directly to him and Vic, 'Hey, you lunatic.'

The flesh at the back of Ragle's neck began to crawl. He pretended to concentrate on his sandwich; across from him Vic, sweating and pale, did the same.

'Hey,' the boy said.

The waitress said, 'Cut it out, or out of here for you.'

To her, the boy said, 'Necktie-fellow.' Again he stuck his thumbs in his ears. The waitress did not seem impressed.

I can't stand it, Ragle thought. I can't live through this. The driver was right. To Vic he said, 'Let's go.'

'Fine,' Vic said. He arose, grasping his sandwich, bent down to drink the last of his coffee, and then started for the door.

Now the check, Ragle thought. So we're doomed. We can't win.

'We have to get going,' he said to the waitress. 'Never mind the pie. How much?' He groped in his coat pocket, a futile gesture.

The waitress added up the bill. 'Eleven-Nine,' she said.

Ragle opened his wallet. The two boys watched. So did the waitress. When they saw the money, the paper banknotes, the waitress said, 'Oh, dear. I haven't seen paper money in years. I guess it's still good.' To the first of the boys she said, 'Ralf, does the government still redeem those old paper notes?'

The boy nodded.

'Wait,' the waitress said. She recomputed the bill. 'That'll be one-forty,' she said. 'But I'll have to give you your change in tokes. If that's all right.' Apologetically, she dug a handful of small plastic wafers from the register, and as he gave her a five-dollar bill she handed back six of the wafers. 'Thank you,' she said.

As he and Vic left, the waitress seated herself with a paper-bound book and resumed her reading at a flattened page.

'What an ordeal,' Vic said. They walked along, both of them eating the last of their sandwiches. 'Those kids. Those ghastly damn kids.'

Lunatic, Ragle thought. Did they recognize me?

At the corner he and Vic stopped. 'What now?' Vic said. 'Anyhow, we can use our money. And we've got some of theirs.' He lit his cigarette lighter to inspect one of the wafers. 'It's plastic,' he said. 'Obviously a substitute for metal. Very light. Like those wartime ration tokens.'

Yes, Ragle thought. Wartime ration tokens. Pennies made out of some nondescript alloy, not copper. And now, tokes. Tokens.

'But there's no blackout,' he said. 'They have their lights on.'

'It's not the same any more,' Vic said. 'Lights was when – ' He broke off. 'I don't understand,' he said. 'I remember World War Two. But I guess I don't, do I? That's the whole point. That was fifty years ago. Before I was born. I never lived through the thirties and forties. Neither did you. All we know about it – they must have taught us.'

'Or we read it,' Ragle said.

'Don't we know enough now?' Vic said. 'We're out. We've seen it.' He shuddered. 'They nad their teeth filed.'

Ragle said, 'That was almost pidgin English they were talking.'

'I guess so.'

'And African tribal markings. And garments.' But they looked at me and one of them said, *Hey, you lunatic.* 'They know,' he said. 'About me. But they don't care.' Somehow, that made him feel more uneasy. Spectators. The cynical, mocking young faces.

'It's surprising they're not in the army,' Vic said.

'They probably will be.' To him, the boys had not appeared old enough. More like sixteen or seventeen.

As he and Vic stood on the corner, footsteps echoed along the dark, deserted street.

Two shapes approached them.

'Hey, you lunatic,' one of them said. Leisurely, the two boys emerged in the street light of the intersection, their arms folded, their faces blank and impersonal. 'Hold you-self stop-stop.'

13

The boy on the left reached into his robe and produced a leather case. From it he selected a cigar and a small pair of gold scissors; he cut off one end of the cigar and placed the cigar in his mouth. His companion, with equal ritual, brought forth a jewelled cigar lighter and lit his friend's cigar.

The boy smoking the cigar said, 'Necktie-fellows, you carry dead chuck-chuck. Wait-lady, she make foulupgoweewee.'

The money, Ragle understood. The waitress shouldn't have accepted it. The boys had told her to, but they had known what the driver had known; it was no longer legal tender.

'So what?' Vic said, also following their broken jargon.

The boy with the jewelled lighter said, 'Bigchiefs, they fixee. No? No? So.' He held out his hand. 'Bigchief fixee, necktie-fellows fixee fat chuck-chuck.'

'Give him some of the tokens,' Vic said, under his breath.

Ragle counted four of the six tokes into the boy's open hand.

The boy bowed from the waist; his topknot grazed the side-walk. Beside him his companion stood impassively upright, ignoring the transaction.

'You necktie-fellows, you got woojy?' the boy with the lighter said emotionlessly.

'Necktie-fellows eyeball on pavement,' the boy with the lighter said. Both he and his companion nodded. Now they had taken on a sombre air, as if something important had entered into the questioning. 'Flop-flop,' the boy with the cigar lighter said. 'Right, necktie-fellows? Flop-flop.' He clapped his hands, back to back, like a seal. Both Ragle and Vic watched in fascination.

'Sure,' Vic said.

The two boys conferred. Then the first, puffing on his cigar and scowling, said, 'Dead chuck-chuck for plenty woojy. You go joe no?'

'No,' his companion put in quickly, striking him on the chest with the flat of his hand. 'Baby go joe no chuck-chuck. Flop ina flop, ina flop-flop. Necktie-fellows flop-flop youself.' Wheeling, he started off, craning his neck and weaving his head from side to side.

'Wait a minute,' Ragle said, as the other boy prepared to do the same. 'Let's talk it over.'

Both boys halted, turned and regarded him with amazement.

Then the boy with the cigar held out his hand. 'Dead chuck-chuck,' he said.

Ragle got out his wallet. 'One bill,' he said. He handed the boy a dollar bill; the boy accepted it. 'That's plenty.'

After the boys had again conferred, the one with the cigar stuck up two fingers.

'Okay,' Ragle said. 'Do you have any more ones?' he asked Vic.

Digging into his pocket Vic said, 'Be sure you want to go along with this.'

The alternative, as he saw it, was to remain on the street corner, with no idea where they were or what to do. 'Let's take a chance,' he said, accepting the bills and passing them over to the boy. 'Now,' he said to the boys. 'Let's have the plenty woojy.'

The boys nodded, bowed from the waist, and stalked away. He and Vic, after hesitating, followed them.

The journey took them down damp-smelling, twisting alleys, across lawns and up driveways. At last the boys led them over a fence and up a flight of steps, to a door. One of the boys rapped on the door. It opened.

'Necktie-fellows quickly walkinachamber,' the boy whispered, as he and his companion squeezed insiae.

Unstable brown light filled the room. To Ragle, it appeared to be a commonplace, rather barren apartment. He saw, through an open door, a kitchen with sink, table, stove, refrigerator. Two other doors had been left shut. In the room sat several boys, all on the floor. The only furniture was a lamp, a table, a television set, and a pile of books. Some of the boys wore the robes, sandals, topknots, and bracelets. The others wore single-breasted suits, white shirts, argyle socks, oxfords. All gazed at Ragle and Vic.

'Here woojy,' the boy with the cigar said. 'You makum sit-sit.' He indicated the floor.

'What did you say?' Vic said.

Ragle said, 'Can't we take the woojy with us?'

'No,' one of the seated boys said. 'Sniff sitinachamber.'

The boy with the cigar opened a door and disappeared into the other room. After a time he returned with a bottle which he handed to Ragle. Everyone watched as Ragle accepted the bottle.

As soon as he had unscrewed the lid, he recognized it.

Vic, sniffing, said, 'It's plain pure carbon tet.'

'Yes,' Ragle said. They've been sitting around sniffing carbon tet, he realized. This is woojy.

'Sniff,' one of the boys said.

Ragle sniffed. Off and on, during his life, he had had occasion to get a noseful of carbon tet. It had no effect on him, except to make his head ache. He passed the bottle to Vic. 'Here,' he said.

'No thanks,' Vic said.

One of the boys in a suit said in a high-pitched voice, 'Necktie-fellows bedivere.'

Everyone smiled cuttingly.

'That's a girl,' Vic said. 'That one there.'

Those in suits, oxfords, shirts and argyles were girls. Their hair had been shaved right to their scalps. But, by their smaller, more delicate features, Ragle recognized them as girls. They wore no make-up. If one of them hadn't spoken, he would not have known.

Ragle said, 'Pretty sissy woojy.'

The room became silent.

One of the girls said, 'Necktie-fellow, him play strange fruit by-an-by.'

The faces of the boys had darkened. At last one of the boys

arose, walked over to the corner of the room, and picked up a tall slim cloth bag. From the bag he slipped a plastic tube with holes spaced along it. He placed one end of the tube in his nose, covered the holes with his fingers, and then humming, began to play a tune on the tube. A nose-flute.

'Sweet flute-flute,' one of the girls, in her suit, said.

The boy lowered the flute, wiped his nose with a small coloured cloth which he drew from his sleeve, and then said in the general direction of Ragle and Vic, 'How's it feel being a lunatic?'

The jargon has lapsed, Ragle thought. Now that they're sore. The others in the room, the girls especially, stared at Ragle and Vic.

'A lunatic?' one of the girls said faintly. 'Really?' she asked the boy.

'Sure,' the boy said. 'Necktie-fellows lunatic.' He smirked. But he, too, looked uneasy. 'Isn't that right?' he demanded.

Ragle said nothing. Beside him Vic ignored the boy.

'You by yourselves?' another boy asked. 'Or are there any more of you around?'

'Just us,' Ragle said.

They stared at him wildly.

'Yes,' he said. 'I admit it.' It seemed to command respect from them, unlike anything else. 'We're lunatics.'

None of the kids moved. They sat rigidly.

One of the boys laughed. 'So necktie-fellows lunatic. So what?' Shrugging, he too went over and got his nose-flute.

'Strike up the flute-flute,' a girl said. Now three flutes had started to whine.

'We're wasting our time here,' Vic said.

'Yes,' he agreed. 'We better leave.' He started to open the door, but as he did so, one of the boys removed the flute from his nose and said,

'Hey, necktie-fellows.'

They stopped.

The boy said, 'MP after you. You go outadoor, MP catch.' He resumed his fluting. The others nodded.

'You know what MP do with lunatic?' a girl said. 'MP give dose of c.c.'

'What's that?' Vic said.

All of them laughed. None of them answered. The fluting and humming continued.

'Necktie-fellows pale,' a boy said, between breaths.

Outside, on the stairs, a tread made the floor shake. The fluting ceased. A knock.

They have us now, Ragle thought. No one in the room moved as the door opened.

'You darn kids,' a raspy voice muttered. A grey-haired elderly woman, immense in a shapeless silk wrapper, peered into the room. She had furred slippers on her feet. 'I told you no piping after ten o'clock. Cut it out.' She glared at them all, from half-shut eyes. At that point she noticed Ragle and Vic. 'Oh,' she said, with suspicion. 'Who are you?'

They tell her, Ragle thought, and then she flounders back down the steps in a state of panic. And the tanks – or whatever the MPs come in – arrive at the bottom. Ted the driver has had plenty of time, by now. So has the waitress. So has everyone.

Anyhow, he thought, we've been out and we've seen that it is 1998, not 1959, and a war is in progress, and the kids now talk like and dress like West African natives and the girls wear men's clothing and shave their heads. And money as we know it has dropped out somewhere along the line. Along with diesel trucks. But, he thought with sudden pessimism, we didn't learn what it's all about. Why they set up the old town, the old cars and streets, kidded us for years . . .

'Who are these two gentlemen?' the elderly woman inquired.

A pause, and then one of the girls, with a mischievous grin, said, 'Looking for rooms.'

'What?' the old woman said, with disbelief.

'Sure,' a boy said. 'They showed up here looking for a room to rent. Stumbling around. Don't you gotcha porch light on?'

'No,' the old woman said. She got out a handkerchief and wiped at her soft, wrinkled forehead; under the pressure the flesh yielded. 'I had retired.' To Ragle and Vic, she said, 'I'm Mrs McFee. I own this apartment house. What kind of rooms did you want?'

Before Ragle could think of an answer, Vic said, 'Anything will do. What do you have?' He glanced at Ragle, showing his relief.

'Well,' she said, beginning to waddle back out on to the stairs, 'if you two gentlemen will follow me, I'll just show you.' On the stairs, she gripped the railing and swung her head to peer back at them. 'Come on,' she said, gasping for breath. Her face had swollen with exertion. 'I've got some very attractive property. You wanted something together, the two of you?' Eyeing them doubtfully, she said, 'Let's step into my office and I can chat with you about your employment and – ' she started on down again, step by step – 'other particulars.'

At the bottom, with much muttering and gasping she located a light switch; a bare bulb winked on, showing them the path that led along the side of the house to the front porch. On the porch an old-fashioned cane rocking chair could be seen. Old-fashioned even from their standpoint. Some things never change, Ragle thought.

'Right in here,' Mrs McFee called. 'If you will.' She disappeared into the house; he and Vic trailed after her, into a cluttered, dark, clothy-smelling living room filled with bric-a-brac, chairs, lamps, framed pictures on the walls, carpets, and, on the mantel, greeting cards by the score. Over the mantel, knitted or woven in many colours, hung a streamer with the words:

ONE HAPPY WORLD BRINGS BLESSINGS
OF JOY TO ALL MANKIND

'What I'd appreciate knowing,' Mrs McFee said, lowering herself into an easy chair, 'is if you're regularly employed.' Leaning forward she tugged a massive ledger from a desk, on to her lap.

'Yes,' Ragle said. 'We're regularly employed.'

'What sort of business?'

Vic said, 'Grocery business. I operate the produce section of a supermarket.'

'A what?' the old woman gasped, twisting her head to hear. In its cage a black and yellow bird of some variety squawked hoarsely. 'Be quiet, Dwight,' she said.

Vic said, 'Fruits and vegetables. Retail selling.'

'What sort of vegetables?'

'All kinds,' he said, with annoyance.

'Where do you get them?'

'From truckers,' Vic said.

'Oh,' she said, grunting. 'And I suppose,' she said to Ragle, 'you're the inspector.'

Ragle said nothing.

'I don't trust you vegetable men,' Mrs McFee said. 'There was one of you around – I don't think it was you, but it might have been – last week. They looked good, but oh my, I would have died if I'd eaten any. They had r.a. written all over them. I can tell. Of course, the man assured me they didn't grow top-top; came from way down in the cellars. Showed me the tag that swore they grew a mile down. But I can smell r.a.'

Ragle thought, *Radio-activity*. Produce grown up on the surface, exposed to fallout. There've been bombings, in the past. Contamination of crops. Understanding rushed over him; the scene of trucks being loaded with food grown underground. *The cellars*. Dangerous peddling of contaminated tomatoes and melons . . .

'No r.a. in our stuff,' Vic said. 'Radio-activity,' he said under his breath, for Ragle's benefit.

'Yes,' Ragle said.

Vic said, 'We're – from a long distance from here. We just got in tonight.'

'I see,' Mrs McFee said.

'We've both been ill,' Vic said. 'What's been happening?'

'What do you mean?' the old woman said, pausing in her task of flipping the pages of her ledger. She had put on a pair of horn-rimmed glasses; behind them her eyes, magnified, had a shrewd, alert glint.

'What's been happening?' Ragle demanded. 'The war,' he said. 'Will you tell us?'

Mrs McFee wet her finger and again turned pages. 'Funny you don't know about the war.'

'Tell us,' Vic said fiercely. 'For Christ's sake!'

'Are you enlisters?' Mrs McFee said.

'No,' Ragle said.

'I'm patriotic, but I won't have enlisters living in my house. Causes too much trouble.'

We'll never get a straight story from her, Ragle thought. It's hopeless. We might as well give up.

On a table rested an upright frame of tinted photographs, all of a young man in uniform. Ragle bent to examine the photographs. 'Who is he?' he said.

'My son,' Mrs McFee said. 'He's stationed down at Anvers Missile Station. I haven't seen him in three years. Not since the war began.'

That recently, Ragle thought. Perhaps the same time that they built the –

When the contest began. Where Will the Little Green Man Be Next? Almost three years . . .

He said, 'Any hits, down there?'

'I don't understand you,' Mrs McFee said.

'Never mind,' Ragle said. Aimlessly, he roamed about the room. Through a wide arch of dark-shiny wood he could see a dining room. Solid central table, many chairs, wall shelves, glass cupboards with plates and cups. And, he saw, a piano. Wandering over to the piano he picked up a handful of the sheet music resting on the rack. All cheap popular sentimental tunes, mostly to do with soldiers and girls.

One of the tunes had the title:

LOONIES ON THE RUN MARCH

Carrying the sheet music back with him, he handed it to Vic. 'See,' he said. 'Read the words.'

Together, they read the verse under the music staff.

> You're a goon, Mister Loon,
> One World you'll never sunder.
> A buffoon, Mister Loon,
> Oh what a dreadful blunder.
> The sky you find so cosy;
> The future tinted rosy;
> But Uncle's gonna spank - you wait!
> So hands ina sky, hands ina sky,
> *Before it is too late! !*

'Do you play, mister?' the old woman was asking.

Ragle said to her, 'The enemy – they're the lunatics, aren't they?'

The sky, he thought. The Moon. Luna.

It wasn't himself and Vic that the MPs hunted. It was the enemy. The war was being fought between Earth and the Moon. And if the kids upstairs could take him and Vic for lunatics, then lunatics had to be human beings. Not creatures. They were colonists, perhaps.

A civil war.

I know what I do, now. I know what the contest is, and what I am. I'm the saviour of this planet. When I solve a puzzle I solve the time and place the next missile will strike. I file one entry after another. And these people, whatever they call themselves, hustle an anti-missile unit to that square on the graph. To that place and at that time. And so everyone stays alive, the kids upstairs with their nose-flutes, the waitress, Ted the driver, my brother-in-law, Bill Black, the Kesselmans, the Keitelbeins. . . .

That's what Mrs Keitelbein and her son had started telling me. Civil Defence . . . *nothing but a history of war up to the present.* Models from 1998, to remind me.

But why have I forgotten?

To Mrs McFee he said, 'Does the name Ragle Gumm mean anything to you?'

The old woman laughed. 'Not a darn thing,' she said. 'As far as I'm concerned Ragle Gumm can go jump in a hat. There isn't any one person who can do that; it's a whole bunch of people, and they always call them "Ragle Gumm". I've known that from the start.'

With a deep, unsteady breath, Vic said, 'I think you're wrong, Mrs McFee. I think there is such a person and he really does do that.'

She said slyly, 'And be right, day in day out?'

'Yes,' Ragle said. Beside him, Vic nodded.

'Oh come on,' she said, screeching.

'A talent,' Ragle said. 'An ability to see a pattern.'

'Listen,' Mrs McFee said, 'I'm a lot older than you boys. I can remember when Ragle Gumm was nothing but a fashion designer, making those hideous Miss Adonis hats.'

'Hats,' Ragle said.

'In fact I still have one.' Grunting, she rose to her feet and lumbered to a closet. 'Here.' She held up a derby hat. 'Nothing but a man's hat. Why, he got them wearing men's hats just to

163

get rid of a lot of old hats when men stopped buying them.'

'And he made money in the hat business?' Vic said.

'Those fashion designers make millions,' Mrs McFee said. 'They all do; every one of them. He was just lucky. That's it – luck. Nothing but luck. And later when he got into the synthetic aluminium business.' She reflected. 'Aluminide. That was luck. One of these fireball lucky men, but they always wind up the same way; their luck runs out on them at the end. His did.' Knowingly, she said, 'His ran out, but they never told us. That's why nobody sees Gumm any more. His luck ran out, and he committed suicide. It's not a rumour. It's a fact. I know a man whose wife worked for the MPs for a summer, and she told him it's positive; Gumm killed himself two years ago. And they've had one person after another predicting those missiles.'

'I see,' Ragle said.

Triumphantly, Mrs McFee told him, 'When they made him put up – when he accepted that offer to come to Denver and do their missile predicting for them, then they saw through him; they saw it was just bluff. And rather than stand the public shame, the disgrace, he – '

Vic interrupted, 'We have to leave.'

'Yes,' Ragle said. 'Good night.' Both he and Vic started toward the door.

'What about your rooms?' Mrs McFee demanded, following after them. 'I haven't had a chance to show you anything.'

'Good night,' Ragle said. He and Vic stepped out on to the porch, down the steps to the path, and to the sidewalk.

'Will you be back?' Mrs McFee called from the porch.

'Later,' Vic said.

The two of them walked away from the house.

'I forgot,' Ragle said. 'I forgot all this.' But I kept on predicting, he thought. I did it anyhow. So in a sense it doesn't matter, because I'm still doing my job.

Vic said, 'I always believed you couldn't learn anything from popular tune lyrics. I was wrong.'

And, Ragle realized, if I'm not sitting in my room working on the puzzle tomorrow, as I always do, our lives may well be snuffed out. No wonder Ted the driver pleaded with me. And no wonder my face was on the cover of *Time* as Man of the Year.

'I remember,' he said, stopping. 'That night. The Kesselmans. The photograph of my aluminium plant.'

'Aluminide,' Vic said. 'She said, anyhow.'

Do I remember everything? Ragle asked himself. What else is there?

'We can go back,' Vic said. 'We have to go back. You do, at least. I guess they needed a bunch of people around you, so that it would look natural. Margo, myself, Bill Black. The conditioned responses, when I reached around in the bathroom for the light cord. They must have light cords, here. Or I did, anyhow. And when the people at the market ran as a group. They must have worked in a store here, worked together. Maybe in a grocery store out here, the same job. Everything the same except that it was forty years later.'

Ahead of them a cluster of lights burned.

'We'll try there,' Ragle said, increasing his pace. He still had the card Ted had given him. The number probably got him in touch with the military people, or whoever it was who had arranged the town in the first place. Back again . . . but why?

'Why is it necessary?' he asked. 'Why can't I do it here? Why do I have to live there, imagining I'm back in 1959, working on a newspaper contest?'

'Don't ask me,' Vic said. 'I can't tell you.'

The lights transformed themselves into words. A neon sign in several colours, burning in the darkness:

WESTERN DRUG AND PHARMACY

'A drugstore,' Vic said. 'We can phone from there.'

They entered the drugstore, an astonishingly tiny, narrow, brilliantly lit place with high shelves and displays. No customers could be seen, nor a clerk; Ragle stopped at the counter and looked around for the public phones. Do they still have them? he wondered.

'May I help you?' a woman's voice sounded nearby.

'Yes,' he said. 'We want to make a phone call. It's urgent.'

'You better show us how to operate the phone,' Vic said. 'Or maybe you could get the number for us.'

'Certainly,' the clerk said, sliding around from behind the counter in her white smock. She smiled at them, a middle-aged woman wearing low-heeled shoes. 'Good evening, Mr Gumm.'

He recognized her.

Mrs Keitelbein.

Nodding to him, Mrs Keitelbein passed him on her way to the door. She closed and locked the door, pulled down the shade, and then turned to face him. 'What's the phone number?' she said.

He handed her the card.

'Oh,' she said, reading the number. 'I see. That's the switchboard for the Armed Services, at Denver. And the extension is 62. That – ' She began to frown. 'That probably would be somebody in the missile-defence establishment. If they'd be there this late they must virtually live there. So that would make them somebody high up.' She returned the card. 'How much do you remember?' she said.

Ragle said, 'I remember a great deal.'

'Did my showing you the model of your factory help you?'

'Yes,' he said. It certainly had. After seeing it, he had got on to the bus and ridden downtown to the supermarket.

'Then I'm glad,' she said.

'You're hanging around,' he said, 'to give me systematic doses of memory. Then you must represent the Armed Services.'

'I do,' she said. 'In a sense.'

'Why did I forget in the first place?'

Mrs Keitelbein said, 'You forgot because you were made to forget. The same way you were made to forget what happened to you that night when you got up as far as the top of the hill and ran into the Kesselmans.'

'But it was city trucks. City employees. They grabbed me. They worked me over. The next morning they started ripping out the street. Keeping an eye on me.' That meant the same people who ran the town. The people who had built it. 'Did they make me forget in the first place?'

'Yes,' she said.

'But you want me to remember.'

She said, 'That's because I'm a lunatic. Not the kind you are, but the kind the MPs want to round up. You had made up your mind to come over to us, Mr Gumm. In fact, you had packed your briefcase. But something went wrong and you never got to us.

166

They didn't want to put an end to you, because they needed you. So they put you to work solving puzzles in a newspaper. That way you could use your talent for them . . . without ethical qualms.' She continued to smile her merry, professional smile; in her white clerk's smock she could have been a nurse, perhaps a dental nurse advocating some new technique for oral hygiene. Efficient and practical. And, he thought, dedicated.

He said, 'Why had I made up my mind to come over to you?'

'Don't you remember?'

'No,' he said.

'Then I have things for you to read. A sort of reorientation kit.' Stooping, she reached behind the counter and brought out a flat manila envelope; she opened it on the counter. 'First,' she said, 'the January 14, 1996 copy of *Time*, with your picture on the cover and your biography inside. Complete, in so far as public knowledge about you goes.'

'What have they been told?' he said, thinking of Mrs McFee and her garble of suspicions and rumours.

'That you have a respiratory condition that requires you to live in seclusion in South America. In a back-country town in Peru called Ayacucho. It's all in the biography.' She held out a small book. 'A grammar school text on current history. Used as the official text in One Happy World schools.'

Ragle said, 'Explain the "One Happy World" slogan to me.'

'It's not a slogan. It's the official nomenclature for the group that believes there's no future in interplanetary travel. One Happy World is good enough, better in fact than a lot of arid wastes that the Lord never intended man to occupy. You know of course what "lunatics" means.'

'Yes,' he said. 'Luna colonists.'

'Not quite. But it's there in the book, along with an account of the origins of the war. And there's one more thing.' From the folder she brought out a pamphlet with the title:

THE STRUGGLE AGAINST TYRANNY

'What's this?' Ragle said, accepting it. The pamphlet gave him an eerie feeling, the strong shock of familiarity, long association.

Mrs Keitelbein said, 'It's a pamphlet circulated among the

thousands of workers at Ragle Gumm, Inc. In your various plants. You haven't given up your economic holdings, you understand. You volunteered to serve the government for a nominal sum – a gesture of patriotism. Your talent to be put to work saving people from lunatic bombings. But after you had worked for the government – the One Happy World Government – for a few months, you had an important change of heart. You always did see patterns sooner than anyone else.'

'Can I take these back to town?' he said. He wanted to be ready for tomorrow's puzzle; it was in his bones.

'No,' she said. 'They know you got out. If you go back they'll make another try at wiping out your memories. I'd rather you stayed here and read them. It's about eleven o'clock. There's time. I know you're thinking about tomorrow. You can't help it.'

'Are we safe here?' Vic said.

'Yes,' she said.

'No MPs will come by and look in?' Vic said.

'Look out the window,' Mrs Keitelbein said.

Both Vic and Ragle went to the drugstore window and peered out at the street.

The street had gone. They faced dark, empty fields.

'We're between towns,' Mrs Keitelbein said. 'Since you set foot in here we've been in motion. We're in motion now. For a month now we've been able to penetrate Old Town, as the Sea-bees call it. They built it, so they named it.' Pausing, she said, 'Didn't it ever occur to you to wonder where you lived? The name of your town? The county? State?'

'No,' Ragle said, feeling foolish.

'Do you know where it is now?'

'No,' he admitted.

Mrs Keitelbein said, 'It's in Wyoming. We're in western Wyoming, near the Idaho border. Your town was built up as a reconstruction of several old towns which got blown away in the early days of the war. The Seabees recreated the environment fairly well, based on texts and records. The ruins that Margo wants the city to clear for the health of the children, the ruins in which we planted the phone book and word-slips and magazines, is a bit of the genuine old town of Kemmerer. An archaic county armoury.'

168

Seating himself at the counter, Ragle began to read his biography in *Time*.

14

In his hands the pages of the magazine opened, spread out, presented him with the world of reality. Names, faces, experiences drifted up at him and resumed their existences. And no men in overalls came slipping in at him from the outside darkness; no one disturbed him. This time he was allowed to sit by himself, gripping the magazine, bent over it and absorbed in it.

More with Moraga, he thought. The old campaign, the 1987 presidential elections. And, he thought, *win with Wolfe*. The winning team. In front of him the lean, bumbling shape of the Harvard law professor, and then his Vice-President. What a contrast, he thought. Disparity responsible for a civil war. And on the same ticket, too. Try to capture everybody's vote. Wrap it all up . . . but can it be done? Law professor from Harvard and ex-railroad foreman. Roman and English law, and then a man who jotted down the weight of sacks of salt.

'Remember John Moraga?' he asked Vic.

Confusion stirred on Vic's face. 'Naturally,' he muttered.

'Funny that an educated man could turn out to be so gullible,' Ragle said. 'Cat's paw for the economic interests. Too naïve, probably. Too cloistered.' Too much theory and too little experience, he thought.

'I don't agree with you,' Vic said in a voice that grew abruptly hard with conviction. 'A man dedicated to seeing his principles carried out in practice, despite all odds.'

Ragle glanced up at him in astonishment. The tight expression of certitude. Partisanship, he thought. Debates in the bars at night: I wouldn't be caught dead using a salad bowl made out of Luna Ore. Don't buy Lunar. The boycott. And all in the name of principles.

Ragle said, 'Buy Ant-Ore.'

'Buy at home,' Vic agreed, without hesitation.

'Why?' Ragle said. 'What's the difference? Do you think of the

Antarctic continent as home?' He was puzzled. 'Lun-Ore or Ant-Ore. Ore is ore.' The great foreign policy debate. The Moon will never be worth anything to us economically, he thought to himself. Forget about it. But suppose it is worth something? What then?

In 1993 President Moraga signed into law the bill that terminated American economic development on Luna. Hurray! Zeeeeep! Zeeeeep!

Fifth Avenue ticker-tape parade.

And then the insurrection. The wolves, he thought.

' "Win with Wolfe",' he said aloud.

Vic said fiercely, 'In my opinion a bunch of traitors.'

Standing apart from the two of them, Mrs Keitelbein listened and watched.

'The law clearly states that in case of presidential disability the Vice-President becomes full and acting President,' Ragle said. 'So how can you start talking about traitors?'

'Acting President isn't the same as President. He was just supposed to see that the real President's wishes were carried out. He wasn't supposed to distort and destroy the President's foreign policies. He took advantage of the President's illness. Restoring funds to the Lunar projects to please a bunch of California liberals with a lot of starry-eyed dreamy notions and no practical sense –' Vic gasped with indignation. 'Mentality of teenagers yearning to drive fast and far in souped-up cars. See beyond the next range of mountains.'

Ragle said, 'You got that from some newspaper column. Those aren't your ideas.'

'Freudian explanation, something to do with vague sexual promptings. Why else go to the Moon? All that talk about "ultimate goal of life". Phony nonsense.' Vic jabbed his finger at him. 'And it isn't legal.'

'If it isn't legal,' Ragle said, 'it doesn't matter if it's vague sexual promptings or not.' You're getting your logic muddled, he thought. Having it both ways. It's immature and it's against the law. Say anything against it, whatever comes to your mind. Why are you so set against Lunar exploration? Smell of the alien? Contamination? The unfamiliar seeping in through the chinks in the walls . . .

170

The radio shouted, '. . . desperately ill with a kidney disorder, President John Moraga at his villa in South Carolina declares that only with painstaking scrutiny and the most solemn attention to the best interests of the nation will he consider – '

Painstaking, Ragel thought. Kidney disorders always painstaking, or rather painsgiving. The poor man.

'He was a hell of a fine President,' Vic said.

Ragle said, 'He was an idiot.'

Mrs Keitelbein nodded.

The group of Lunar colonists declared that they would not return funds they had received and which the Federal agencies had begun billing them for. Accordingly, the FBI arrested them qua group for violation of statutes dealing with misuse of Federal funds, and, where machinery rather than funds were involved, for unauthorized possession of Federal property et cetera.

Pretext, Ragel Gumm thought.

In the dim evening the lights of the car radio illuminated the dashboard, his knee, the knee of the girl beside him as both he and she lay back together, entwined, warm, perspiring, reaching now and then into a bag of potato chips resting on the folds of her skirt. He leaned forward once to sip beer.

'Why would people want to live on the Moon?' the girl murmured.

'Chronic malcontents,' he said, sleepily. 'Normal people don't need to. Normal people would be satisfied with life as it is.' He closed his eyes and listened to the dance music on the radio.

'Is it pretty on the Moon?' the girl asked.

'Oh Christ, it's awful,' he said. 'Nothing but rock and dust.'

The girl said, 'When we get married I'd rather live down around Mexico City. Prices are high, but it's very cosmopolitan.'

On the magazine pages between Ragle Gumm's hands, the article reminded him that he was now forty-six years old. It had been a long time since he had lounged with the girl in the car, listening to dance music on the radio. That was a very sweet girl, he thought. Why isn't there a picture of her here in the article? Maybe they don't know about her. Part of my life that didn't count. Didn't affect mankind. . . .

In February of 1994 a battle broke out at Base One, the nominal capital of the Lunar colonies. Soldiers from the nearby missile base were set upon by colonists, and a five-hour pitched encounter was fought. That night, special troop-transporting ships left Earth for Luna.

Hurray, he thought. Zeeeeep! Zeeeeep!

Within a month a full-scale war was under way.

'I see,' Ragle Gumm said. He closed the magazine.

Mrs Keitelbein said, 'A civil war is the worst kind possible. Family against family. Father against son.'

'The expansionists – ' With difficulty, he said, 'The lunatics on Earth didn't do very well.'

'They fought a while, in California and New York and in a few large inland cities. But by the end of the first year the One Happy Worlders had control here on Earth.' Mrs Keitelbein smiled at him with her fixed, professional smile; she leaned back against a counter, her arms folded. 'Now and then at night, lunatic partisans cut phone lines and blow up bridges. But most of those who survived are getting a dose of c.c. Concentration camps, in Nevada and Arizona.'

Ragle said, 'But you have the Moon.'

'Oh yes,' she said. 'And now we're fairly self-sufficient. We have the resources, the equipment. The trained men.'

'Don't they bomb you?'

She said, 'Well, you see, Luna keeps one side away from the Earth.'

Yes, he thought. Of course. The ideal military base. Earth did not have that advantage. Eventually, every part of Earth swam into the sights of the watchers on the Moon.

Mrs Keitelbein said, 'All our crops are grown hydro – hydroponics, in tanks under the surface. No way they can be contaminated by fallout. And we have no atmosphere to pick up and carry the dust. The lesser gravity permits much of the dust to leave completely . . . it just drifts away, into space. Our installations are underground, too. Our houses and schools. And – ' she smiled – 'we breathe canned air. So no bacteriological material affects us. We're completely contained. Even if there're fewer of us. Only a few thousand, in fact.'

'And you've been bombing Earth,' he said.

'We have an attack programme. Aggressive approach. We put

172

warheads into what used to be transports and fire them at Earth. One or two a week . . . plus smaller strikes, research rockets which we have in quantity. And communication and supply rockets, small stuff good for a few farmhouses or a factory. It worries them because they can never tell if it's a full-size transport with a full-size H-warhead, or only a little fellow. It disrupts their lives.'

Ragle said, 'And that's what I've been predicting.'

'Yes,' she said.

'How well have I done?'

'Not as well as they've told you. Lowery, I mean.'

'I see,' he said.

'But not badly, either. We've succeeded in randomizing our pattern more or less . . . you get some of them, especially the full-size transports. I think we tend to fuss with them to a greater degree because we have only a limited number. We tend to unrandomize them. So you sense the pattern, you and your talent. Women's hats. What they'll be wearing next year. Occult.'

'Yes,' he said. 'Or artistic.'

'But why'd you go over to them?' Vic demanded. 'They've been bombing us, killing women and children – '

'He knows why now,' Mrs Keitelbein said. 'I saw it on his face as he read. He remembers.'

'Yes,' Ragle said. 'I remember.'

'Why did you go over to them?' Vic said.

'Because they're right,' Ragle said. 'And the isolationists are wrong.'

Mrs Keitelbein said, 'That's why.'

When Margo opened the front door and saw it was Bill Black outside on the dark porch, she said,

'They're not here. They're down at the store, taking a rush inventory. Something about a surprise audit.'

'Can I come in anyhow?' Black said.

She let him in. He shut the door after him. 'I know they're not here.' He had a listless, despondent manner. 'But they're not down at the store.'

'That's where I saw them last,' she said, not enjoying telling a lie. 'And that's what they told me.' Told me to say, she thought to herself.

Black said, 'They got out. We picked up the driver of the truck. They let him off a hundred or so miles along the road.'

'How do you know?' she said, and then she felt rage at him. An almost hysterical resentment. She did not understand, but she had a deep intuition. 'You and your lasagne,' she said chokingly. 'Coming over here and spying, hanging around him all the time. Sending that tail-switching wife of yours over to rub up against him.'

'She's not my wife,' he said. 'They assigned her because I had to be set up in a residential context.'

Her head swam. 'Does – she know?'

'No.'

'That's something,' Margo said. 'Now what?' she said. 'You can stand there smirking because you know what it's all about.'

'I'm not smirking,' Black said. 'I'm just thinking that at the moment I had my chance to get him back I thought to myself, That must be the Kesselmans. It's the same people. Simple mix-up on the names. I wonder who conjured up that. I never was too good on names. Maybe they found that out. But with sixteen hundred names to keep track of and deal with – '

'Sixteen hundred,' she said. 'What do you mean?' And her intuition, then, grew. A sense of the finiteness of the world around her. The streets and houses and shops and cars and people. Sixteen hundred people, standing in the centre of a stage. Surrounded by props, by furniture to sit in, kitchens to cook in, cars to drive, food to fix. And then, behind the props, the flat, painted scenery. Painted houses set farther back. Painted people. Painted streets. Sounds from speakers set in the wall. Sammy sitting alone in a classroom, the only pupil. And even the teacher not real. Only a series of tapes being played for him.

'Do we get to know what it's for?' she said.

'He knows. Ragle knows.'

She said, 'That's why we don't have radios.'

'You'd have picked things up on a radio,' Black said.

'We did,' she said. 'We picked you up.'

He grimaced. 'It was a question of time. Sooner or later. But we expected him to keep sinking back into it, in spite of that.'

'But someone came along,' Margo said.

'Yes. Two more people. Tonight we sent a work crew to the

house – that big old two-story house on the corner – but they're gone. Nobody there. Left all their models. They gave him a course in Civil Defence. Leading up to the present.'

She said, 'If you have nothing else to say, I wish you'd leave.'

'I'm going to stay here,' Black told her. 'All night. He might decide to come back. I thought you'd prefer it if Junie didn't come with me. I can sleep here in the living room; that way I'll see him if he does show up.' Opening the front door he lifted a small suitcase into the house. 'My toothbrush, pyjamas, a few personal things,' he said, in the same dulled, spiritless voice.

'You're in trouble,' she said. 'Aren't you?'

'So are you,' Black said. Setting the suitcase down on a chair he opened it and began to lay out his possessions.

'Who are you?' she said. 'If you're not "Bill Black".'

'I am Bill Black. Major William Black, United States Board of Strategic Planning, Western Theatre. Originally I worked with Ragle, plotting out missile strikes. In some respects I was his pupil.'

'So you don't work for the city. For the water company.'

The front door opened and there stood Junie Black, in a coat, holding a clock. Her face was puffy and red; obviously she had been crying. 'You forgot your clock,' she said to Bill Black, holding it out to him. 'Why are you staying here tonight?' she said in a quavering voice. 'Is it something I did?' She glanced from him to Margo. 'Are you two having an affair? Is that it? Was that it all the time?'

Neither of them said anything.

'Please explain it to me,' Junie said.

Bill said, 'For god's sake, will you beat it. Go on home.'

Sniffling, she said, 'Okay. Whatever you say. Will you be home tomorrow, or is this permanent?'

'It's just for tonight,' he said.

The door shut after her.

'What a pest,' Bill Black said.

'She still believes it,' Margo said. 'That she's your wife.'

'She'll believe it until she's been reconstructed,' Bill said. 'So will you. You'll keep on seeing what you've been seeing. The training is all there, on a nonrational level. Impressed on your systems.'

'It's awful,' she said.

'Oh, I don't know. There are worse things. It's an attempt to save your lives.'

'Is Ragle conditioned, too? Like the rest of us?'

'No,' Black said, as he laid out his pyjamas on the couch. Margo noticed the loud colours, the flowers and leaves of bright red. 'Ragle is in a little different shape. He gave us the idea for all this. He got himself into a dilemma, and the only way he could solve it was to go into a withdrawal psychosis.'

She thought, Then he really is insane.

'He withdrew into a fantasy of tranquillity,' Black said, winding the clock that Junie had brought over. 'Back to a period before the war. To his childhood. To the late 'fifties, when he was an infant.'

'I don't believe a thing you're saying,' she said, resisting it. But she still heard it.

'So we found a system by which we could let him live in his stress-free world. Relatively stress-free, I mean. And still plot our missile intercepts for us. He could do it without the sense of load on his shoulders. The lives of all mankind. He could make it into a game, a newspaper contest. That was our tip-off, originally. One day, when we dropped into his headquarters at Denver, he greeted us by saying, "I've almost got today's puzzle finished." A week or so later he had gotten a full-scale retreat fantasy going.'

'Is he really my brother?' she said.

Black hesitated. 'No,' he said.

'Is he any relation to me?'

'No,' Black said, with reluctance.

'Is Vic my husband?'

'N-no.'

'Is anybody any relation to anybody?' she demanded.

Scowling, Black said, 'I – ' Then he bit his lip and said, 'It so happens that you and I are married. But your personality-type fitted in better as a member of Ragle's household. It had to be arranged on a practical basis.'

After that, neither of them said anything. Margo walked unsteadily into the kitchen and reflexively seated herself at the table there.

Bill Black my husband, she thought. Major Bill Black.

In the living room, her husband unrolled a blanket on the couch, tossed a pillow at one end, and prepared to retire for the night.

Going to the living room door, she said, 'Can I ask you something?'

He nodded.

'Do you know where the light cord is that Vic reached for, that night in the bathroom?'

Black said, 'Vic managed a grocery store in Oregon. The light cord might have been there. Or in his apartment there.'

'How long have you and I been married?'

'Six years.'

She said, 'Any children?'

'Two girls. Ages four and five.'

'What about Sammy?' In his room, Sammy slept on, his door shut. 'He's no relation to anybody? Just a child recruited somewhere along the line, like a movie actor to fill a part?'

'He's Vic's boy. Vic and his wife.'

'What's his wife's name?'

'You've never met her.'

'Not that big Texas girl down at the store.'

Black laughed. 'No. A girl named Betty or Barbara; I never met her, either.'

'What a mess,' she said.

'It is,' he said.

She returned to the kitchen and reseated herself. Later, she heard him switch on the television set. He listened to concert music for an hour or so, and then she heard him switch the set off, and then the living room light, and then get under the blanket on the couch. Later on, at the kitchen table, she involuntarily dozed.

The telephone woke her up. She could hear Bill Black flailing about in the living room, trying to find it.

'In the hall,' she said groggily.

'Hello,' Black said.

The clock on the wall above the kitchen sink told her that the time was three-thirty. Lord, she thought.

'Okay,' Black said. He hung up the phone and padded back into the living room. Listening, she heard him dress, stuff his things away in the suitcase, and then the front door opened and shut. He had left. He had gone.

Not waiting, she thought, rubbing her eyes and trying to wake up. She felt stiff and cold; shivering, she got to her feet and stood before the oven, trying to get warm.

They're not coming back, she thought. At least, Ragle isn't coming back. Or Black would wait.

From his bedroom, Sammy called, 'Mommy! Mommy!'

She opened the door. 'What's the matter?' she said.

Sitting up in bed, Sammy said, 'Who was that on the phone?'

'Nobody,' she said. She entered the room and bent down to tuck the covers over the boy. 'Go back to sleep.'

'Did Dad get home yet?'

'Not yet,' she said.

'Wow,' Sammy said, settling back down and already drifting back into sleep. 'Maybe they stole something . . . left town.'

She remained in the bedroom, seated on the edge of the boy's bed, smoking a cigarette and forcing herself to stay awake.

I don't think they'll be back, she thought. But I'll wait up anyhow. Just in case.

'What do you mean they're right?' Vic said. 'You mean it's right to bomb towns and hospitals and churches?'

Ragle Gumm remembered the day he had first heard about the Lunar colonists, already called lunatics, firing on Federal troops. Nobody had been very much surprised. The lunatics, for the most part, consisted of discontented people, unestablished young couples, ambitious young men and their wives, few with children, none with property or responsibility. His first reaction was to wish that he could fight. But his age forbade that. And he had something much more valuable to volunteer.

They had put him to work plotting the missile strikes, making his graphs and patterns of prediction, doing his statistical research, he and his staff. Major Black had been his executive officer, a bright individual eager to learn how the plotting was done. For the first year it had gone properly, and then the weight of responsibility had gotten him down. The sense that all their lives depended on him. And at that point the army people had decided to take him off Earth. To put him aboard a ship and transport him to one of the health resorts on Venus to which high government officials went, and at which they wasted much time. The climate on Venus, or perhaps the minerals in the water, or the gravity – no one could be sure – had done much to cure cancer and heart trouble.

For the first time in his life he found himself leaving Earth. Journeying out into space, between planets. Free of gravity. The greatest tie had ceased to hold him. The fundamental force that kept the universe of matter behaving as it did. The Heisenberg Unified Field Theory had connected all energy, all phenomena into a single experience. Now, as his ship left Earth, he passed from that experience to another, the experience of pure freedom.

It answered, for him, a need that he had never been aware of. A deep restless yearning under the surface, always there in him, throughout his life, but not articulated. The need to travel on. To migrate.

His ancestors had migrated. They had appeared, nomads, not farmers but food-gatherers, entering the West from Asia. When they had reached the Mediterranean they had settled down, because they had reached the edge of the world; there was no place left to go. And then later, hundreds of years later, reports had arrived that other places existed. Lands beyond the sea. They had never gotten out on to the sea much, except perhaps for their abortive migration to North Africa. That migration out on to the water in boats was a terrifying thing for them. They had no idea where they were going, but after a while they had made that migration, from one continent to another. And that held them for a time, because again they had reached the edge of the world.

No migration had ever been like this. For any species, any race. From one planet to another. How could it be surpassed? They made now, in these ships, the final leap. Every variety of life made its migration, travelled on. It was a universal need, a universal experience. But these people had found the ultimate stage, and as far as they knew, no other species or race had found that.

It had nothing to do with minerals, resources, scientific measurement. Nor even exploration and profit. Those were excuses. The actual reason lay outside their conscious minds. If he were required to, he could not formulate the need, even as he experienced it fully. No one could. An instinct, the most primitive drive, as well as the most noble and complex. It was both at once.

And the ironic thing, he thought, is that people say God never meant for us to travel in space.

The lunatics are right, he thought, because they know it has nothing to do with how profitable the ore concessions can be made to be. We're only pretending to mine ore on Luna. It's not a political question, or even an ethical one. But you have to answer something when someone asks you. You have to pretend that you know.

For a week he bathed in the warm mineral waters at the Roosevelt Hot Springs on Venus. Then they shipped him back to Earth. And, shortly after that, he started spending his time thinking back to his childhood. To the peaceful days when his father had sat around the living room reading the newspaper and the kids had watched Captain Kangaroo on T V. When his mother had driven their new Volkswagen, and the news on the radio hadn't been about war but about the first Earth satellites and the initial hopes for thermonuclear power. For infinite sources of energy.

Before the great strikes and depressions and civil discord that came later.

That was his last memory. Spending his time meditating about the fifties. And then, one day, he found himself back in the fifties. It had seemed a marvellous event to him. A breath-taking wonder. All at once the sirens, the c.c. buildings, the conflict and hate, the bumper strips reading ONE HAPPY WORLD, vanished. The soldiers in their uniforms hanging around him all day long, the dread of the next missile attack, the pressure and tension, and above all the doubt that they all felt. The terrible guilt of a civil war, masked over by greater and greater ferocity. Brother against brother. Family against itself.

A Volkswagen rolled up and parked. A woman, very pretty smiling, stepped out and said,

'*Almost ready to go home?*'

That's a darn sensible little car they've got, he thought. They made a good buy. High resale value.

'*Just about,*' *he said to his mother.*

'I want to get a few things in the drugstore,' his father said, closing the car door after them.

Trade-in on electric razors, he thought as he watched his mother and father go off toward the drug department of Ernie's Shopping Centre. Seven-fifty for your old razor, regardless of make. No ominous preoccupations : the pleasure of buying. Above his head the shiny signs. Colours of shifting ads. The brightness, the splendour. He wandered about the parking lot, among the long pastel cars, gazing up at the signs, reading the words in the window displays. Schilling drip coffee 69c a pound. Gosh, he thought. What a buy.

His eyes took in the sight of merchandise, cars, people, counters ; he thought, What a lot to look at. What a lot to examine. A fair, practically. In the grocery department a woman giving away free samples of cheese. He wandered that way. Bits of yellow cheese on a tray. The woman holding the tray out to anyone. Something for nothing. The excitement. Hum and murmur. He entered the store and reached out for his free sample, trembling. The woman, smiling down at him, said,

'What do you say?'

'Thank you,' he said.

'Do you enjoy this?' the woman asked. 'Roaming around here in the different stores while your parents are shopping?'

'Sure,' he said, munching on the cheese.

The woman said, 'Is it because you feel that everything you might need is available here? A big store, a supermarket, is a complete world in itself?'

'I guess so,' he admitted.

'So there's nothing to fear,' the woman said. 'No need to feel anxiety. You can relax. Find peace, here.'

'That's right,' he said, with a measure of resentment at her, at the questioning. He looked once more at the tray of food.

'Which department are you in now?' the woman asked.

He looked around him and saw that he was in the pharmacy department. Among the tubes of toothpaste and magazines and sunglasses and jars of hand lotion. But I was in the food part, he thought with surprise. Where the samples of food are, the free food. Are there free samples of gum and candy here? That would be okay.

'You see,' the woman said, 'they didn't do anything to you, to your mind. You slipped back yourself. You've slipped back now, just reading about it. You keep wanting to go back.' Now she did not have a tray of cheese samples. 'Do you know who I am?' she asked in a considerate voice.

'You're familiar,' he said, stalling because he could not recall.

'I'm Mrs Keitelbein,' the woman said.

'That's so,' he agreed. He moved away from her. 'You've done a lot to help me,' he said to her, feeling grateful.

'You're getting out of it,' Mrs Keitelbein said. 'But it'll take time. The pull on you is strong. The tug back into the past.'

The Saturday-afternoon crowd swarmed on all sides of him. How nice, he thought. This is the Golden Age. The finest time to be alive. I hope I can live like this always.

His father, beckoning to him from the Volkswagen. Armload of parcels. 'Let's go,' his father called.

'Okay,' he said, still wondering, still seeing everything, unwilling to let it all go by him. In the corner of the parking lot heaps of colour-ful paper that had blown there, wrappers and cartons and paper bags. His mind made out the patterns, the cigarette packages crumpled up, the lids to milkshake cartons. And in the debris lay something of value. A dollar bill, folded. It had blown there with the rest. Bending, he sorted it out, unfolded it. Yes, a dollar bill. Lost by someone, probably a long, long time ago.

'Hey, look what I found,' he called to his father and mother, running toward them and the car.

Conference, ending in, 'Can he keep it? Would it be right?' His mother, concerned.

'Never be able to locate the owner,' his father said. 'Sure, keep it.' He tousled the boy's hair.

'But he didn't earn it,' his mother said.

'I found it,' Ragle Gumm chanted, clutching the bill. 'I figured out where it was; I knew it was there with all that other junk.'

'Luck,' his father said. 'Now, I know fellows that can walk along and spot money on the pavement any day of the week. I never can. I bet I never found a dime in the gutter all my life.'

'I can do that,' Ragle Gumm chanted. 'I can figure it out; I know how.'

Later, his father relaxing on the couch in the living room, relating

tales about World War Two, his part in the Pacific phase. His
mother washing dishes in the kitchen. The tranquillity of the house . . .

'*What are you going to do with your dollar?*' *his father asked.*

'*Invest it,*' *Ragle Gumm said.* '*So I'll have more.*'

'*Big businessman, eh?*' *his father said.* '*Don't forget about corporation taxes.*'

'*I'll have plenty left over,*' *he said confidently, leaning back the way his father did, hands behind his head, elbows stuck out.*

He savoured this happiest of all moments of life.

'But why so inaccurate?' he asked Mrs Keitelbein. 'The Tucker car. It was a terrific car, but – '

Mrs Keitelbein said, 'You did ride in one, once.'

'Yes,' he said. 'Or at least I think so. When I was a kid.' And, at that point remembering, he could feel the presence of the car. 'In Los Angeles,' he said. 'A friend of my dad's owned one of the prototypes.'

'You see, that would explain it,' she said.

'But it never was put into production. It never got beyond the hand-built stage.'

'But you needed it,' Mrs Keitelbein said. 'It was for you.'

Ragle Gumm said, '*Uncle Tom's Cabin.*' It had seemed perfectly natural to him, at the time, when Vic had shown them all the brochure from the Book-of-the-Month Club. 'That thing was written a century before my time. That's a really ancient book.'

Picking up the magazine article, Mrs Keitelbein held it out to him. 'A childhood verity,' she said. 'Try to remember.'

There, in the article, a line about the book. He had owned a copy, read the book over and over again. Battered yellow and black covers, charcoal-like illustrations as lurid as the book itself. Again he felt the weight of the thing in his hands, the dusty, rough pressure of the fabric and paper. Himself, off in the quiet and shadows of the yard, nose down, eyes fixed on the text. Keeping it with him in his room, rereading it because it was a stable element; it did not change. It gave him a sense of certainty. A sense that he could count on it to be there, exactly as it had always been. Even the crayon markings on the first page that he had made, his scrawled initials.

'Everything in terms of your requirements,' Mrs Keitelbein

said. 'What you needed, for your security and comfort. Why should it be accurate? If *Uncle Tom's Cabin* was a necessity of your childhood, it was included.'

Like a daydream, he thought. Keeping in the good. Excluding the undesirable.

'If radios infringed, then there were no radios,' Mrs Keitelbein said. 'Or at least there weren't supposed to be.'

But such a natural thing, he realized. They overlooked a radio every now and then. They kept forgetting that in the illusion the radio did not exist; they kept slipping up in just such trifles. Typical difficulty in maintaining daydreams . . . they failed to be consistent. Sitting at the table playing poker with us, Bill Black saw the crystal set and did not remember. It was too commonplace. It did not register; he had his mind on more important matters.

In her patient way, Mrs Keitelbein went on, 'So you recognize that they built for you – and placed you in – a safe, controlled environment in which you could do your job without doubt or distractions. Or the realization that you were on the wrong side.'

Vic said savagely, 'The *wrong* side? – the side that was attacked!'

'In a civil war,' Ragle said, 'every side is wrong. It's hopeless to try to untangle it. Everyone is a victim.'

In his lucid periods, before they had taken him from his office and established him in Old Town, he had evolved a plan. He had carefully assembled his notes and papers, packed his possessions, and prepared to leave. In a roundabout manner he had managed to make contact with a group of California lunatics at one of the concentration camps in the Midwest; doses of reorientation training had not yet affected them or their loyalties, and from them he had gotten instructions. He was to meet with a free, undetected lunatic in St Louis, at a particular time, on a particular day. But he had never arrived there. The day before, they had picked up his contact, gotten the information from him. And that was that.

In the concentration camps, the captured lunatics underwent a systematic brainwashing, but of course it was never called that. This was education along new lines, a freeing of the individual from prejudices, malformed convictions, from neurotic obsessions and fixed ideas. It helped him mature. It was knowledge. He came forth a better man.

When Old Town had been built, the people who entered it and became part of its life underwent the technique used in the camps. They volunteered. All but Ragle Gumm. And on him the camp technique fastened the last elements of his withdrawal into the past.

They made it work, he realized. *I withdrew and they followed right along after me. They kept me in sight.*

Vic said, 'You better think this out. It's a big thing, to go over to the other side.'

'He already has made up his mind,' Mrs Keitelbein said. 'He did that three years ago.'

'I'm not going with you,' Vic said.

'I know that,' Ragle said.

'Are you going to walk out on Margo, your own sister?'

'Yes,' he said.

'You're going to walk out on everybody.'

'Yes,' he said.

'So they can bomb us and kill us all.'

'No,' he said. Because after he had volunteered, left his private business and gone to work at Denver, he had learned something that the top officials of the government knew that had never been made public. It was a well-guarded secret. The lunatics, the colonists on Luna, had agreed to come to terms in the first weeks of the war. They insisted only that a sizeable effort be maintained toward further colonization, and that lunatics not be subjected to punitive action after hostilities had ceased. Without Ragle Gumm the government at Denver would yield on those points. The threat of missile attacks would be enough. Public feeling against the Lunar colonists did not go that far; three years of fighting and suffering for both sides had made a difference.

Vic said, 'You're a traitor.' He stared at his brother-in-law. Except, Ragle thought, I'm not his brother-in-law. We're not related. I did not know him before Old Town.

Yes, he thought. I did know him. When I lived in Bend, Oregon. He operated a grocery store, there. I used to buy my fresh fruit and vegetables from him. He was always puttering about the potato bins in his white apron, smiling at the customers, worrying about spoilage. That was the extent to which we knew each other.

Nor have I got a sister.

But, he thought, I will consider them my family, because in the two years and a half at Old Town they have been a genuine family, along with Sammy. And June and Bill Black are my neighbours. I *am* walking out on them, family and relatives, neighbours and friends. That is what civil war means. In a sense it's the most idealistic kind of war. The most heroic. It means the most sacrifices, the fewest practical advantages.

I'm doing it because I know it is right. It comes first, my duty. Everyone else, Bill Black and Victor Nielson and Margo and Lowery and Mrs Keitelbein and Mrs Kesselman – they all have done their duty; they have been loyal to what they believe in. I intend to do the same.

Sticking out his hand he said to Vic, 'Good-bye.'

Vic, his face wooden, ignored him.

'Are you going back to Old Town?' Ragle said.

Vic nodded.

'Maybe I'll see you all again,' Ragle said. 'After the war.' He did not believe that it would last much longer. 'I wonder if they'll keep up Old Town,' he said. 'Without me in the centre.'

Turning, Vic walked off, away from him, to the door of the drugstore. 'Any way to get out of here?' he said loudly, his back to the two of them.

'You'll be let out,' Mrs Keitelbein said. 'We'll drop you off on the highway and you can arrange for a ride back to Old Town.'

Vic remained by the door.

It's a shame, Ragle Gumm thought. But it has been that way for some time, now. This is nothing new.

'Would you kill me?' he said to Vic. 'If you could?'

'No,' Vic said. 'There's always the chance you'll switch back again, to this side.'

To Mrs Keitelbein, Ragle said, 'Let's go.'

'Your second trip,' she said. 'You'll be leaving Earth again.'

'That's right,' Ragle said. Another lunatic joining the group already there.

Beyond the windows of the drugstore a shape tilted on its end, to launching position. Vapours boiled up from its bottom. The loading platform coasted over to it and locked in place. Halfway up the side of the ship a door opened. A man stuck his head out, blinked, strained to see in the night darkness. Then he lit a coloured light.

The man with the coloured light resembled Walter Keitelbein to a striking degree. As a matter of fact, he *was* Walter Keitelbein.

ABOUT THE AUTHOR

Philip K. Dick was born in Chicago in 1928, but lived most of his life in California. He began reading science fiction when he was twelve, and was never able to stop. Among the most prolific and eccentric of s-f writers, Dick's many novels and stories all blend a sharp and quirky imagination with a strong sense of the surreal. *The Man in the High Castle*, perhaps his most painstakingly constructed and chilling novel, won the Hugo Award in 1963. His other novels include *The Penultimate Truth* and *The Three Stigmata of Palmer Eldritch*.

Philip K. Dick died in 1982.